LOVE & LIMITATIONS

COLLECTED STORIES

J. SCOTT COATSWORTH

Published by
Other Worlds Ink
PO Box 19341, Sacramento, CA 95819

 Created with Vellum

*I dedicate "Love & Limitations" to my husband Mark, whose love
has helped me shatter my own limitations.*

CONTENTS

Foreword   vii

I Only Want to Be With You   1
The Boy in the Band   28
Translation   91
Slow Thaw   124
Ten   199
Thanks for Reading!   231
The River City Chronicles   232

About the Author   237
Also by J. Scott Coatsworth   239

FOREWORD

"Love & Limitations" is my fourth short story collection, some of which were originally published in anthologies, and one of which is being published here for the first time.

All of the stories herein are MM Romance or Romance adjacent. Some are bright and cheerful, others more melancholy and sad, but each one has its own light. I have also included a little info at the end of each story as to when it was written and why.

I hope you enjoy it!

I ONLY WANT TO BE WITH YOU

THE DOORBELL RANG.

Derrek groaned, pulling his blanket up over his head. "Leave me alone, Tony."

Tony from work had stopped by three times to check on him after he'd taken the week off to plan his mother's funeral. It was starting to get obnoxious. Tony kinda had a thing for black guys. Derrek *really* didn't have a thing for him.

"It's not Tony." The voice was deeper, warmer than Tony's. It didn't *scream* gay accountant.

Oh shit. Derrek was in no shape for company, but it was *Ryan.* Ryan Kessler.

Ryan was practically family. They'd been friends for five years, ever since they'd met at a grief support group. "Coming." He threw the blanket under the couch and checked himself in the mirror, trying to force his hair into some semblance of *combed.* Then he dragged himself to the door.

Derrek clearly wasn't *Ryan's* type. Yet somehow, they'd formed a singular friendship.

"Hey, sport." Ryan stood there in his full glory, looking like that gay soccer player from Spain? Portugal? Cristiano Ronaldo. Clean cut, tanned, and beautiful.

Seriously, Derrek was pretty sure that Ryan glowed and that birds chirped when he entered a room. It all might have been in his head.

It didn't matter, anyhow. *Ryan is with Alex.*

Ryan held up a paper bag and pulled out a round container. "Brought you some soup from the Chicken Pie Shop."

"You brought me soup?" Derrek sniffed himself surreptitiously. He hadn't bathed in three days, since his mother's funeral.

"Yeah. I'm sorry I wasn't here sooner. Work had me in San Francisco for training. I just got in last night and heard your voicemail." Ryan hugged him. "I'm so sorry, Derr."

"Thanks. It's been a rough week. Want to come in?" Derrek took the container.

"Sure." He followed Derrek inside.

"Hey, you hungry? I can't eat all of this myself."

"Yeah, I haven't had dinner yet."

"What about Alex?"

"He said he would be home late. He has a work thing tonight."

Derrek tried not to roll his eyes. "Wanna stick around and eat with me, then? The soup smells great. I haven't really had much of an appetite, since mom passed."

"What happened?"

Derrek shook his head. "They don't know. She was at work, and she just... fell." He hadn't been there, but his mind had latched onto that image. The look of horror on her face, the long collapse... he grabbed the edge of the kitchen counter and squeezed it hard. *Oh God, why do I have to keep seeing it?* "They think it was a stroke."

Ryan's arms wrapped around him and pulled him close. "They didn't do an autopsy?"

Derrek tried to ignore the effect Ryan had on him. This wasn't the time. "We didn't want one. I mean... what's the point?" He sighed. "She looked so beautiful—her face made up and her hair done, wearing one of her favorite bright blue blouses. But she was... I don't know... hollow, somehow? Not like herself at all."

Ryan nodded. "My grandma was like that. Like it wasn't even her." He pulled a chair out and gestured for Derrek to sit. "Relax.

I'll heat this up for us." He put the soup in one of Derrek's cranberry Pyrex bowls.

Derrek watched Ryan work, setting the table with ceramic bowls and a couple spoons. *He knows where everything is.* "I'm sorry I'm such a mess. I haven't felt like showering. Like doing much of anything, really." He rubbed his eyes. *I do need a shower.* "I have to go back to work tomorrow."

"You're entitled to be a mess. Are you sure you're ready for work?" Ryan microwaved the soup, glancing at Derrek over his shoulder.

"Honestly, I think it will be a good distraction." He was ready to throw himself into something, and at least at work he got a paycheck for it. "The Grind has been really good about giving me the time off."

"What do you want to drink?" Ryan poked his head into the fridge. "Eeeeew."

"What?"

"I don't think milk's supposed to look like that."

"Like what?"

"Like cottage cheese?" He held up the container.

Derrek snorted in spite of himself. "Sorry. I haven't gotten to the store in a few days. Or a week, maybe. It's hard to remember."

"How about some wine?"

"Perfect."

Ryan found a couple of wineglasses, and uncorked a bottle of red wine from Derrek's modest under-the-sink collection, mostly housewarming gifts brought by friends.

The microwave beeped, and Ryan served the soup, ladling it steaming into the two bowls.

It smelled heavenly.

"Best chicken soup in San Diego," Ryan said with a grin. "At least Yelp says so."

"Well, if Yelp says it's true..." Derrek managed a weak smile. "I'm sorry. I'm not very good company right now."

"Hey, *I'm* the company. You're the guest of honor. Or something like that. Eat!"

Derrek took a sip of the chunky soup. "Oh my God, that's good." It was full of carrots, potato, and big chunks of white chicken meat. He hadn't realized how hungry he was.

Ryan grinned. "Yeah, it really is."

Derrek gulped it down. "So," he asked between spoonfuls. "Does Alex know you're here?"

Derrek nodded. "Yeah. I told him."

"And he was okay with it?"

Ryan was silent.

"Ryan, does Alex mind that you came to see me?"

Ryan shrugged. "He'll get over it."

Jesus, Mary, and Mamma Mia. "Ryan..."

"It'll be okay. *Really.* I needed to come, to check in on you, to make sure you were all right." He reached out to touch Derrek's hand. "It's what friends do."

Derrek squeezed his hand. "I'm glad you came. Can I make a confession?"

"Sure?" Ryan raised an eyebrow.

"I might not mind if your being here pisses Alex off, a little."

Ryan laughed. "He'll be fine. He owes me. He didn't tell me you'd called until I got home."

They talked for hours. At first it was about Derrek's mother, and all the good things Derrek remembered about her. Then they moved on to David and Will, the men they'd loved and lost.

Derrek couldn't believe it had been five years already.

Finally, they moved on to their hopes and dreams for the future. Derrek wanted to be a full-time writer. Ryan wanted to open his own coffee shop.

Derrek yawned and glanced at his phone. "Oh shit, it's after midnight."

Ryan gave him a sly smile. "I know that look. It's time for me to go home."

Derrek nodded. "Yeah, probably. Work tomorrow, remember?"

"The Monday before Thanksgiving?"

Derrek laughed ruefully. "Yeah, I have to get back to it. Coffee waits for no man."

"You're gonna be okay." Ryan gathered the dirty dishes and carried them to the sink.

"Oh, don't worry about those. I'll wash them tomorrow. Just soak them."

"You sure?"

"Yeah." It was nice having someone there. Someone to talk to. "Thanks so much for coming. It means the world to me." *Alex doesn't know what he has.*

"You have plans for Thanksgiving?"

Derrek nodded. "My sister invited me over on Thursday, but I'm not sure I want to go."

"Yeah, I get that. It's still raw."

"It's just—"

"Hey, I *know*. Why don't you come over to our place? I'm making dinner, and Chet and Michael are coming too."

Spend the holiday with Ryan? How could he say no? And yet... "I don't know. Wouldn't I be a fifth wheel?" He wasn't sure he wanted to be around Alex, either.

"*I'd* like to have you there." Ryan's voice was warm and inviting.

Derrek trembled a little. "Okay. I'll come."

"Perfect. Stop by around three?" He kissed Derrek on the cheek.

"Will do." Derrek watched Ryan walk out the door again, going back to Alex.

He sighed. Then he locked it and went to bed alone.

Derrek looked human again—a little sad around the eyes, maybe, but clean. Presentable as company.

Alex and Ryan lived over in North Park, in a cute little Mission home that was probably worth close to a million bucks these days. It was Alex's place—nothing in it reflected Ryan's tastes, as far as Derrek could tell.

This is a bad idea. He could still cancel—tell Ryan he was sick. Tell him his sister had insisted that he come. Claim he was overcome with grief.

Tell him... tell Ryan he was scared to death that everyone would see how he felt about him.

His phone buzzed.

See you soon, sport.

Derrek sighed. It was time to get off the couch and back into the real world.

See you soon.

It was already a quarter after three when he arrived. He let himself in through the side gate and followed the sound of voices into the backyard. Alex was holding court at the table on the brick-paved porch behind the Mission-style home. It was a warm San Diego fall evening. Strings of white lights running up the trunks of the trees illuminated the yard with an enchanting glow.

"Hey, Derrek!" Chet squealed and jumped up, running to give him a big hug. Chet was one of the few guys Derrek knew who was more nelly than he was.

"Hey, Chet. How are you guys?" Chet smelled like lavender and vanilla.

"We're good." He grinned. "The store's going gangbusters—we're having a hard time keeping up the inventory."

Michael gave him a hug. "So sorry to hear about your mother." Michael was six foot four, almost a foot taller than Chet. He'd grown a full dark beard since the last time Derrek had seen him.

"Thanks. She always liked you guys." He brushed Michael's beard with his hand. "I like the mountain man look."

Michael laughed. "Thanks. I've been working from home lately. I'm afraid I've gotten a little lazy."

Derrek turned to face his nemesis. "Hey, Alex."

Alex nodded. "Hey." The man smiled, but it didn't reach his eyes. "So glad you were free on such short notice."

"Me too. Kind of you to make room at your table." He refused to be baited. "Where's Ryan?"

"He insisted on cooking. I figured we'd just have it catered, but he has this *thing* about Thanksgiving." He dismissed the "thing" with a wave of his hand.

"I think I'll pop in and see how he's doing."

"Suit yourself." Alex turned back to his other guests. "Have you guys been to *Cocks* yet? They have the cutest bartenders..."

Poor Ryan, doing the whole meal alone. Derrek used to spend Thanksgiving Day with his mom and sister, and they'd all cook the meal together. A sting of pain shot through his gut.

Derrek shook his head, and went inside.

Ryan pulled the turkey out of the oven. It was beautiful and golden, and the smell... He inhaled deeply, anticipating how good it was going to taste.

He basted it with some of the juice from the bottom of the pan. As he slipped it back into the oven, another timer went off.

Shit, which one is that? The bean casserole in the other oven? The cranberries on the stove?

His mom had always made this look so easy, but she was out of town on a cruise in the Mediterranean with his stepfather Bill.

"Hey!" Derrek poked his head into the kitchen.

"Hey!" Ryan closed the oven door and turned to give Derrek a hug. "Happy Thanksgiving. How are you feeling?" Another timer went off. "Jesus Christ."

Derrek laughed. "Here, let me help." He stirred the cranberry sauce, sniffing it. "This smells delicious—did you make it from scratch?" He moved it to the back burner, and moved on to the second oven.

"Yup, Grandma Tula's recipe."

"The casserole looks good too. I'm gonna sprinkle a little water on it to keep it moist." He grabbed a cup from the cabinet by the sink.

"You're good at this." *He knows where everything is.* Thank God Derrek had come.

"My mom and sister and I used to do this together every year." He sniffed the air. "The turkey smells fantastic." Derrek peered out the blinds at the backyard. "Alex is in rare form tonight."

"Sorry about that. He had a bad day." Alex had been having *a lot* of bad days lately.

Derrek frowned. "I think he hates me."

Ryan laughed. "Hate's a strong word." He pulled the rolls out of the fridge and put them on a cookie sheet, brushing them with melted butter.

"Ryan..."

"Yeah. He *kinda* hates you. I'm sorry. He knows we talk, and he's the jealous type." He shrugged. "It just means he loves me." He put the rolls in the oven, on the shelf under the turkey. "Look, it'll blow over." He kissed Derrek's cheek. "Having you to talk to—to come to when things are rough—it means the world to me, sport." Derrek didn't know how good a guy he was.

"Glad I could help?"

"You have no idea how much." If only Alex liked to cook half as much as Derrek did. "You're going to make someone a great husband, you know."

Derrek stiffened. "Um, thanks. Can I set the table?"

"Sure? The dishes are in the cupboard in the dining room. The Fiestaware."

"Got it." Derrek backed out of the room as if he was afraid to turn his back on Ryan.

What was that all about?

Derrek sat back in his chair, feeling stuffed. "That was an amazing dinner, Ryan."

Alex sighed. "The turkey was a bit overcooked, but you'll do better next year. Or we'll just have it catered. Like I *suggested* last week." He kissed Ryan.

Derrek looked away.

Chet jumped in to smooth over the awkwardness. "It really *was* good, Ryan. Thanks so much for inviting us over."

"Oh, it's okay. We're always really honest with each other." Alex flashed his shit-eating grin, the one he used when he wanted to charm your ass off.

Like all those the times you came home late, and told Ryan you were at the office?

Ryan was staring at his plate glumly.

"Would you clear the table?" Alex kissed Ryan's cheek. "He's much better at clean-up." He laughed, and Derrek *hated* him in that moment. Ryan deserved so much better.

"I'm sorry. I have to go." He didn't need to sit here and watch this farce play itself out. He pushed his chair back loudly and pulled on his jacket.

"You don't have to leave..." Ryan got up, but Alex pulled him back down into his chair.

"He's probably got better things to do. Thanks for coming, Derrek."

Chet gave him a quick hug. "See you soon, sweetie."

"Thanks for an *interesting* evening." One day, Ryan would see Alex for what he was. He had to, right?

Derrek let the gate slam behind him.

Ryan stood outside of Derrek's apartment building. It was a warm early December evening, and cars sped by on their way home from work.

Not seeing Derrek was killing him. Not being able to talk with him, not hearing from him by text or email... he'd always been able to blow off steam with Derrek, to use him as a sounding board. Derrek had been his best friend, ever since they'd met in that bleak moment of his life just after David had died.

Derrek and Alex just didn't mix.

Over the last week, ever since Thanksgiving, really, Derrek hadn't returned his calls.

Ryan had tried to give him space. Really, he had. He'd kept himself busy around the house, and then at work, managing to only glance at his phone once an hour. Okay, maybe once every fifteen minutes.

Now he *really* needed to talk with Derrek. He needed his friend back.

Whatever was going on with Derrek, Ryan had to fix it.

The doorbell rang.

Derrek sighed, putting *Ally McBeal* on pause. He'd found it on Hulu, and had been binge-watching the show all week—it helped to keep his mind off his mother, and off Ryan. He'd spent his evenings curled up on his couch in his pajamas.

Work had been boring as hell—his career at the Everyday Grind was a dead-end—and he'd been hoping to just zone out after he'd finished a couple hours of writing.

Tonight was supposed to be his.

Derrek padded to the entryway, humming "I Only Want to Be With You." He peered out at the hallway of his old apartment building. "Oh shit." He flattened his back to the door with a thump, hoping Ryan hadn't seen the darkening of the peephole as he'd looked through, or the shadow of his feet under the door.

He'd been happy with his decision to take himself out of the middle of Ryan and Alex's dysfunctional relationship. His life was simpler, and that was good, right?

"I know you're in there. I can hear you breathing."

Stupid fucking thin doors. He *hated* living in an apartment. "Just a sec," he called. "I'm... I'm naked here." He was *not* going to let Ryan Kessler see him in his Superman pajamas.

"Take your time. It's not like I haven't seen it before." He sounded upset.

Yeah, at the gym, maybe. Derrek raced to his bedroom, pulled off the pajamas and stuffed them into his hamper. He pulled out a pair of jeans, the one he'd worn to the Farmer's Market that morning. They smelled wearable. A bright orange t-shirt from the closet completed the ensemble. It said "yeah, I'm gay, but I'm enjoying a quiet evening at home with Calista Flockhart." Or something like that. *Gotta let my flame burn bright.*

He opened the door to let Ryan in.

"Hey, sport." His friend smirked. "Been out hunting?"

Derrek looked down to see Pikachu grinning up at him. "I... sorry. It's laundry day."

"Fair enough." Ryan brushed by him into the apartment.

He'd been working out. He smelled really good, his musk an incredible aphrodisiac. Derrek closed his eyes. *Stop it. He's taken.*

Unlike Ryan, Derrek wasn't one of those guys who could pass for straight. He was defiantly, obviously gay. Even when he tried to turn it down low, little bursts of the rainbow invariably slipped out between his teeth.

"Sorry to bother you... were you going out?"

Derrek shook his head. "Hardly. I was planning a bit of a night in."

"Ah. A porncation, huh?"

"Um... *Ally McBeal*, actually."

"They made a porno out of that?" Ryan grinned, and Derrek felt warm all over.

"No. The TV series. Dancing baby, Oogachaka, fresh bowl. I used to watch it with mom and my sister when I was a kid."

"Ah, gotcha." He rubbed his eyes. "I'm sorry to barge in. You just took off last week at Thanksgiving—"

"I'm sorry. I didn't want to stick around to see the way Alex treats you."

"Well, crap." Ryan sat down on Derrek's red leather couch, slipping off his shoes and sinking his toes into Derrek's white alpaca rug.

"What's up?" Ryan always came to him when he needed someone to confide in, a shoulder to cry on. Sometimes Derrek wondered how Ryan could share all these intimate things with him, and then go back to his boyfriend afterward—especially when that boyfriend was Alex. It was kinda fucked up.

Ryan sighed. "It's Alex. He did it again."

"Did what? Hey, can I get you a beer?" Derrek was more of a

wine kind of guy, but he kept a case of Modelo Especial on hand at all times for Ryan. Just in case.

"Sure."

"Keep talking." Derrek went into the kitchen to grab a couple beers.

"He didn't come home last night. You know, the usual shit. 'My cell phone died.' 'I got stuck at the office.' 'I got pulled over and they arrested me for possession and I got thrown in jail.'"

Derrek handed him a beer. "What was it this time?"

"The last one. Only he couldn't show me any kind of ticket or paperwork." He sipped on the beer. "I made him give me his cell phone, and some other guy's been texting him all morning."

Why do you stay with him? Derrek would never say that out loud. "That doesn't sound good."

"I know, right?" Ryan took another sip. "I ran out and went to Mo's."

"To get drunk?"

Ryan nodded. "I only had one beer. I just sat there, looking at all the guys, and wondering... 'Was it you? Were *you* the one who fucked my boyfriend?' And I just kept getting more sadder..."

"Sadder."

"What?"

"It's just 'sadder,' not 'more sadder.'" *The curse of being a writer.* "Sorry, it doesn't matter. Go on."

"Yeah. Sadder. I just..." He stopped, and downed the last of his beer, and set the bottle down on Derrek's coffee table.

Derrek discretely slipped a rainbow coaster under it. "You just what?" God, Ryan was beautiful, sitting there on Derrek's couch arms with his legs spread out. Like Derrek's own personal God. *If only he were here for* me.

Ryan shrugged. "I just wish I could find a guy who wasn't such a complete asshole, you know?"

Bingo. Derrek's heart beat a little faster, but he kept his calm. "You really know how to pick 'em."

"Geez, I guess." He leaned forward and put his elbows on his knees and his hands on his chin. "I just... it shouldn't be like this."

"No. It shouldn't. The way Alex treats you—"

"Do you ever think about Will?"

That caught him by surprise. Derrek glanced over at the picture of the two of them, that last Christmas before Will had died. He'd already started to lose weight then, as the chemo had taken its toll. "Every day."

"Was he *good* to you?"

"Yeah, he was." Derrek hugged himself tight, remembering what it had felt like to be in Will's arms. "He was there whenever I needed him. Even when he was sick, he would always ask me if *I* was okay."

"I wish I could have met him." Ryan got up and started to pace. "David was like that too. The night of the accident, he told the paramedics to check me first. He was bleeding inside, but he was more worried about me..." He stopped, covering his mouth with his hand. "God, I wish I'd known." Ryan sank down on the couch next to him.

Ryan's cologne was subtle, but it worked its magic on Derrek.

"Can I stay here for the night? I could take the couch." His eyes were wet. "I *really* don't want to see Alex right now."

"Sure." The thought of Ryan sleeping over made Derrek's heart almost stop. *Shake it off, Derrek. Shake it off.*

"That's great. Thanks." Ryan kissed his cheek, then stretched his arms and yawned. "Would you mind if I crash now? I was up all night last night, waiting for Alex to get home."

"Sure. Let me get you a pillow and a blanket." Derrek pulled out one of the quilts from the hall linen closet. He'd bought it at his mother's church—it was one of the ones the women there prayed over after they finished it. Mostly he'd liked it for the mix of pinks and purples in the fabric.

Then he grabbed a pillow and pillowcase. "I don't know why you stay with him. There are so many other guys who—"

A long snore stopped him. Ryan was already fast asleep.

Derrek put the pillowcase on and lifted up Ryan's head, laying it gently back down on the pillow. Then he covered Ryan with the blanket. "Good night, my sweet prince."

He kissed Ryan on the forehead.

Ryan stirred but didn't wake.

They could talk more about it in the morning. Maybe he could get Ryan to see what an ass Alex really was. How much Ryan deserved to have something better. Someone better.

Derrek took a cold shower and went to bed to read for a while. About half past eleven, he finally drifted off into a restless sleep.

When he got up the next morning, Ryan was gone. In his place on the couch, Derrek found a note:

Thanks so much for last night's talk. Alex called. I'm going home.

Ryan filed his last report for the day and shut down his computer.

It was half past seven. He'd found himself staying at work later and later—ostensibly because of his heavy workload. But in reality, he was avoiding Alex.

Alex, who had apologized up and down for his latest affair. Alex, who had promised to never let it happen again.

Ryan *wanted* to believe him. Alex was a good guy. Ryan saw things about him that no one else did, in their quiet moments together. And yeah, maybe he had a point, that gay guys *were* different from heterosexuals. That it was harder for them to be faithful.

It was that last part that really gave Ryan a heartache.

He sighed, leaning back in his chair with his arms behind his neck.

Alex had *sounded* sincere.

Ryan wanted to believe that he could change. That Alex could be the kind of guy he longed for. Someone like David.

Since that last visit, he and Derrek had kept up their communication, mostly by text.

Their exchanges had been casual. Talk about the weather. About holiday plans. About how bad traffic was on the Five.

Ryan sighed.

It was time to go home. If they could just make it through

Christmas—one more week—maybe some of the pressure of the holidays would be off, and they could figure out a way forward.

He grabbed his jacket and headed out of the office.

Just one more week.

Derrek lit his apple cinnamon candle and placed it on the fireplace mantel. Two more days until his first Christmas without his mom.

He closed his eyes and said a little prayer to her, wherever she might be.

He and Ryan had settled firmly into the friend zone. Bit by bit, Derrek was accepting that he and Ryan would never be a *thing*. They mostly texted these days, and Derrek was okay with that. It gave him a little needed distance.

He bit his tongue whenever Ryan mentioned Alex, who was either the best thing ever or the devil incarnate.

Derrek even started to enjoy their regular text exchanges, looking forward to when his phone broke out into "I Only Want to Be With You"—getting his little fix of Ryan.

Then, a week before Christmas, all communications had ceased.

It was probably for the best.

He headed to bed, determined to forget all about his handsome, unattainable friend.

Knock knock knock.

Derrek looked up from his pillow, confused. He glared blearily at the alarm clock. It flashed 2:23 AM.

It took a minute for things to percolate in his brain. Someone was pounding on his front door. Who in the *flaming balls* was banging on his door in the early morning on Christmas Eve?

Bam bam bam.

Cursing under his breath, Derrek got out of bed and pulled on his silk robe, lashing it around his waist. "I'm coming!" Mrs. Foster was going to give him hell in the morning for all the noise.

He peered through the peephole. It was Ryan.

Derrek opened the door and ushered him inside, looking down the hall to see if anyone else had noticed. There was no one in sight —he was in the clear.

Ryan was a bit tipsy. He also had a suitcase with him.

"Oh hell." He maneuvered Ryan over to the couch and took the suitcase away.

Derrek's phone rang. "Hello?"

"What the hell is going on over there?" a woman's voice demanded, scratchy with a couple hundred years of cigarette smoke. He pictured his neighbor in her fluffy slippers with her gray hair up in big pink curlers and a snarl on her face.

"Sorry, Mrs. Foster. I was just moving some boxes and dropped a couple on the hardwood floor."

"In the middle of the night?" She sounded suspicious.

"I know, I know. I'm sorry. Won't happen again." He hung up, concerned that Ryan might start making more noise if he wasn't supervised.

Ryan looked up at him, his eyes bloodshot. "Hey."

"What happened?" Derrek sank down into his leather armchair.

Ryan paused, as if he had to really think about it. "He left me again. I think for good."

"Why?" Not that Alex needed a reason. He was a fucking asshole.

"He read my texts. With you."

"Ah."

Ryan was clearly too drunk to have this conversation in a reasonable way. "Let's get you to bed. We can talk more in the morning."

"Okay. I'm just so sad. Sadder. More sadder. You know?"

"Yeah. I know. Let's get those shoes off." As he unlaced Ryan's topsiders, he sighed. This was hardly the way he'd imagined undressing his best friend.

"Thanks, Derrek. You're a good guy. You know that?"

Knife to the gut. "Yeah, let's get your shirt and pants off." He unbuttoned Ryan's white shirt, exposing the gorgeous chest underneath. *Why did I think someone like him could ever be interested in me?*

Next came the pants, and of course he was wearing his Under Armor.

Derrek looked away as he levered Ryan up onto the couch. He got out one of his blankets and a pillow, and got Ryan comfortable on the couch.

Ryan whispered something.

"What was that?" Derrek leaned in closer.

"I said, I wish I was with you instead." Then he closed his eyes and fell asleep. Soon he was snoring loudly.

Those were the words he'd longed to hear, but not when Ryan was stone drunk.

Derrek stared down at his friend, thinking how familiar this scene was.

One day, maybe you'll figure out that he's no good for you. When you're sober.

Derrek awoke to the smell of scrambled eggs and bacon.

He sat up in bed, confused—his fridge was basically empty. He'd been planning a Trader Joe's run the day after Christmas.

Pulling on his jeans and a rainbow tie-dyed t-shirt, he padded out into his living room.

"Hey, sport!" Ryan grinned at him from the kitchen, where he was stirring something in a skillet on the stove. "Thanks for taking care of me last night."

"Eggs," Derrek said. By which he meant "Where did you get the eggs? I didn't have any in the fridge."

"Oh, I went to the little corner store. They're really nice."

"Coffee."

"Take a seat, and I'll bring you some."

He speaks Morning Derrek.

Ryan set the skillet off to the side and came around the island to bring him a steaming cup of *awake.*

Derrek took it and sipped at it gratefully. "Thanks."

"And here are some eggs to go with it." Ryan slid a plate of fluffy yellow happiness filled with bits of bacon in front of Derrek.

"Oh my God, this looks heavenly." Derrek breathed in the *eggy cheddary bacony* goodness.

"It speaks in full sentences!" Ryan smiled weakly, sliding into the chair across the table from him.

"Yeah, it takes me a while to become *me* in the mornings." The coffee was perking him up quickly. "I could get used to this, you know."

"You're welcome." Ryan grinned. "Merry Christmas Eve."

They ate mostly in silence. Ryan looked lost in thought, picking at his plate.

Derrek wanted to give him some space. He really *could* get used to this, he decided. Maybe things were shifting between them. "Hey, wanna hang out today? I don't really have any plans. We could talk."

Ryan shook his head. "Sorry, can't."

"I can come with you to Alex's place to get your things, if you want." Derrek had planned to go to his sister's house for dinner, but he could always bail for a good cause.

Ryan stared at him for a minute, then shook his head. "Probably a bad idea. I'm going to go see Alex. Maybe we can work this thing out."

"Unfuckingbelievable." Derrek shoved his chair backward and shook the table, spilling his coffee all over the surface and Ryan's shirt.

"What the hell's wrong with you?" Ryan grabbed a napkin and started wiping his white shirt furiously.

"Are you fucking serious?" *How can you go back to Alex again? What was it going to take to open Ryan's eyes?*

"Serious about what?" Ryan pulled off his shirt and went to rinse it under the sink.

Derrek ignored his perfect chest. *"This guy—"*

"Alex."

"*Alex.*" God, he hated saying that name. "He walks all over you. He cheats on you. He treats you like *shit*. And you just keep on fucking taking it." Derrek's vision was red with rage.

"It's not all his fault. There's trouble in every relationship."

"Don't." Derrek's voice came out ice cold.

"Don't *what?*" Ryan stared at him across the kitchen island.

"Don't give me that bullshit. There's trouble, and there's *trouble.* Alex is capital T *Trouble.*" He'd known it since the day they'd met at Ryan's party, the year before.

"I need to try to work things out—"

Derrek was sick of it. Sick of the back and forth. Sick of being Ryan's go-to shoulder to cry on. "Do whatever the hell you want. Just don't expect me to be here to talk you down the next time he walks out on you, or tells you what a worthless piece of shit you are."

"God, Derrek. You're so... so—"

"So what?"

"So goddamned *naive.* You think *everyone* deserves true love. The perfect relationship. Sometimes we have to work at it. Sometimes it's difficult."

"I had it." Derrek's vision blurred. "I had it with Will, and I still miss him so damn much."

"Five fucking years later, and you still wear his ring." Ryan glared at him. "I had it with David, too. But he's gone. Will and David are both *gone.*"

Derrek gritted his teeth. "Yes, they are. And maybe I *am* naive. But I haven't given up hope."

"Well, good for you."

"You're fucking *blind,* Ryan. You can't see how much you're really worth." Derrek grabbed his dishes, including the overturned coffee cup, and threw them in the sink. Then he stormed back into his bedroom and slammed the door.

A few minutes later, he heard the front door bang shut.

Derrek threw his keys down on the table in the entryway.

His sister Lilah had been concerned for him. She had her husband Brian and her two kids to get her through the holidays, now that Mom was gone. "You're all alone," she'd said, wrapping him in her shawl and patchouli musk. "You need someone in your life."

She was right. He *hated* being alone during the Christmas season.

Derrek went to the kitchen and poured himself a glass of white wine.

He'd never been good at doing the whole bar scene. White guys there always asked him how long his cock was. Like *that* stereotype was always true. And he had always had a hard time approaching guys he liked, no matter their color.

Will had been special. Will had come looking for *him*.

They'd met on the beach at Coronado. Derrek's dark skin had been smothered under three layers of sunblock, protected by a towel and a huge rainbow beach umbrella, wearing sunglasses big enough to make Elton John jealous. He was kind of anal about the whole *avoiding the sun* thing.

Will had been playing volleyball with some friends.

The ball had flown into Derrek's lap and Will had followed it there, flashing him the biggest smile when he'd handed the ball back sheepishly. *And the rest, as they say, was history.*

Derrek carried the glass into the bedroom and set it down on his nightstand.

He rummaged through his closet, finding the old Nike shoebox where he'd saved his most precious possessions. He set the box on the bed and stared at it for a long moment, taking another swig of his wine. Then, like ripping off a Band-Aid, he pulled off the lid.

The ring box was on top.

Derrek opened it. Inside was a white gold band matched to the one that he still wore on his ring finger. They'd bought them to celebrate their wedding, back in 2008. He and Will had been just twenty-three, but they'd known even then that they'd spend a lifetime together. *How wrong we were.*

He closed the lid gently, and set the ring box aside.

Next was one of Will's shirts. It was an old t-shirt, tattered at the edges that he used to wear to the gym. Derrek pulled it up to his face and inhaled deeply. God, how he missed Will's scent.

Next, a photo of Will in Junior High.

Will had given it to him for his birthday, after a particularly nasty fit of self-doubt and recrimination, brought on by an encounter with Derrek's father early on in their relationship. Derrek's dad had accused him of being a "pansy-ass faggot."

"God, I wish I was more like you," Derrek had said in the car on the way home from his parents' house.

"What do you mean?" Will's luminous brown eyes had warmed his heart, taking away some of the sting of the night.

"Maybe if I was more athletic. More masculine. More... manly. Maybe he would accept me."

"Ah."

Derrek had glared at him. "What do you mean, 'ah'?"

Will grinned. "I wasn't always an all-American boy, you know."

"Yeah?"

"Yeah. I had glasses and braces and a bad case of acne until sophomore year." He laughed. "I was a total geek."

Derrek snorted. "I'd like to see that."

"I'll show you when we get home."

Now Derrek stared down at the old tattered photo of Will's teenaged face, and wished for the hundredth or maybe thousandth time that Will could be with him again. *If you were here, you'd tell me I'm a freakin' idiot for waiting around.*

Will would want him to be with someone again.

He pulled the ring off his finger, staring at it. No matter what happened, he would always have his memories of that day, on the beach at Coronado, when they'd made it official between them.

He kissed the photo, and put it back in the box.

Then he set his ring inside the ring box with Will's, and put the whole thing away in his closet.

So what if things hadn't worked out with Ryan? There was *someone* out there for him. Will would make sure of that, wherever he was.

Derrek lay on his sofa in his pajamas, staring at the shifting lights on his Christmas tree for a couple hours, until he finally fell asleep.

Derrek was tired of being sad.

He was tired of sitting at home, crying over his mother's death.

He was tired of mooning over a guy he could never have.

It's Christmas Day, for God's sake. He'd read in the paper about an outdoor ice-skating rink at the Hotel del Coronado—and he figured it was a good way to get into the holiday spirit.

Will had always loved Coronado.

Derrek pulled out one of his mother's knitted scarves that he hardly ever got to wear in warm and sunny San Diego, and hopped on a bus for the ride over to Coronado. It was filled with people in holiday clothing, the bus driver smiled at him and wished him a Merry Christmas, and a couple grandmothers in bright red Rudolph sweaters waved at him and giggled.

A group in the back of the bus started up a round of Christmas carols, working their way from "Frosty the Snowman" to "Good King Wenceslas".

Derrek shrugged. *What the hell.* He joined in, and it lasted all the way to his stop outside the hotel. Derek grinned at all the good cheer.

When the bus pulled up in front of the del Coronado, he disembarked, feeling a whole lot better. About himself. About his life. About Christmas.

He walked through the hotel lobby and down the long hallway to the seaside of the hotel, past the toy store and the other expensive boutique shops.

There it was. An impossibility—a wide swath of ice sparkling under the Southern California sun, looking out over the warm blue waters of the Pacific.

Will would have *loved* this.

Derrek rented a pair of skates, and soon he was gliding around the rink, his troubles forgotten, weaving in and out of the couples who skated slowly together hand in hand. His mother used to take him skating on Christmas Day—they'd get a hot chocolate, lace on their shoes, and then glide around the rink together while his sister, who hated ice-skating, sat on the sidelines and scowled.

For the first time since the funeral, he remembered his mother with joy instead of sadness.

The sun shone down on the improbable scene, making up for the chill of the ice beneath his skates. It was a beautiful day.

As afternoon edged into evening, Derrek turned in his skates and got back on the bus, glancing back at the hotel as it disappeared around the bend. *Thanks, Mom. Thank you, Will, for a perfect day.*

Ryan sat on the bench in Balboa Park, staring up at the park's iconic pink tower. His mind was in turmoil.

He'd crashed in a hotel room the night before, crushed by what Derrek had said to him. Derrek, the one guy in the whole world who really *knew* him, who always listened to him when he needed to talk, who was the true constant in his life.

At first, he'd been really pissed at Derrek for not telling him how he felt. Surely it would have been better to have it all out in the open between them. They had always told each other everything before, hadn't they?

Then it had hit him. Derrek hated Alex, but he'd been trying to support Ryan all this time.

Because Derrek had feelings for him. *He loves me.*

The realization shook Ryan to his core. *Jesus, I'm a fucking idiot.* He'd never imagined someone like Derrek could love someone like him. Someone so beautiful and intelligent and classy. Someone with such warmth and love in his heart. A writer with a poet's soul. *I don't deserve him.*

Ryan knew well enough what he was—a good-looking guy with nothing much else to offer. In fifteen years, he'd be a middle-aged desk jockey with receding hair who'd be lucky if he had anyone to come home to at night.

Derrek loves *me.*

Ryan sat there for the rest of the afternoon, trying to figure out what to do.

You can't see how much you're really worth.

Derrek was right. Derrek *saw* him in a way that Alex never had. *Why do I give Alex this power over me?*

Ryan took a deep breath. It was time for that to change. David would want him to stand up for himself. *I deserve better.*

But with Derrek... it was complicated. What if they tried to be together and it didn't work out? Would he lose his best friend forever?

In the end, as the sun set on Christmas afternoon, he made up his mind. He wasn't sure it was the right choice, but if not, he'd figure out a way to live with the consequences.

He got up off the bench and set off to find Alex.

The bus was mostly empty, and the ride home was much quieter. Derrek stared out at the bay as they crossed over the Coronado Bridge, high above the water. The sun was setting, and it blazed a fiery path across the water. The light winked out as they descended into the city streets of San Diego.

In half an hour, he arrived at his home stop.

The street was dark, lanterns casting pools of light every twenty feet. He trudged back up the hill to his apartment building, his hands in his pockets. It was a cool fifty-five degrees out, practically arctic weather by San Diego standards. He shivered.

As he rounded the corner, he saw someone sitting on the stoop of his building. He squinted. "Ryan?"

His friend stood, his face carefully neutral, his hands in his pockets. "Hey, Derr."

"Hey."

They faced each other, a good ten feet between them, in the dim light of the street lamps and apartment windows.

"That was quite an explosion yesterday," Ryan said at last.

Derrek blushed. "I know." He sighed. "Look, I'm sorry. I was just upset about everything and it came out—"

Ryan shook his head. "No, I'm glad you said it. I wish you'd told me a long time ago."

Derrek frowned. "You are?" *What's happening here?*

Ryan took a tentative step toward him. "Yeah. You were right, and I am fucking blind." He took a deep breath. "I have to ask you something."

Here it comes. He's gonna ask me how the hell I thought I could have a chance with someone like him. "Go ahead."

"You like me, don't you?" He looked anxious.

Derrek laughed. "Of course I do. We're friends."

"No. I mean you... *like* me. Right?" He looked more nervous than Derrek had ever seen him. The words hung in the air between them for a long moment.

"Yes." This time Derrek took a step forward. "I have since... well, since I met you. But it seemed so inappropriate. Will had just died. And you—"

"Yeah. I'd just lost David too."

Derrek took a deep breath. "Okay. So... you're here because?" Maybe Ryan was finally ready to leave Alex. Maybe Derrek's Christmas wish would come true. *Yeah, and maybe Santa Claus left me a million dollars in my stocking last night.*

Derrek held out his hands. "I wanted to explain. And apologize."

Of course. Ryan was always the gallant one. Derrek felt like he'd just been socked in the gut. "Oh. Okay. Well, that's very kind of you. I hope you have a nice rest of your Christmas evening." Derrek just wanted to get away from Ryan, lock the door behind him. He brushed past Ryan, but the man took his arm.

"Wait. Please." Ryan's voice cracked.

"What?"

"I'm sorry. That came out wrong."

Their noses were inches apart, Ryan's eyes searching his. "Explain." Derrek's hands twitched.

"You asked me why I stayed with Alex." He took Derrek's hand. "This is hard for me."

Derrek squeezed his hand. "You can tell me anything."

"When I was in high school, I was a total geek. Glasses, acne, skinny as a rail."

"But... you're gorgeous."

Ryan laughed. "Thanks. That means a lot, coming from you." Then his look turned serious again. "The kids on the football team used to beat the crap out of me every day, calling me *faggot* and worse."

Derrek stared at him. "Holy shit."

"It was years before I *started* to feel good about myself again. I started working out. I didn't want to let them do that to me anymore. And in senior year I beat the crap out of the Captain of the football team when he tried pulling his shit on me."

"You never told me."

"I was embarrassed. I thought you'd think less of me. That you'd see me... like they saw me. As a silly weak little faggot." He looked away. "I never really told anyone."

"Jesus. You're one of the best, most amazing guys I've ever known." Derrek couldn't believe what he was hearing.

Ryan looked down at the ground. "Thanks." When he looked back up at Derrek, his stare was intense. "The thing is, it never even occurred to me that *you* were interested in *me*. That you could be, I mean. That I was *worthy* of your interest."

Derrek laughed. "Holy shit, of course you are. And of course I am. How can't you see that?"

Ryan sighed. "When Alex treated me like shit, I felt like I deserved it."

"Past tense?" Derrek held his breath.

Ryan nodded. "I took a long time to think things over today. Then I went to see him. He said he wanted to see me, to patch things up."

Derrek's heart stopped. "What did you say?"

Ryan grinned. "I told him to go to hell."

Derrek laughed, a deep, satisfying sound. "Holy crap, you

didn't." His heart started again, and quickly made up for lost time. "What did he say?"

"I didn't wait to hear." Ryan ran his hand along Derrek's cheek, his look tender. "I was an idiot, but now I've figured it all out." He stared into Derrek's eyes. "I only want to be with you."

"Are you sure? What if—"

Ryan shut him up with a kiss.

Derrek finally let himself surrender. He kissed Ryan back hungrily, surreptitiously pinching himself to be sure he wasn't dreaming. He'd waited five years for this moment, and now he wanted to live in it forever.

Their heartbeats merged, their fingers intertwined, and his nerve stiffened. And that wasn't all.

When they parted, Ryan laid a hand on his cheek. "Merry Christmas, Derrek."

"Merry Christmas." Derrek leaned forward and whispered, "Do you want to come up?" in his best husky voice.

Ryan grinned. "I thought you'd never ask."

I wrote this one in response to a call for submissions from Mischief Corner Books for queer holiday stories. In addition to the Vonda Sheppard tune from Ally McBeal, it was inspired by a line in Vanessa William's song Save the Best for Last, which for copyright purposes I won't quote directly, but which basically said "Why are you being such an idiot with that guy while telling me about all of your hopes and dreams?" MCB published it, and earlier this year I got the rights back, giving me the chance to share it all over again with you, my favorite readers.

THE BOY IN THE BAND

Prologue

RYAN SWUNG the door to the roof of the Bank of America building open, his hand going reflexively to his back pocket to pull out his cigarettes and the lighter he'd slipped into the pack. His husband Andy *hated* that he smoked, but it had been a difficult year, capped by the death of his father after a long fight with lung cancer.

He was well aware of the irony.

He liked to come up to the rooftop for a quick smoke at lunchtime. It was the second-tallest skyscraper in Tucson, with panoramic views of "A" Mountain and the Santa Catalina, Rincon and Santa Rita Mountains. He worked on the fourteenth floor as an accountant, a thankless job in a viewless cubicle. Up here, for a few moments, he was free.

Today however, he wasn't alone. Someone was standing on the ledge of the building, looking down at Stone Avenue sixteen stories below.

He slipped the cigarette pack back into his pocket. "Hey there," he said gently, afraid to startle the person. It was a young man... maybe fifteen? Sixteen? A teenager, at any rate.

The boy glanced back at him over his shoulder, and then turned back to look at the ground far below once again.

Ryan thought about going to get help—a cop? His boss? But he was afraid the boy might jump before Ryan came back with help.

Engage him.

That's what they always did on TV, right? They talked the guy down off the ledge. Ryan had always wanted to be a cop, to help people, but he'd never gotten up the guts to go for it. Now was his chance.

"Nice day." He edged a little closer. "You come up here often?" He needed to keep the boy's attention, to get him to think about something, anything besides jumping.

"I've seen better." The boy glanced back at him again, frowning, then looked away. He was blond, with startlingly blue eyes.

Ryan nodded. "I can see that." He took another small step toward the stranger. "Look, I'm not a counselor or anything. But you wanna talk about it? I *am* a good listener."

The boy shook his head. "Nothing much to talk about. And don't come any closer."

Kid's on a rooftop, ready to jump, and there's nothing to talk about? "Look, can I be honest with you?"

The boy shrugged. "Sure."

"I'm Ryan. I just came up here for a quick smoke. And you... what's your name?"

The boy didn't respond.

"Okay. I'm guessing you're here for something a little more... permanent. Am I right?"

The kid snorted. "You're a fucking genius."

Ryan grinned in spite of himself. "Not really. Just an accountant. But here's what I'm thinking. Once you jump, it's over, right?"

The boy's shoulders stiffened, and Ryan was afraid he was going to leap off the roof right then and there. His stomach twisted in fear and he gathered himself to leap after the boy, to try to grab him by his grey hoodie.

Then the boy's shoulders slumped. "I guess."

Ryan released his breath in a huff. "Good, we agree on that, at least." He tried to remember how they did this in the movies, but memory failed him. He was on his own here. "Okay, here's what I suggest. I've got some time to kill." He winced at the unfortunate choice of words. "Once you make that jump, your time is up. So what if you come down from there, and we talk a bit?"

"There's nothing left to talk about."

"Bullshit. Something brought you up here. Something happened to bring you to this rooftop, to this moment. Look, if we talk and you still want to go through with it, I won't stop you. You can jump, and all you've lost is a few moments of time. Right?"

The boy seemed to consider it. "How do I know you'll keep your word?"

That one stumped Ryan. "You don't," he admitted. "But I can't keep an eye on you every moment of every day. I don't even know your name. So if I stop you this time, you can always try again, some other time." Not that he could live with himself if this kid did something permanent.

"It's Justin."

"What?"

"You asked what my name was. It's Justin."

"Justin. Okay." That was something. "So what do you say?" He held out his hand, painfully aware how out of his depth he was.

Justin stood there for an agonizingly long time, silent, now staring out at the city spread out across the valley instead of at the street below.

Ryan took that as a good sign.

"Okay. I'll talk. But I'm staying up here."

Ryan exhaled and withdrew his hand. "Okay, fair enough." He took a deep breath. *Keep your voice calm.* "Want to tell me what brought you up here?"

Monday

Justin startled awake.

He was sitting on a green bus seat, bouncing up and down as the school bus rattled along the pot-hole filled road. Outside, monsoon clouds threatened rain, with low, rumbling thunder following a fork of lightning that arched across the sky.

He sat up in the middle of a full-fledged food fight as a school of Goldfish flew by overhead, dropping crumbs in their wake, eliciting return fire of a flight of stick pretzels that arched past him like miniature arrows.

The other students were screeching and laughing raucously. Justin closed his eyes, wishing the ride would be over. He just wanted to blend in, to get through the first day of his Junior Year unnoticed.

The bus slammed to a halt, throwing him roughly against the padded seat in front of him.

"I said knock it off, you little rats." The bus driver, Marilyn Manson, was a heavyset woman in her fifties, with deeply carved wrinkles next to her mouth and curly concrete-gray hair. She was every bit as scary as the singer with whom she shared a name—and Justin only knew that because his mother had one of his golden oldie albums.

"Zane Jepsen, back in your seat." Her voice was low and gravelly—from a lifetime of smoking, Justin assumed.

The football player sat down, eyes narrowed.

"And you!"

Justin saw to his terror that she was pointing at him. "Me?" It came out in a weird high-pitched squeak.

The other kids laughed.

"Yes, you. I saw you throw those pretzels. You're coming with me." She grabbed him by the ear and hauled him out of his seat and up the aisle.

The laughter turned into a roar.

Justin blushed. He'd done nothing to deserve this. He'd been asleep. *Whatever.*

He'd hoped his first day back at school would pass unremarkably, that the other kids wouldn't recognize him. After all, he wasn't *Jenny* anymore.

He'd worked hard to change his appearance. The testosterone had deepened his voice a little. He'd cut his hair and dyed it black, and bound up his breasts underneath a black t-shirt. Still the world, in all its twisted so-called wisdom, saw fit to single him out.

The bus driver pushed him into the empty front seat. "Look, you may be new here, but that's no excuse for that kind of behavior. You're on *my* bus. You will sit here quietly and behave yourself until we get to school. *Do you understand?*"

"Yes, ma'am." He tried to lower his voice, but he was only partly successful.

The busload of kids behind him tittered again.

"That's enough from all of you," she said, glaring at them. The laughter quieted to occasional giggles.

Mrs. Manson sat down and started up the bus once again.

Justin sunk down in the seat, hoping the other kids would forget about him. He pulled out his school-issued iPad and stared at the reflection in the black screen.

He wasn't that person anymore, the gender he'd been assigned at birth. Not that he'd ever really felt like *her* to begin with.

It had been hard enough coming out to his mother. She had screamed and slapped him hard across the face, and had refused to talk with him at all for *three whole days*. That was when she'd started drinking again. Not that things had been all that great between them before—she'd been a mean dry drunk.

He pulled out his wallet. "Justin Bailor, Junior, La Cañada High School class of 2021." He'd forged her signature to get the school to change his ID.

The bus pulled into the school parking lot. Justin stared out at the new solar panels they'd installed over the stalls. Looked like he wasn't the only one who'd changed over the summer.

The bus slammed to a halt in front of the school. "Principal's office with you," the driver said, glaring at him.

As he got off the bus, he caught Zane staring at him, a puzzled look on the football captain's face.

Justin looked away quickly.

He stuffed his iPad back into his backpack and rushed out of sight into the admin office, closing the door quickly behind him. He'd never been close to Zane, but Zane had known Jenny, at least a little. *So much for laying low.*

Justin sat in the admin office for ten minutes, a lump in his throat.

"Justin Bailor," a woman called from the Principal's office.

He got up and entered her office, his stomach clenching.

Principal Krebbs was a tall Black woman with close-cropped hair, a neat gray suit, and gold-framed glasses. She stared at him over the top of those frames. "Justin Bailor." She clicked on her mouse, glancing at her computer screen, "Ah, I knew that name sounded familiar. I didn't expect to see you in here. At least not on your first day. Marilyn says you were making trouble on the bus."

"No, ma'am," he said softly. "I was just trying to blend in. I don't know why she—"

She crossed her hands in front of her on her desk. "Look, can I be frank with you?"

He nodded.

"I understand the position you're in, and I promise to do everything I can to help you ease back into school life after your transition, but you're going to have to learn a harsh lesson." She took off her glasses and sat back, appraising him. "As someone who is different, you have to be better than *everyone else.*" She took off her glasses and sat back with a sigh. "I learned it early, as a black woman. You can't give them any reason to come after you, because they will. That means being on your best behavior, all the time."

"I guess so." *Not that I did anything wrong.* Anything at all.

She stared at him for a moment longer, as if weighing his soul. "I don't want any more trouble from you. Are we clear?"

"Yes, perfectly." Justin was proud that he was able to keep his voice from trembling.

"I know it's got to be hard on you, so I'll cut you a little slack. But don't test me. You're still a student, just like every other one of the miscreants in this school."

Justin swallowed hard. "Th… thank you, Ms. Krebbs."

"Here's your schedule." She handed him a sheet of paper. "The teachers have all been advised as well, but per your mother's request, we have not told the other students." She turned back to her screen. "You can go now."

He nodded, and grabbed his backpack and cleared out of the office, hoping no one else would see him leave.

He wished he could stop being trans for one day, and just be Justin.

Ryan sat at the front of the bus, hoping Christian Simms and his friends wouldn't bother him today. Hoping he could get off the bus and run to class before one of them caught him and started pushing him around and calling him names. Queer. Faggot. Little Bitch.

The bus pulled to a halt in front of the school, and he jumped up and hopped down the steps, heading for the sanctuary of Mrs. Devlin's English classroom at a dead run…

It had been like that for almost a year. Until Andy.

Looking at this kid before him now, he had a sudden sense of kinship. Being trans must have been just as hard on Justin as being gay had been for him. Maybe harder.

"High school was the shits for me too." Such a long time ago, but thinking about it again now, it could have been yesterday. "Coming out was hard enough. I can't imagine what it must have been like for you, to transition in high school." He looked at the boy with newfound respect. "And without your mother's support."

Justin nodded. "I don't think I realized how hard it would be."

"I know. I came out in high school, and it was the most difficult thing I ever did, but also the most liberating. It was a long time ago, though."

Justin looked back at him. "You're gay?"

"As a three dollar bill."

"What's that?"

Ryan frowned. "It just means super queer."

"Uh, sure." Justin nodded. "What was it like... way back then?" His voice was low and dull, but Ryan thought he heard a spark of interest.

"Coming out? Almost impossible. I felt like I was the only gay kid in the whole school."

"It's not like that at La Cañada," Justin said with a sigh. "There are a number of gay kids. But I think I'm the only trans one."

Ryan nodded. "I remember that feeling." The kid was awfully close to the drop-off. "Look, you're making me crazy nervous, standing up there. Can I at least convince you to step down off the ledge?" He stepped back a bit. "I'll give you plenty of room."

Justin turned to look at him, and the sadness there ripped at Ryan's gut. At last, Justin nodded. "Okay, but stay back."

"I'm like a statue." He wondered what was going through Justin's head. Things must have gotten really bad for the kid to be up here, considering this. He reached for something, anything to say. What came out had been buried deep for years. Decades, even. "I thought about killing myself, once." He hadn't thought about that year in a long time.

"Yeah?" Justin stepped down from the ledge onto the roof of the building, slumping down into a crouch. with his back to the low wall.

Better. "Yeah. This wrestler named Christian Simms used to taunt me in school, and one day he snuck up behind me and pulled down my pants in front of the whole class. Another time, his friends held me down while they wrote the word 'faggot' across my face in permanent marker."

"Holy shit." Justin looked at Ryan with newfound respect. "What stopped you?"

"Someone convinced me there was still a lot to live for." He sighed, remembering how Andy had talked him down. Not from a literal building, but close enough. "I was lucky. So tell me what happened next. What brought you up on this roof?" He had to keep the kid talking.

Justin looked down at the rooftop and sighed. "The first day of school was bad enough. Tuesday was much worse…"

Tuesday

29... 14... 36.

Justin turned the combination lock, to the right, back past the first number to the left, and back to the right to the third one. It clicked open. He pulled out his lunch bag and looked inside—there was a peanut butter and jelly sandwich and a Ziplock bag full of potato chips.

He took out the sandwich and sighed. His mother had forgotten the jelly again. She'd been on one of her benders the night before, already hungover when he got up, laying on the couch with her eyes glazed over. It was a wonder she'd managed to get out of bed to get him out the door that morning.

He shrugged. *I'll make do.* That seemed to be his life motto these days.

He left it inside his locker and closed the door, and looked around.

The hallway traffic had thinned out, but a few kids were still passing by, mostly ignoring him. No one seemed to have recognized him. Yet.

Two more fucking years. He could do two more years. Then he could get a job and pay for his surgeries and get away from all of these ignorant assholes.

He had to piss before he went to his Trigonometry class. He glanced uneasily at the boy's restroom.

Zane and his henchmen Chet and Brian stood by the bathroom door, talking and laughing raucously. As Justin watched, Brian said something stupid—poor guy had never managed more than a C-minus average—and Zane punched him hard in the shoulder. It was so... law of the jungle. They were the big ugly apes, fists scraping the ground when they weren't pounding their hairy chests.

They might as well have been a different species.

He could wait. Thank God Zane wasn't in his Trig class.

Justin found his way to the classroom and took a seat at the back of the room, where he was less likely to be noticed. He was glad his trip to the Principal's office hadn't made him late for class. The less attention he drew, the better.

He'd spent most of the summer since he'd started on testosterone practicing being a regular guy. Watching TikTok videos about how to walk like one, talk like one, even growling like a gorilla and scratching his crotch, like Zane and his friends.

He scowled a lot too. He wasn't sure, exactly, what else cis guys did to look like guys, but they did scowl. All the time.

The T had lowered his voice, a little, but it sounded more like a gay guy's voice than John Hamm's. He was still waiting for his facial hair to start coming in, but many of his cis peers weren't shaving yet, either, so he figured he was okay on that count.

"Okay, we're gonna do roll call," Mr. Jones said, clearing his throat. "Everyone sit down please."

There was some mumbling, but soon everyone was seated.

"Damon Aquila."

"Here."

"Molly Ashton."

"Here."

"Jonathan Avila."

When his name came up, Justin lowered his voice a little. "Here." No one seemed to notice.

Once everyone was accounted for, the teacher turned on the smart board. "Please get out your iPads."

Justin took out his tablet and took notes as Mr. Jones laid out the course study plan for the year.

He waited as long as he could, but he really had to go. When he couldn't stand it any longer, he raised his hand.

"Yes, Justin?"

"I need to use the restroom." He tried not to fidget. "Can I be excused?"

Mr. Jones nodded. "This once. But next time, make sure you use the bathroom during class breaks."

Justin nodded. "Thank you." He slipped out of the room, aware that the whole class was watching him. *Way to be inconspicuous, idiot.*

He ran down the hallway to the bathroom. Luckily for him, it was deserted this time.

He went into one of the stalls, and closed the door behind him. He'd ordered a Stand To Pee packer to use at the urinal, so he wouldn't have to sit in one of the stalls like a girl. He'd found it on Amazon using his mother's account—that was going to be fun to try to explain to her—but the package had gotten lost somewhere around Denver and hadn't made it in time for school.

He was just starting to feel relief when the bathroom door burst open and someone came in. Three someones.

"I fucking hate math."

Justin knew that voice. It was Brian Timmins.

"It's all just bullshit today anyhow." Justin heard the sound of a lighter, and then the smell of cigarette smoke filled the room.

He had to get back to class, or Mr. Jones would send him to the principal's office again, this time for skipping. But he didn't want to deal with three football players, especially not alone, and in the boys' restroom.

So he lifted his feet quietly off the floor and waited.

"My dad got sent off on another tour." Zane spat. "My mom had a fit when she found out."

"Crap, man, that sucks." Brian's voice sounded different. Like he actually gave a shit. "How many is that now?"

"Four so far. My mom wants him home, but I think he hates it here with us."

"You gonna join up when you get out of this place?"

"Hell, I don't know." Zane was quiet for a moment, and the sound of water splashing in the sink filled the room. "My mom would be fucking pissed, but she's always telling me I don't have any skills or any common sense. At least in the Army you get to go places. They pay you decent and shit, and you don't owe anyone."

Justin couldn't afford to wait any longer. He flushed the toilet and hurried out, washing his hands.

"Hey, new kid," Zane said, sizing him up. "You look familiar. Do I know you?"

Justin shook his head. "I don't think so." He dried his hands and rushed out, aware of Zane's eyes boring into his back. He hurried back to his trig class.

"Nice of you to rejoin us, Mister Bailor," his teacher said when he slid back into his desk chair.

"Sorry, the bathroom down the hall was closed. I had to go to another one."

Mr. Jones studied him for a moment over the rims of his glasses, but then shrugged and let it go. "For the second semester, we'll be starting with chapter 12..."

Justin was starving. He grabbed his lunch from the locker, and made his way to the snack bar to get a soda. There was already a long line—he'd be better off trying the vending machine in the cafeteria.

He turned and ran right into someone, spilling the guy's Pepsi all over his new shirt. "Shit! I'm so sorry." He knelt to pick up the cup.

Other kids were laughing around him. Justin was sure it was directed at him. He seemed to be the butt of all the school jokes today.

"Hey, you okay?" The guy he'd bumped into was kneeling beside him, picking up his lunch bag to hand it back to him. He was cute, with short dark hair, big brown eyes, and a handsome but totally-not-gorilla-like face.

"I'm sorry about that. It was my fault." He held out his hand with a grin. "Noah Wiseman," he said with a broad smile.

Justin grinned back, forgetting for a moment all the shitty things that had happened so far that day, and that his shirt was soaking wet. "I'm Ju-Justin. You're tall."

Noah nodded, laughing. "Yes. Yes I am, JuJustin." He helped Justin up to his feet.

"It's just Justin." *God, I'm such an idiot.* His face was burning.

Noah grinned again. "Nice to meet you. Are you new here too? You look a little overwhelmed."

"Um, kind of? Yeah? No?" Justin didn't quite know how to answer that one.

Noah laughed. "Well, okay then. I am. I just moved to Tucson from San Diego."

"Well... welcome."

Noah smirked. "Thanks. See you around." He waved and disappeared into the crowd.

Justin watched him go, wishing he'd said something less stupid. *'You're tall?' Really?*

Then he surveyed the damage. His shirt was soaked with Pepsi —he'd have to go rinse it off in the bathroom, in the middle of lunch.

Fuck.

Maybe he could use the one in the P.E. changing room. It should be empty over lunchtime.

The area in front of the gym was empty. Justin ducked inside and opened the door to the changing room. "Hello?"

No one answered—he was all alone. He was so glad there was no Physical Education requirement for juniors. He slipped into the locker room and headed for the showers. He set his lunch down on the closest bench and pulled off his shirt.

His breasts were bound tightly underneath—and his chest binder was soaked. He frowned at his breasts, wishing for the ten thousandth time they weren't there. He'd clean the binder when he got home.

Peeking once more around the corner into the locker room to be sure he was still alone, he turned on the faucet and washed his shirt. Then he grabbed a clean towel to dry it off as best he could. At least he'd gotten the worst of the soda out before it stained.

He was pulling the damp shirt back on over his shoulders when he heard a door open and close. He came out of the shower to find Mr. Jeffries, one of the P.E. teachers, staring him in the face.

"I, uh, had to wash my shirt. Someone spilled soda on it."

"You're Jenny. Jenny Bailor, right?"

"Um, it's *Justin*, Sir." Being deadnamed like that hit him in the gut. The teachers were supposed to be supportive, weren't they? He felt a little nauseous.

"You were born a girl." The coach punched him in the shoulder with a fat finger. "Far as I'm concerned, ain't nothing changed. I don't want to see you in the *boy's* locker room again. We clear? You gotta go, you use the girls'."

"Yes, sir." Justin grabbed his lunch and ran past the teacher, trying not to cry.

Real men don't cry.

"Ryan Baker," Mr. Davis called.

"Queer." Christian Simms snickered, high-fiving his friends.

"Fucking asshole," Ryan said.

"That's enough out of you, Mr. Baker."

Ryan jumped out of his seat. "But he called me queer."

"You have to grow a thicker skin, Mr. Baker. The real world's not going to coddle you."

Ryan couldn't believe what he was hearing. "You can't be fucking serious. He just called me a queer. You heard that, right?"

"One more outburst like that and I'm sending you to the principal's office."

Ryan couldn't believe his ears. He sat down, trying not to let his emotions overcome him.

Real men don't cry.

Some things never change. Ryan wanted to reach out to Justin, to pull him close and hug him tight. "The coach shouldn't have treated you like that."

Justin put his head down between his knees. "It was so fucking humiliating." His voice was so soft Ryan almost didn't hear it.

"I can imagine."

"Can you?" He looked up, and his eyes were wet. "Sometimes, just for a minute, I forget I'm trans. Like, I'm just some regular guy, you know? As if the rest is all just some weird nightmare. I'm just *me.* And then someone comes along and rubs it in my face."

Ryan nodded. "It's like that for all of us exceptional people."

"Exceptional?" Justin's forehead creased.

Ryan grinned. "Yeah. See, I have this theory. There are millions of people who were born to lead everyday lives—to marry someone of the opposite sex. To settle down, get a good job, have two and a half kids... you know, what they call 'normal life.' But there are some of us who just can't fit inside a normal life. We're bigger than that, more colorful, with dreams and ideas that keep trying to burst out of the standard little cardboard box. So we're exceptional. And we have it hard at first, because we don't fit in, but sooner or later we spread our wings and fly."

Justin managed a weak grin. "Exceptional. I like that."

"Sometimes someone tries to shove you back into the box. They don't like it when others don't fit their preconceived notions of who other people should be. But you have to resist it with all your might."

"Maybe so," he said back, looking up at the afternoon sky.

"So what happened the next day?"

Wednesday

Justin sat at the back of his Biology class and glanced at the clock. It was already 1:30—one more class and the pep rally, and he'd be free for the day. With luck, his mom would be out, drinking or with one of her "boyfriends". The less they saw of each other, the better.

He pulled out his iPad and waited for Ms. Mertz to do the roll-call. She was his oldest teacher—he was pretty sure she'd been here when his mother had gone to school. She'd been out the first two days of school sick, and didn't look so good today.

"Davis Jones?"

"Here."

"Tamaya Lashmi?"

"That's me."

"Jenny Bailor?"

Holy fuck. Justin's face turned red. She didn't... she couldn't have... she hadn't just deadnamed him in front of the whole class. There was no way that had just happened.

"Jenny? Jenny Bailor?" She looked up from her desk, her brow knitted, looking around at all the students over the rims of her gold-framed glasses.

"It's... it's Justin." He could feel the eyes of the entire class on him.

"Oh yes. I see that." She nodded. "It's Justin now, not Jenny. I am so sorry, Justin. What amazing times we live in, huh?" She laughed, fanning herself in comical fashion with her hand, and then went back to the roll call.

The damage was done.

All around him, the students were whispering and pointing at him:

"I thought he looked familiar..."

"Didn't Jenny transfer to Coliseum?"

"Damn, it really is her."

His face was flushed.

Ms. Mertz seemed oblivious to what she had just done. "Okay, students, please flip to the first chapter of your textbooks. Today we'll be discussing viruses..."

Justin looked down at his iPad and tried to ignore the whispers and furtive looks from the other students.

His Biology class let out, and the students poured into the halls. He watched the other kids from his class as they started spreading the news, like when a virus ruptured its cell walls and spread throughout the host's body. In minutes, the whole school would know, infected by his classmates.

He'd expected it would get out eventually, but had hoped he'd have at a least couple weeks to settle in first. *Fuck fuck fuck fuck fuck fuck fuck.*

He sighed and headed to the band room. Every surreptitious glance, every whispered comment around him seemed to be about him, though there was no way the rumor could have spread that fast. Was there?

Then he saw someone posting on SnapChat.

He groaned. *Everyone* would know in a matter of minutes.

He had other things to worry about, though. The first pep rally of the year was here.

Justin pushed open the double doors of the band room, and headed to his locker to get out his uniform. He pulled the dark green jacket with its gold piping on over his uniform over his still-wet t-shirt.

"Sorry I'm late!" The voice seemed to echo across the room. Justin looked up and caught a glimpse of Noah, grinning like a madman.

Holy crap, Noah was a band geek? How had Justin not noticed him in band that morning?

Sure enough—Noah had his uniform draped over his shoulder, and a pair of drumsticks sticking out of his back pocket.

Justin's ears went red. Drummers were the coolest kids in the band... well, them and the trumpet players. He'd been flirting with a drummer!

He turned away, hoping Noah wouldn't recognize him, and pulled on his white pants with their green and gold stripe running down each side. *Act casual. He'll go away.*

"Hey there... Justin, is it?"

No such luck. Justin looked up into Noah's warm brown eyes. "Um... yeah. Yeah, I think so."

He sank down into the green plastic chair next to Justin. "I just got my uniform. They said I needed white shoes." He pointed at his black and white Vans. "Got any shoe polish?"

Justin cursed himself for running out. "No... sorry—"

"No problem. I'll get some from someone else." He winked at Justin and then he was gone again.

Justin growled under his breath. *Stupid stupid stupid. Cute boy talks to you, and you get so tongue tied you don't even know your own name.*

And what if someone noticed how attracted he was to the new kid?

Justin assembled his flute, getting ready for the march across campus. He was regretting his choice of instrument, and not for the first time. *Real* men didn't play flutes.

It lent itself a little too readily to jokes. He'd decided on it in Junior High. He'd watched his friend lugging his French horn to school every day on the bus. Stevie had been a scrawny little kid, and the instrument case was almost as big as he was. He would strap it to a skateboard every day with a couple of bungee cords to roll it to the bus stop, and then wrestle it up onto the bus.

Justin was no fool. He'd vowed to pick the smallest instrument possible, and since the junior high band didn't have any piccolos, he'd ended up a flute player.

"Everyone ready?" their teacher and band leader called. Last year, Mr. Masters had led the school's band to its first Superior award in ten years at Band Day. He seemed determined to do it again this year. He winked at Justin. He was the one teacher in whom Justin had confided, the year before.

Justin liked being in the band. He wasn't very good—maybe because he never practiced—but it was like being part of an army. He felt safe when he was among them, even if most of them didn't know who he was anymore.

He pulled on his green cap with the white feather, aware that he looked like an utter *band geek*, but at least he wasn't alone.

They formed up a column of four students abreast, woodwinds first, followed by brass, with the drum corps at the back. Then they marched out of the band room together.

He put on his stern marching face as they emerged from the hallway into the sunshine. It was a good thousand feet through the campus from the Fine Arts Building to the Multiple Purpose Room where the rally would be held. The way was lined with other students watching the spectacle.

The drums started up behind him, and Andy felt their power. The other kids in the school lined the sidewalk, and the drums beat a steady rhythm:

Bah dah dum dum dum da dum,
Bah dah dum dum dum da dum dum dum...

It was a jolt of pure percussive energy, and it always made Justin happy.

The sidewalks between the Fine Arts Building and the MPR were covered with corrugated metal sheets to keep off the sun, and they trapped and amplified the sound of the drums until it seemed to fill all of Justin's world.

Noah was somewhere behind him, playing one of those drums.

Justin saw Zane, the football player, standing in the crowd ahead of them. *Tranny*, he whispered, his mouth twisted with disgust. His foot caught Justin's leg, sending him falling hard to the ground. His flute flew out of his hands to clatter on the concrete in front of him.

The band behind him ground to a halt.

Everyone was laughing. Well, everyone but the band members. The drums faded off to nothing.

Marina Marazzi, one of the clarinet players, held out her hand, her face dark with anger. "You okay?"

He nodded. "Just clumsy."

She shot a look at Zane. "Clumsy my ass. Here." She handed him his flute, and he looked it over to be sure it was ok. Nothing seemed damaged.

His left hand had been scraped up on the rough concrete, but he'd live.

"Everything alright back here?" Mr. Masters appeared alongside the column.

"Yes sir," Justin said, forcing a smile. "I just tripped, that's all."

"Be more careful. We can't risk losing one of our best flute players."

Justin flushed with embarrassment. He was far from the best. "Won't happen again, Mr. Masters."

Mr. Masters smiled. "Then let's get going. Drummers?"

The sound started up again, and the band pressed forward.

Bah dah dum dum dum da dum...

It wasn't easy being a trans kid in 2019.

Standing in the middle of the practice field, Ryan listened to the band teacher's instructions.

They'd all gotten better at this, slowly but surely. He remembered the day Mr. Morris had called out "Left", and the band had split down the middle as half went left and half went right.

The band kids didn't care who or what he was. They didn't care that he had a crush on Dimitri Velenov, the blond trumpet player who was a senior while he was a freshman.

He remembered his clarinet, and the band in their white band hats with the blue, like a red, white, and blue army of geeks, marching across the field together.

Justin had gone quiet. His face was ashen.

Ryan gave him a little space. It was hard being *different* in high school, no matter what that difference was. If it hadn't been for Andy, it might have been him up on the rooftop, once upon a time. It had been, actually. Only it hadn't been a rooftop, exactly.

"I just wanted to be normal," Justin said at last.

Ryan snorted. "Good luck with that. Not one of us is 'normal'. There's no such thing."

Justin looked at him, an eyebrow raised.

"Don't believe me? I'll bet every last one of those kids in your school has something... different about him or her. For me, it was the whole gay thing." He closed his eyes, remembering. "I had my own Zane, you know. His name was Christian Simms, and he beat the crap out of me a couple times."

"Yeah?"

"Yeah." He sighed. "Funny thing is, Chris came out himself, five years later. Even looked me up and apologized for the way he acted toward me in school."

Justin still looked doubtful.

"This bully of yours, Zane? His father's off on combat duty, right?"

Justin nodded. "Yeah, I think so."

"And your friend, Marina—maybe she's a lesbian. And one of the other kids probably has asthma, or diabetes. There are probably a few who have OCD, or phobias, or are on the spectrum, or some other *thing* they don't want the rest of the school to know about. Point is, nobody's normal." He stared at Justin, trying to figure out where the kid's head was. "What do you really want out of life?" he asked at last.

Justin thought about it for a long time. Finally, he said "I just want to be me."

Ryan nodded. "That's more like it." The kid was talking. Thinking. Much better than jumping. "Now what happened next?"

Thursday

Justin came out of his American History class, his last class. He'd managed to get through the day without incident—so far. He headed back to his locker, ready to grab the rest of his stuff and call it a day.

A bunch of other students were gathered around it.

He pushed his way through the crowd and stopped when he saw the word "Tranny" scrawled in black permanent marker across the metal face of the locker.

The other students laughed nervously, and then Zane grabbed him and slammed him up against the wall. "Hey there, little faggot."

That didn't even make sense, but Justin was in no position to argue word choice.

The other kids melted back, leaving a big space between themselves and the bully and his victim.

"Let... me... go." Justin struggled, but he was no match for the football player.

One hand around his neck, the bigger teen punched him in the gut with his other fist. "That's what we do to tranny faggots around here."

Justin wheezed, trying to breathe.

"Let him go, Zane." A girl's voice.

"What's it to you, Marina?"

She pushed him hard, shoving him away from Justin. "You're a fucking ass."

His throat suddenly free, Justin took a grateful breath of air.

"Just teaching *it* a lesson." Zane smirked.

God, I fucking hate you. He touched his throat, where Zane's huge hand had pinned him to the wall.

For her answer, Marina hauled off and punched him hard across the jaw, knocking him to the ground. The other kids gasped and laughed.

She turned to check on Justin. "Hey, you okay?"

"I think so..." He breathed shallowly, still struggling for air.

"Come on. I'll take you to the principal's office."

"No!" He shook his head vehemently. "That will only make it

worse." Indeed, Zane was glaring at him, rubbing his jaw. The bully had just been embarrassed in front of the whole school. By a girl. Anything Justin said or did would exacerbate the situation.

"Come on then. Let's get out of here." She helped him up and shot a dirty glance back at Zane.

The crowd dispersed as they made their way outside into the fresh air.

"Thanks for helping me." Justin blushed. *Some man I am. I can't even take care of myself.*

"'S'okay. I hate the way they're all talking about you. Don't let assholes like Zane get you down. In five years they'll be gas station attendants and we'll be... well, something better."

Justin laughed. "Thanks. I needed that." Thank God school was over. He was dying to get out of there. "I gotta go."

She raised an eyebrow. "Hey, you want a ride? Not sure it's safe on the bus for you today."

He nodded. "I'd like that." He'd been bracing himself for the jeers on the ride home.

"Where do you live?"

"Out near Magee and First. Up by the mountain."

She nodded. "Come on. That's not too far from my house."

Marina stood out in more ways than one. She was tall. Like, really tall for a girl. And she was one of the only Black kids in the school.

She drove a beat-up old tan minivan. "It was my mom's car, before she got her new Prius," she explained with a grin.

They climbed into the car. It was hot, but for a moment the heat felt good.

"Seatbelts, please. My parents only let me drive if I'm belted in."

"I don't have a car." For some reason, Justin felt very safe with her.

She started the car, and they rumbled out of the parking lot, past all the other kids leaving on foot and by bike and skateboard.

He looked at the school as they passed by, and sighed heavily. He'd just have to come back and do all of this again the next day.

"I hate that the jocks treat kids like us that way." She glanced at him.

"Like us?" She was nothing like him.

"Yeah. The outcasts. The queer kids."

Justin stared at her. "You're gay?"

Marina smirked. "Well, lesbian. I like girls." She glanced over at him. "You're *trans*, right?"

Justin shrugged. "Yeah. Turn left up here." He looked over at her. "How come you never talked to me... before?"

She grinned. "You weren't all that interesting, back then."

Justin decided to take that as a compliment. "Thanks, I think."

"You know what I mean."

"I guess so." They were getting close to his place. "Hey, you can drop me off here."

Marina looked around at the empty desert. "In the middle of nowhere? No way. I'm taking you to your place."

Justin blushed. He didn't want her to see his home. "Really, it's okay—"

"Forget it. I'll drop you at your front door."

He gave up. "Okay. Make a right here."

Laney turned smoothly into his trailer park. It was an old place in a ragged patch of desert, in the shadow of the Catalina Mountains.

He looked around. "Oh, that's it, up there on the left." The trailer was badly in need of repainting, patches of rusted metal poking out from under the old white paint. One of the windows was broken and covered over with a piece of plywood. The front yard was filled with weeds. He hated living there.

"A real fixer-upper." She winked. "Want me to give you a ride tonight, for the game?"

"That would be great, thanks! Five o'clock?" He grabbed his backpack from the floor and climbed out of the car. "Um... thanks, Marina. I owe you one."

She grinned. "I'll remember that."

He closed the door and waved as she took off. He stared in wonder at the car as it kicked up a cloud of dust.

He'd made a friend.

He used the key in his pocket to let himself into the trailer, and made his way back to his room and threw his backpack on his bed. The old walls were covered with posters, including one of Captain America and Bucky and another of Steven Universe.

He pulled his iPad out and checked his Tumblr. There was a smattering of new comments, mostly asking if he really was a "tranny". A couple people had left helpful suggestions for him that seemed anatomically unlikely, if not impossible.

A car pulled into the gravel driveway, making a loud grinding sound.

He glanced out the window. His mother was getting out of the car and coming around to the front door.

"Crap." He hopped onto his bed and pulled his headphones on, and streamed his favorite Nineties grunge music from Pandora. Maybe if his mom saw that he was occupied, she'd leave him alone.

No such luck.

"What the hell is this?" she screamed as she entered his room, brandishing an open Amazon box.

Resigned, he pulled off his headphones and let them fall around his neck. "I don't know. I can't see what you're holding."

She pulled something out of the box. It was the Stand to Pee packer he had ordered, shaped like a penis. "Now you're having sex toys sent to the house? What the hell is wrong with you?" She slapped him hard upside the head with it.

"It's not a sex toy—"

"Like hell it's not." She glared at him for a moment, and then her anger seemed to collapse like a house of cards. "I just don't know what I did wrong with you."

Justin took a deep breath, not rising to the bait. "There's *nothing* wrong with me."

"Look at you. You were such a pretty girl, Jenny—"

"It's *Justin* now."

"Not to me. You'll always be Jenny to me." She threw the STP packer down on the bed. "Ruin your own life if you want to. But you aren't going to do it under my roof. I want you out of here."

"But mom!" Surely she was joking. For all of its faults, this was his home. *Where would I go?*

"Don't *but mom* me. You made your choice. Now I'm making mine. I want you gone by tonight." She slammed his door behind her, a bottle of cheap red wine in her other hand.

He stared at the door in shock.

What the hell just happened? His own mother had just kicked him out? Where the hell was he going to go?

Cursing under his breath, he started gathering his things, the few that he cared about, anyhow. He made a pile on his bed—his phone, his trophy for little league baseball, some clothes, and his teddy bear, Oscar. *Maybe I'm better off getting out of this hell hole.*

When Marina arrived at five to pick him up, he had everything that meant anything to him packed in a duffel bag, along with his band uniform on a hanger.

He left without looking back.

"Your mother and I think it's best you leave our house, Ryan."

Ryan stared across the dining room table at his father as if the man had gone crazy. "You can't... you're my parents."

"Are you still claiming that you're a... a... a homosexual?"

"The word's 'gay', Dad."

His father ignored him. "As long as you insist on acting this way, we think it's best that you find another place to live."

This couldn't be happening. "Where am I going to go?"

"You should have thought about that first." His father's voice was calm, but Ryan could feel the tension behind it.

"When?" was all he said.

"By tomorrow night. And Ryan..."

"What?"

"If you change your mind... our door is always open."

"Doesn't really sound like it, does it?" Ryan slammed his bedroom door in his father's face, and sank down on the bed, closing his eyes to keep himself from crying.

Ryan's heart was breaking for the poor kid—he knew exactly what it was like to get thrown out on your ass. He wanted to give Justin a big hug.

Instead, he stood his ground. The kid needed space, and Ryan didn't want to push him.

His own mother had been supportive after she'd gotten over the shock of it, but his father never had come around. How could you turn on your own flesh and blood like that? "My mother hates me for it," he said softly.

"I'm sure that's not true. Maybe she just doesn't understand you—"

"She *hates* me. I'm just her dependent meal ticket." He shuddered, and Ryan's heart broke for him a little more. "When I was seven, I told her I was really a boy. She told me to take it back, to say I was a girl. She told me I would go to hell if I didn't."

Ryan frowned. No one should talk to their kids that way.

"The way she stared at me... she took my hand and held it over the burner on the stove. When I refused, she hissed 'Saaaaay it!'—I still remember her stale breath."

"Oh God." Ryan already hated this woman he'd never met.

"She pushed my hand down onto the hot metal. I screamed 'I'm not a boy!' and she stopped." He shuddered. "That was the last time I brought up my gender with my mother. She's mellowed out since then. The alcohol knocks her out for a couple days, sometimes." He frowned. "I never thought she'd kick me out."

"No one should ever be treated like that." He'd report this woman to Child Protective Services, if he could find out who she was.

It was at that moment that Ryan *knew*, as sure as he knew his own name. that he had been brought up here for a reason. He wasn't a believer. But something greater than him had sent him here.

He still wanted to take this poor kid into his arms, to hug him and tell him everything would be all right, but the space between them was like a wall.

He had to keep Justin talking. "So what did you do next?"

Thursday Night

"Planning on moving into the band room?" Marina asked, eyeing the duffel bag as she threw open the car door for him.

"Something like that." He shoved it into the back seat along with his uniform and then got into the minivan. "Glad it's a home game tonight."

She nodded. "Bet it's gonna be a spectacle!"

"Probably." He just hoped it wasn't at his expense.

She started the car, and soon they were flying down the road toward La Cañada. "Did you practice much?"

Justin shook his head. "Not really. It was a weird afternoon." He didn't want to talk about it—he'd worry about where he was going to end up for the night later.

They pulled into the school parking lot and Marina found a shady spot under one of the solar panels. It was still hot out, the pavement almost crackling underfoot.

Zane and his friends were hanging out by his Tesla. Justin frowned. How did a high school senior get a Tesla?

"Playing the skin flute again, faggot?" Zane Jepson snarled as they walked past. His laughter echoed after them as they made their way to the band room.

"Fucking asshole." Marina glared back at Zane. "Don't listen to him, Justin. He's an idiot."

He found a seat in the band room, the wide, tiered space where the band met to practice. He pulled on the polyester white pants with the green stripes that ran up both sides. He already had his white socks on, and he followed them with a pair of white loafers.

He frowned. One of his shoes had a big grass stain at the toe. "Anyone got some extra polish?"

Marina threw him a bottle. He reached for it, but it slipped out of his grasp and landed with a thud on Jason Sutter's lap. "Here you go," the trumpet player said with a grin.

"Thanks." Justin covered up the stain with a dollop of polish, and handed the bottle back to her.

His green jacket went over his white t-shirt, traced in front with gold lines in a design he'd always thought looked like a fancy rib cage. He wasn't sure who had picked the school colors, but he supposed it could have been worse. *Maybe pink with purple were already taken.*

Next he slipped on his white gloves. He shoved his duffle bag into his band locker. He had no idea where he would go when the evening was over. Maybe he could hide in the bathroom and spend the night in the band room. *Time enough to worry about that later.*

The place was a flurry of activity, with band members dressing, tuning their instruments, and practicing bits of the song for the night —"Firework."

Justin looked around and found Noah in one corner, playing the drums. He beelined to the drummer's side. He threw his uniform over a chair and pulled on the jacket over his shirt. "That sounds amazing." He blushed, shucking his pants and changing as quickly as possible in case anyone was looking.

"Thanks!" Noah stopped playing and grinned at him. "Just something I've been working on."

Justin pulled on his green and gold cap with its fuzzy white feather in front, completing the ensemble. He grimaced. It was more like a feather boa on a wire. "Why did you move here? To Tucson, I mean."

Noah tucked his drumsticks into his belt loop. "My moms. One of them got a job with the city.

"Moms?"

"Yeah, I have two." Noah frowned. "You have a problem with that?"

"No!" He was surprised at the question. He leaned in to whisper, "I'm—"

"Everyone form up," Mr. Masters called loudly from the front of the room. The other kids quieted down. "We're gonna march over to the game."

"Got to go. Talk to you later." Noah touched his shoulder, then grabbed his drum to take his place in line.

Justin stashed his regular clothes in his band locker, staring after Noah longingly.

The football stands were packed. The band had its own section, but the rest of the seats were filled with students and parents for the biggest game of the year, the showcase match between La Cañada and their chief rival, Coliseum High School. The Warriors against the Gladiators.

It was a warm evening, the air still and expectant.

Justin sat with the other woodwinds, casting surreptitious glances at the drummer boys in the back at the top of the grandstands. Noah saw him and grinned at him once. Justin turned quickly away, hoping no one else had noticed.

"He's cute," Marina whispered in his ear, glancing back at Noah.

"Don't look at him!" Justin squeezed her hand, shooting her a worried smile.

The whistle blew, and the quarterback on the Gladiators' team hiked the ball and fell back, looking for an open receiver. His linemen protected him as he threw a long pass.

The ball went up, up, up, and the whole crowd went silent.

Then it plummeted into the hands of one of the other Gladiators, who ran it forward twenty yards. In two more minutes, the visiting team scored the first touchdown of the game.

It went downhill from there.

By the time halftime rolled around, the Warriors were down twenty-one to seven, and the coach was pacing up and down the sidelines like a man awaiting his own execution. He pulled his team together for a pep talk.

"We're up," Mr. Masters called. The band filed down from the stands onto the field while most of the crowd left for popcorn and candy from the snack bar and a quick bathroom break.

They found their places. The smell of grass was strong from the blades broken and smashed during the first half.

Justin took his place and the lights came up. The grandstands started to fill up again. Mr. Masters lifted his hands, starting them off with a flourish.

A brassy version of "Firework" blasted out of the band's myriad instruments, and their formation began to move and blend and twist, the band leaders imaginative choreography playing out like art on the field.

Sometimes Justin wished he could see the routine from above. He loved watching the other schools at the annual Battle of the Bands at the University of Arizona, and this one would look *amazing*.

Halfway through the song, the music stopped as suddenly as it had begun. Everyone in the band all began to run wildly back and forth across the field.

The crowd gasped.

In exactly eight beats, they were all in their new spots, bodies forming the Arizona state flag.

Marina flashed him a big grin.

At that moment, Justin loved being a part of the marching band more than anything else ever. *I wish this could last all night.*

They wrapped up the show and slipped off the field single file, to the wild applause of the audience in the stands.

"Hey Justin!" Noah came running up to him, his drum bouncing with his enthusiasm. "That was fucking amazing." He smiled, and Justin's world lit up.

"It was something, wasn't it?" He grinned back, his face hotter than the Arizona sun.

Noah took his hand. "Wanna go see a movie this weekend?"

Oh God, how I want to. But did Noah know? What if they kissed? What if it turned into something more?

Justin glanced over at the bench.

Zane was sitting there, staring at the two of them holding hands, his black eyes boring through them like coals.

Justin shuddered and pulled away from Noah. "No. I'm busy. I have a lot of homework—"

Noah frowned. "You can just say no. You don't have to lie to me if you don't want to go."

"It's not—"

"It's not what?"

Justin stared at him helplessly.

Noah snorted and shook his head, then turned away and disappeared into the crowd.

Justin stared after him, refusing to look at Zane again.

He would not give the football player the satisfaction of seeing that he was angry. Or afraid.

Justin waited in the parking lot for Marina. She'd disappeared into the bathroom with Jasmine, one of the clarinet players, and he was starting to feel stood up.

He'd changed into his street clothes, and had left his band uniform in his locker.

The light above him was flickering on and off, lending the whole scene a creepy horror film vibe.

"Well, if it isn't my favorite little faggot."

Justin froze. He knew that taunting voice. His hands started shaking.

"Whatcha doin' there, *faggot?*"

"I'm not a faggot," he said under his breath.

"What did you say, *faggot?*" Zane said it right in his ear.

"I said I'm not a faggot, *asshole.*" He elbowed the football player out of his way and turned to run. He couldn't believe he'd said that out loud, but it was done, and he was no physical match for Zane.

Zane hauled him back by the shirt collar and slammed Justin into a car with so much force that the window cracked.

Oh God, I hope it's the window.

In the intermittent light, two other shapes approached like hyenas out of the darkness. Chet Colson and Brian Timmins, Zane's friends and teammates.

They stood over him, examining their prey.

Zane unzipped his jeans.

Justin couldn't help but look—it was like watching a car wreck. Even in the moonlight, it was impressive, but he felt no desire at all.

His heart was beating three hundred times a second, and cold sweat slicked his arms.

"Wanna suck my cock, little tranny faggot boy? I saw you looking at me on the field."

His friends laughed.

Justin's throat was dry. "No. I don't."

"Like I'd let you, you little prick." He zipped up his jeans and grabbed Justin by the throat. "We oughta put an end to little cock-suckers like you."

"Please... just let me go." Justin was shaking all over now, and his crotch was warm. He'd wet his pants from fear. "I... I won't tell anyone."

"I don't think so." He pulled back his fist and hit Justin squarely in the gut.

The air rushed out of his lungs and he fell to the ground, gasping for air.

The three boys were laughing above him. Justin closed his eyes, willing it to end. Praying to be anywhere but here...

"What the fuck are you doing?" someone asked.

"Just messing with this faggot. Hey, it's the other one!"

Pain radiated through Justin's stomach. Still, he managed to open his eyes, squinting past Zane's silhouette.

"Damn straight, I'm a faggot, but I'm not afraid of your fucking bullshit."

Noah? Justin edged up into a sitting position, clutching his gut.

"Looks like we get to fuck up two of you tonight." Zane took a swing at Noah, but the drummer danced back, grabbing the football player's arm and pulling him forward to slam against the door of an old Ford truck.

Zane shook himself off with a growl like a bear. He charged at Noah, who danced out of his way again. Zane slammed headlong into another car and fell to the ground dizzily.

Chet and Brian charged the newcomer together.

Noah roundhouse-kicked Chet in the jaw, sending him sprawling. He pivoted to grab Brian in an arm lock, tightening his grip around the bully's neck. "You little shits leave me and my friend alone, or I'll snap you in half. Got it?"

Chet moaned, apparently unable to speak.

"Don't think I can't do it, either." He let go of Brian, and kicked him in the ass.

Chet ran off into the darkness, cursing, followed by the other two.

Noah knelt beside Justin. "Hey, you okay?"

Justin shook his head. "My stomach hurts. And..." *Don't make me say it.* "I think I wet myself." He expected Noah to back off in disgust.

Instead, Noah helped him up. "It's a natural bodily reaction when we're under attack. Totally not a big deal. Let's get you cleaned up. Your uniform's in your locker, right?"

"Yeah," he croaked. "I don't want anyone to see me like this."

Noah nodded. "Ok, what if I take you back to my place? My moms are gone for the weekend. You can clean up there. We'll call your folks and tell them you're staying over."

"Okay." Justin was flooded with mixed feelings. A guy he liked had just asked him to spend the night. Never in his wildest dreams had he thought it would happen to him. Of course, it was the worst possible time.

He felt disgusting, dirty, and weak.

Noah must have sensed it. "No funny business. I promise. Just a safe place to clean up and sleep."

Justin nodded. "Okay." He wasn't ready for sex. For intimacy. And he still wasn't sure if Noah *knew*.

So why was he disappointed?

It was his first time.

Back behind the dumpster near the school football field, kissing Andy. The way the other boy's lips responded. His mouth tasted like chocolate milk.

The incredible surge of desire, shame, and primal need.

Even now, thinking about it made Ryan's libido surge and his heart beat faster.

He was no longer alone.

Ryan shook his head. That had been so long ago. He tried to remember how he had felt in that moment, and what his life in the closet had been like.

He recognized the pain and hunger in Justin's eyes. *It was my own.* "You don't have any friends at school, do you? No one who is like you?"

Justin stared at him for a minute, then looked down at the rooftop. "Not really. I think I'm the only one there."

This kid had been given something to deal with that was way beyond his capacity to handle, and then he'd been thrown into the world all alone. "When I was your age," and yes, he cringed at that one, "I felt the same way. I thought I was the only gay kid in school. We didn't have the internet, or cell phones. There were no good gay role models on TV, let alone transgender ones. Laverne Cox was probably just being born."

"How old *are* you?" Justin looked at him with wide eyes.

"Old enough to know better than to tell you." He sighed. "Then this kid named Andy came along. He was new to school, like Noah, and just knowing him changed my life. You probably feel like that about Noah, even though he's not trans. Is he?"

Justin shook his head. "No." He stood up, looking toward the door, and then back at the ledge.

"You haven't finished your story." Ryan stood, trying to forestall Justin before the boy took it into his head to go ahead and do what he came here for. "You promised to tell me the whole thing." His hands shook a little, his nicotine craving kicking in. Now was not the time. He ignored the tremors.

"I promised to talk with you for a little while. That's it."

"Okay, okay. Look, you told me most of your story, and if you...

leave now, I'll never know how it ended. Don't you want at least one person to know who you were? Who you *are?*"

"Maybe…"

"You want to be yourself. You have that chance. Here. With me. I want to know who you are, who you *really* are." He took a chance. "Or was all that talk just bullshit?"

"What?" Justin glared at him, surprise evident on his face.

"Maybe you just want to play the martyr. Maybe you don't want to jump at all."

Justin stared at him as if he'd gone insane.

Ryan felt the sweat bead his brow, nicotine addiction or nerves, it didn't matter. "Come on. Just talk to me."

Justin took one more look at the ledge, and then back at Ryan, and nodded. "Okay." He sat back down.

Ryan breathed a sigh of relief. *Minute by minute.* "So what went wrong? What sent you up here?"

Shattered

Noah helped hose down Justin's feet at the door after he'd removed his shoes and socks, and he rolled up his still-wet jeans to avoid dripping through the house.

He was mortified.

"Don't worry about it." Noah must have seen the look on his face. "I peed my bed last month. I had this dream that I had to go, and I woke up in a wet bed."

Justin laughed, the tension broken. "Thanks." He looked around the house. The walls were a soft coral stucco, with beautiful log beams set into the ceiling. The huge Saltillo floor tiles were covered by serapes, lending the whole place a distinctly Mexican flavor.

Noah led him back to the bathroom. "Get a quick shower. I'll check in on you in a bit."

"Thanks." Justin locked the door behind him. It was Noah's house, and he was pretty sure he was safe here. After what had happened in the parking lot, he needed the extra feeling of protection. Still, he wasn't sure he was ready to deal with the whole trans thing and Noah's possible reaction. *He has to know.*

Then again, he was the new kid in town. Maybe he didn't.

He'd texted his mom to tell her he'd be staying over with Noah, but she hadn't replied. He was pretty sure he knew why.

He took off his clothes, laying the soiled jeans on top of his shirt, placing both on the toilet so he wouldn't soil the rug or the bathroom fixtures. He was a mess. He'd insisted that Noah put something down to protect the passenger car seat of his old Honda Civic. In the end, they'd used the plastic from Noah's band uniform.

He unwrapped his breasts, grimacing at the fleshy appendages. They were a constant reminder of how he'd been born, but they weren't *him.*

He set the STP in the tub to wash it, along with himself.

Then he ran the shower until the water was warm. He stepped inside, pulling the shower curtain closed behind him. He grabbed the bar of Dove and washed himself down, feeling a little better as the stink of urine washed off of him.

"You okay in there?" Noah called from outside.

"Yup. Thanks. I'll be done in a moment." He was glad he'd locked the door.

"Take your time. I found some clothes for you, and I ordered a pizza. Mom left me some spending money."

Justin *was* hungry. He hadn't had anything besides a Twix and a Pepsi at the game. His stomach was feeling a little better where Zane had punched him, though there was the beginning of a bruise there. He'd be tender for days. "Can you leave them by the door?"

"Sure thing."

Justin sighed—if Noah hadn't stepped in, things could have been a lot worse.

He shampooed his hair. It was strange using someone else's soap in someone else's bathroom. He looked down at the long hair in the drain that definitely was not his and wrinkled his nose. Still, beggars and choosers.

He washed his STP, and then rinsed off. At last, he felt presentable. He grabbed the towel Noah had hung for him and dried off. He put the binder back on and wrapped the towel around his waist and chest. Then he cracked the door and grabbed the pile of clothes laying in front of the door in the hallway, and closed the door hurriedly.

He put on the underwear and then the jeans, wondering if they were Noah's. The thought gave him a little thrill. The STP went inside, giving him a respectable bulge. Then the black athletic socks, his binder, and a black t-shirt with a faded Cage the Elephant logo.

He wiped the steam off the mirror with the towels and examined the results. He didn't look half bad, though the jeans were loose and long on him.

He hung the towel up to dry, grabbed his own clothes gingerly, and went in search of Noah. He found his new friend in the living room.

"Hey, you look great!" Noah was wearing matching jeans and a white t-shirt.

Justin blushed. "You think so?"

Noah nodded enthusiastically. "A lot better than those football players."

Justin face went white at the mention of his attackers.

"Sorry." Noah, to his credit, blushed. "Hey, it's over. They lost, *and* they're assholes. Here, give me those."

Justin shook his head. He didn't want Noah touching them. "Just show me where the washer is. I'll put them in myself."

Noah nodded. "Fair enough. We'll wash them tonight. You can wear my clothes home and get them back to me later."

Justin didn't know how to tell Noah that he had no home to go back to. *One thing at a time.*

He followed Noah down the hall, and deposited the stinking clothes into the washer. He ducked back into the bathroom and washed his hands while Noah started the machine.

"Come on. We can hang out... I'll grab you a drink."

Justin followed him into the living room, trying not to stare, and chose a seat on the comfy looking Santa Fe print couch.

Noah returned a moment later to hand him a Pepsi, and popped one open for himself.

Justin plopped down on the couch next to Noah and propped his feet up on the coffee room table. "So, has that happened before?"

"What... oh." Justin blushed. "Not since I was little."

"No. The bullying. The assault."

Justin sipped his soda. "Only once since—"

"You came out?"

Justin nodded. "Something like that."

Noah nodded. "I'm glad to hear it. I'd hate to think you were going through that kind of shit on a regular basis." He sipped his soda, his brown eyes watching Justin closely.

He looked away. "I think Zane's a closet case."

Noah snorted. "Oh, most definitely. I saw how he waved his meat in front of you. Bitch wants it bad."

Justin snickered. "You saw that?"

"Yeah. I didn't want to jump in and make it look like you needed my help. Until he sucker punched you in the stomach. Bullies never fight fair."

"You kicked his ass, though." Justin could still see it in his head. "How did you do that? It was amazing. Like Street Fighter."

"Thanks." Noah gave him the biggest shit eating grin he'd ever seen. "After I came out, my moms took me to this karate place in Oceanside. Taught me how to defend myself. They said no son of theirs was going to get the piss kicked out of him for being a straight-up fairy."

Justin laughed, then sobered when he remembered his own predicament. "My mom... kicked me out today. That's why I had the big duffle bag."

"Holy shit. You could stay here for the night..." He blushed, something Justin found adorable.

The doorbell rang. "Pizza!" Noah jumped up and ran to the door.

Justin watched talking to the pizza delivery guy. Noah was beautiful. And they were here alone, together. He wished that he'd been born a boy on the outside. That he didn't have to navigate this extra layer of crap every time he wanted to get close to someone.

Noah returned with his prize, a large pepperoni pizza with a side of breadsticks. "Go ahead, dig in." He sat in the recliner directly opposite from Justin, grabbing a slice for himself.

"Thanks for what you did. It could have gone a lot worse." Justin took a big bite, which filled his mouth with cheesy garlicky deliciousness.

"You're welcome," Noah said through a mouthful of pizza. "I'm sorry I was a prick at the football game. I'm just not used to hiding who I am. I *do* like you, Justin."

Justin blanched. He wasn't ready for this yet. "Did you... want to...?"

"Want to what?" Recognition flashed across his face. "Oh, no."

Justin sighed and looked away. Even other gay guys didn't want to be with him.

Noah must have noticed. "No, I didn't mean it like that. I'd totally like to get with you."

"Then... what?" Hope rekindled in Justin chest.

"It's just... well, you've never done it before, have you?"

Being around Noah seemed to induce a perpetual state of blushing. "I'm not a virgin—"

"With your hand doesn't count."

"Um... well then, no." There'd been one time before, with Bobby Blake, but that was before, and it hadn't amounted to much.

"And you just had a traumatic night."

Justin nodded. "I guess so." Again, the unexpected disappointment.

"I like you, Justin, but I don't want to be with you like that. Because you think you should. Because someone scared the shit out of you."

"I get it." He got another slice of pizza. "So maybe another time?" After he had a chance to tell Noah his secret.

Noah grinned. "For sure another time."

Justin *liked* this guy too. Really liked him. Noah made him feel... normal. "So what are we going to do all night, then?"

"Talk." Noah got up to sit next to him on the couch. "You *do* like to talk, don't you?"

"I do."

So they did. Justin told Noah all about growing up in Tucson, a liberal city that nonetheless seemed to have no other queer people besides himself. Oh, and the older gay couple who lived down the street from his house that no one ever talked about.

He talked about his mother, her regular bouts with alcoholism, and how she didn't accept who he was.

Noah told him about growing up in San Diego. How he had come out to his moms at twelve, and how they had embraced him and told him it didn't matter one whit. How he missed the beach at Coronado. He also talked about how he wanted to help people when he graduated. Especially queer kids.

Justin grinned. "It must have been really different in San Diego."

"Oh, I don't know. Maybe. It's a Navy town, so there are a lot of homophobic assholes there too. I just never let that stop me." He grabbed another slice of pizza, grazing Justin's arm.

It was like an electric shock. He looked away. "I wish I had your confidence."

"There's nothing wrong with being gay. With liking other guys." He put a hand on Justin's leg, and it felt like he was on fire. "Did your mom tell you it was wrong, the way you felt?"

"Yeah." Justin stared into Noah's blue eyes. Noah was so close, he could almost hear the drummer's heart beating.

"You can't let people like her, like Zane and his crew tell you there's something wrong with who you are." Noah leaned forward and kissed him.

Justin closed his eyes. It felt so good—all those things he'd always wanted. Sparks. Fireworks. A divine shudder down his spine...

Their lips parted. "I really do like you," Noah said. "I know I promised no monkey business..."

Justin's hand reached forward of its own volition and touched Noah's jeans, working its way up his leg to his crotch, feeling the hardness beneath. He closed his eyes and took a deep breath. "Noah... I like you too. Oh God, I like you." He bit his lip. "But I have to tell you something before this goes any further."

Noah sat back, his eyes widening. "What? Did someone hurt you, before?"

"Not exactly." *No way out but through.* "Noah, I'm trans. You knew that, right? The whole school has been talking about it on Instagram and Snapchat."

Noah's eyes went wide. "Wait... you're... you're not...?"

"I'm a guy, just like you. Except on the outside, and one of these days soon—"

Noah's face darkened, and he pushed himself away from Justin. "Why didn't you tell me? I was starting to fall for you."

"I thought you *knew*." Justin fought back tears, held back his anger. Why was it *always* like this? "Everyone knows. After what happened yesterday. I thought you did too, that it didn't matter. Noah, I didn't mean to—"

Noah's expression was flat and unreadable. "I think you should go."

"What? I'm sorry! Look, if we could just talk about this…"

Noah stood and grabbed Justin's duffle bag, thrusting it at him. "I'll bring you your clothes at school tomorrow." He ushered Justin to the door.

"If we could just—"

"You lied to me. I trusted you, and you lied to me." He looked really hurt.

The door slammed, leaving him as alone as he had ever been.

Justin felt like crying. *I'm so sick of this.* He hated being treated like a freak. being rejected, over and over again.

I hate living like this.

Justin walked down the moonlit road, past the palo verdes and creosote bushes and houses that were mostly dark. It was after midnight, and he didn't know where to go.

He'd known transitioning would be hard, but he hadn't expected it to be like this.

Everybody knew, and nobody wanted him—not Noah, and not even his own mother. *No one will ever love me.*

He was fooling himself if he expected to have a normal life, to be like a cis guy. To fool anyone but himself.

I'm a freak.

He came to a park, dark and abandoned, and stared at the playground equipment. There was a plastic jungle gym with a little yellow chamber at top. It would do.

Looking around to make sure no one saw him, he climbed the ladder and eased himself inside. It was a bit tight, but it was shelter.

Justin put down his duffle bag as a makeshift pillow beneath his head and lay down on his back.

He was exhausted, physically and emotionally. His mother had abandoned him, and the way Noah had looked at him still made him want to cry.

Tomorrow, Zane and his friends would be waiting for him at school.

It was too much. He was tired of fighting.

He closed his eyes. He would figure out what to do in the morning. Just then, he needed to sleep.

———

"Say it." His mother glared at him through a drunken haze.

Jenny whimpered. "No." He was seven years old, and this was the day he lost his childhood innocence.

His mother's eyes burned into him like the eyes of a demon as she held his hand over the burner. "You will not backtalk your mother. Say it."

The skin on his fingers was starting to really hurt. He struggled to pull his hand away from the stove, but his mother held it there firmly, her grip on his wrist tightening. "No," he whispered.

"Saaaaay it!" she hissed, her black eyes boring into him, her breath smelling of old cigarettes, and pushed his hand down onto the coil of hot metal.

He screamed, and whimpered though his tears. "I'm... I'm not a boy." He howled the pain flared anew in his burnt hand.

His mother shoved it into a bowl of ice water. "That's right, you're not. Now you remember that, next time you think of spouting this foolishness, Jennifer Ashley Bailor."

Justin awoke with a start.

The morning air was chilly. There was dew on the plastic edges of his little hideaway. He sat up and stretched, wincing at the ache in his back. He wasn't used to sleeping on hard surfaces.

His mother was right, after all. He was a fool. A freak *and* a fool...

He felt a preternatural sense of calm descend upon him. Events had all led him to this place, from when he was a child until the day before. He was no longer scared, or worried, or even bitter. He knew what he had to do.

He climbed down from the jungle gym, leaving his duffle bag behind. He wouldn't need it anymore, after today.

Then he checked his wallet. He had $3.00—plenty for the Sun Tran bus fare into town. There was a stop just down the street.

He walked along the edge of the road, barely shifting as cars whooshed past him at sixty miles an hour, just inches away.

As the sun rose above Shadow Mountain, he sat down at the bus stop to wait. Other passengers showed up one by one—an elderly woman with a walker, a young man with white ear buds, a man in a business suit in tennis shoes.

Justin ignored them all. It wouldn't be much longer.

The bus was late, but he was in no hurry. He paid his fare, and took a seat at the back, staring out numbly at the buildings they passed as the bus made its way down Oracle, toward downtown.

In his mind, he replayed the events of the week, over and over on a loop.

Bus driver. Bathroom. Coach. Roll Call. Deadnamed. Kicked Out. Beaten up. Noah.

Bus driver. Bathroom. Coach. Roll Call. Deadnamed. Kicked Out. Beaten up. Noah.

The words took on a numbing quality inside his head, and eventually they lost all meaning.

Half an hour later, the bus pulled into its stop at the transfer station, in the heart of downtown.

Justin got off the bus and looked around at the skyscrapers surrounding him. *There. That one.*

"Sir, can you spare some change?" The woman was missing a few of her teeth. Her blue eyes looked up at him, hopeful.

He handed her his last dollar.

"God bless you," she called after him.

"Not likely," he said under his breath, as he entered the lobby of the building.

"Can I help you?" the security guard, Ted—at least, according to his name tag—asked him.

"I'm here to see my father. He works on the 12th floor."

Ted smiled and gestured toward the elevators. "Take the one on the left."

"Thanks," Justin said, and managed a perfunctory smile. "Can I use your bathroom?"

"Right back there."

There was one more thing he wanted to do. He went inside and locked the door.

He looked at himself in the mirror, willing himself to be the man he knew he was. The curve of his face was still too feminine, the skin too smooth.

He wanted to be Justin, not Jenny, when they found him. He wanted to break *their* hearts—Zane and his mother and Noah's—just this once.

Nothing changed.

With a resigned shrug, he left the bathroom, and took the elevator up to the top floor.

Justin had expected to have to force the door open, but someone before him had left it unlocked. A pile of abandoned cigarette butts told him the reason.

He was glad he'd never started smoking. *That shit will kill you.*

He crossed the roof and climbed up on the ledge of the building, swaying a little with vertigo as he looked at the street far below. Just one more step and he'd be free.

Just one step.

"Hey there."

Full Circle

"Look, I get it." Ryan desperately needed to *reach* this kid. Their stories were so alike, even though they were separated by three decades. "It seems like things will never get better, but I know what you're going through."

Justin wiped his eyes with the back of his hand. "How could you understand? You're not *like* me." He turned and climbed back up on the ledge, staring down at the street far below.

"I tried to kill myself too. Before my parents kicked me out. " He inched forward just a bit while Justin's back was to him. He couldn't let the kid fall.

"So?"

"I was so depressed about being gay. About how the other kids treated me because I was different, even before I came out." He closed his eyes. That had been a dark time in his life, when he'd truly thought he was beyond redemption. "I didn't see how it was ever going to get any better. I was so sick, so tired. I thought I was a freak."

At that word, Justin looked back at him. "A freak?"

Ryan nodded. He stared at Justin's back, pleading silently with the kid to stay where he was. To not make that leap.

Justin was quiet for a long time. So long that Ryan was beginning to wonder if the kid had heard him.

At last he said, "What stopped you?"

"Let me tell you."

Ryan sat on the bedroom windowsill in his family's apartment, twelve floors up from Lake Street. He'd jimmied the safety window open, and his legs dangled over the void. It would be so easy to just let himself go limp, to let it all go...

Far below, one of the L trains negotiated the turn onto Wells Street, its loud *clackety-clack* announcing its passage to everyone within five blocks. The wind blew chilly off of Lake Michigan, making him shiver.

Just let go. That's all he had to do. Lean forward a bit, and fall... twelve stories should be enough to ensure a quick end.

He was sick, and he was tired. Sick of the kids at Williams Wells making fun of him, screwing with him every day, scrawling *faggot* on his locker, spitting in his food, pushing him from behind without provocation.

Tired of fighting his desires. Of reading the Bible every night and trying to be a better Christian.

Christian.

Christian Simms and his football buddies had stuffed Ryan into a trash can that afternoon, and he'd climbed out covered in moldy food and bits of shredded paper.

Just that morning, he'd finally been feeling good about himself, when he'd worked up the courage to approach Andy Marks, the other gay kid in school, and ask him out on a date.

Andy had rejected him. Maybe he didn't like Ryan the way Ryan liked him. Maybe he already had a boyfriend. It didn't matter.

The day had gone rapidly downhill from there.

He'd been harassed and pushed around by the other kids in school every day for three months, and now that Christmas was approaching, he didn't want to fight it, or them, anymore.

There was a light tap at the door.

"Go away," he said, his heart beating faster. He didn't want his mother to see him like this. He wanted it to be quick and painless, so she wouldn't have to worry about him anymore.

The door opened. "Hey, it's just me, Andy. Your mom said I could—" He stopped, staring at Ryan, framed by the window.

Ryan looked back at his friend. "Hey."

"Hey. What... what are you doing?"

"What does it look like?" Ryan was done with the niceties.

"It looks like you either couldn't stand the heat in here, or you have a death wish."

"Bingo." Ryan didn't really feel like talking. "Why are you here?

You made it pretty clear how you felt about me, earlier. You don't need to stay around to watch the wreckage."

Andy was silent.

"What, nothing to say?" he glanced over his shoulder at his friend. *Ex friend.*

"I came to apologize. You caught me off guard in school today."

"Apologize for what? You don't like me—that was clear enough."

"It's not like that. Look, I was just scared of what the other kids would think. I'm not brave like you." Andy was shaking.

That got his attention. "You think I'm brave?"

"Yeah. The way you insist on being yourself, no matter how much shit it gets you into. You have no idea how much I look up to you for that. You're... exceptional."

"You're just saying that because I'm sitting here on the window ledge, and you don't want me to jump."

Andy laughed nervously. "Maybe. But it's still true."

"I'm sick of being brave, or exceptional, or whatever," Ryan said, hearing the bitterness in his own voice. "Every day, it just gets worse."

"I know." Andy was quiet for a long time.

Maybe it was time to get on with it, before Andy, or anyone else, could stop him. He leaned forward.

"Wait!" Andy's frantic voice froze him.

I don't want to hurt him. "What?"

"I brought a gift for you." He pulled something out of his pocket. Ryan couldn't tell what it was from his perch.

"What is it?"

"You have to come inside to see." He sounded anxious.

No wonder. "Just tell me."

"It's a rainbow bracelet. I made it for you." He held it out like a lifeline. "I'm sorry I said no before. But I do want to go out with you. I want you to show me how to be strong."

Ryan closed his eyes. There it was. The thing he had been waiting to hear, had been hoping for, for years.

But it was too late. Wasn't it? He was so tired. He was sick of being the faggot. The queer one.

Andy must have read his mind. "It's *not* too late, Ryan. Come on inside. Talk to me. You have to let me reach you."

Something in Andy's voice touched him in a way that nothing else had in a long time. The numbness inside him loosened its grip on him, and the pain came roaring back, bringing with it something else. A realization.

I don't want to die.

He pulled his legs back inside his room and got up, and the world wobbled around him. He staggered and fell to the ground and began sobbing uncontrollably.

Andy sat down next to him, his back against Ryan's bed, and pulled him up into his arms. "It's okay," he whispered, rocking Ryan back and forth slowly. "It's all going to be okay."

Ryan felt the warmth of Andy's chest through their shirts. Slowly, sob by small sob, the anguish lessened, absorbed in the cotton of Andy's t-shirt. At last it ended, leaving him hollowed out.

The pain was gone. He had another boy's arms around him. And for the first time in a long time, he felt safe and loved.

"May I?" Andy held up the little bracelet. It was hand-made, the colors of leather intertwined, all six from the LGBT rainbow.

"Please." He sat up and held out his wrist, and Andy tied the laces tight but not too tight.

"It's beautiful. Thank you."

For his response, Andy kissed him.

* * *

"After that, everything changed," Ryan closed his eyes, remembering those amazing days. "Andy was on the soccer team. We would walk down the halls, hand in hand, and no one would say a thing. It was like dating Superman."

"You could have stayed in the closet."

Ryan snorted. "Some guys could. I wasn't one of them. Some of us were born under the pink moon."

Justin snorted, but he managed a slight smile.

Ryan pushed ahead. "I believe that we have more in common

than the things that make us different. That one of us can reach out to another and *connect* and say 'I see you. I understand you. You're not alone anymore'."

The world stood still. The wind had died down, and the sound of the traffic from far below dwindled down to nothing as if the cars had all just vanished.

Justin turned to stare at him.

"You have a choice." Ryan held out his hand. "And for once, you have someone who will stand by your side when you make it." He held Justin's gaze, putting every ounce of love and compassion and understanding he had into that look.

It wasn't going to be enough. He saw Justin waver, saw the doubt flash through his eyes.

"Give me a chance. Please." He held the kid's gaze. "You're not a *freak*, Justin. You deserve to be loved."

Justin stared at him, and for a moment, time really did stand still. The seconds stretched out into minutes, and the world held its breath.

At last, Justin nodded and exhaled, and ever so slowly he stepped down off the ledge.

Ryan pulled the boy down into his arms and hugged him fiercely as Justin began to cry. "I don't want to be a freak."

"You're not." Justin was warm in his arms, sobbing almost uncontrollably. "They're the freaks."

He just held the kid for the longest time, like Andy had done for him all those years ago.

At last, he whispered, "I want to make you a proposal. Come home with me. I'll get us something to eat. You can stay with us tonight. Tomorrow we'll get Child Protective Services out to your house to check on your mother. If she's as bad as you say, I should have no trouble getting you out of there."

"You're not trying to pick me up, are you?" Justin said, sniffling.

Ryan snorted. "You're underage, and a hot mess to boot. Are you kidding?" He held Ryan out at arm's length. "My husband and I have a foster license. And if you're not comfortable after tonight, we'll find another place for you to stay. So what do you say? Do we have a deal?"

Justin nodded, wiping his eyes. "Deal."

"Come on. Let's go home." He'd have to check in with his boss, but he had a lot of personal time coming. Plus he'd need to check with his friend in Social Services. But that could wait. For now he just wanted to get Justin down off the roof.

Home

Ryan was talking to someone on his cell phone. They were in the garage, the cool air a balm after the warmth of the roof.

Justin wasn't sure why, but he trusted this guy. Something had shifted between them during their long talk. Ryan had actually *listened*. He seemed to understand everything Justin was going through.

Justin didn't believe in God. But something had sent Ryan to find him.

Ryan had called him *exceptional*. No one had ever called him that before.

Ryan finished his call. "You ready?"

Justin nodded.

"Let's go."

Ryan's Prius was waiting for them. "Sit in the front with me." His guardian angel cleared off some files from the passenger seat and shoved them into the back of the car. "Buckle up."

When Justin was strapped in, he started the car, and pulled out of the garage.

Justin stared out the window at the cloudless sky, trying to imagine Ryan as a teenager falling head over heels for a boy. He couldn't see it. The man seemed so adult. So grounded.

"I cleared it for you to stay with us tonight. In the morning we'll figure a few things out, okay?"

"Like what?" He hadn't thought much beyond dinner—which sounded good to his rumbling stomach—and a place to sleep.

"Like what happens next for you. I know some friends down at Wingspan—"

"What's that?"

"The LGBT center. If I can get temporary guardianship of you, I want you to meet some other trans folks here in town. Will you do that for me?"

Temporary. Justin nodded. "I'd like that." He hadn't known places like that existed.

"We also need to set some ground rules," Ryan said sternly.

That didn't sound good.

"As long as you're staying with us, you need to be home by nine PM. No exceptions. If you have a problem, you tell me first before you try to do something about it. There will be no secrets between us. You call me whenever you need me."

"I don't have a phone."

"We'll get you a temporary one."

There it was again. *Temporary.*

This new life of his was only that. *Temporary. A mirage.*

In a day, maybe two or three, he'd be thrown back into the old life, and nothing would have changed.

He stared glumly out the window at the businesses as they passed, wondering why he had let this man talk him out of jumping.

Well, he could always find another way out.

"Hey, you've gone all quiet on me. What's going on in that head of yours?"

Justin just sighed.

"Come on, no secrets, remember? What is it?"

Justin shook his head. "Nothing's going to change. You'll get tired of me, and send me home in a day or two."

Ryan veered off the side of the road, kicking up a cloud of dust, and shut it off. He turned to face Justin. "Listen to me. I can't promise you exactly what's going to happen next." His warm brown eyes were fixed on Justin's, as if he were trying to make him believe what he was saying through sheer force of will. "But I will promise you this. You are *never* going back to that old life. Whatever comes next for you, it's going to be a thousand times better. Got it?"

Justin's eyes went wide, and he nodded meekly.

"Sometimes we all need saving. You just have to accept that you're worthy of it."

He restarted the car and pulled back onto the road.

Am I worthy? He wondered about that the rest of the way to Ryan's home.

Ryan pulled the car up into a driveway at the end of a cul-de-sac. The sun had set and it was quickly getting dark—the Prius's lights flashed across a modest tan brick house and carport, and then were extinguished, leaving them in darkness.

"You ready?"

"For what?" At this point he wasn't sure he was ready for anything.

"To meet my husband."

Justin had never met a married gay couple before. "Sure. What's his name?"

"Andy." Ryan grinned. "Come on."

Andy? Surely it couldn't be the same one...

Justin followed Ryan up through the gate at the front of the house. The home was simple but well-maintained, with a row of rose bushes in full bloom along the front.

"Honey, we're home," Ryan called through the screen door, ushering Justin inside.

A guy even taller than Ryan emerged from the kitchen, with short-cropped dark hair and warm brown eyes. "Hi there," he said to Justin. "I'm Andy."

"*The* Andy?" It was like he'd just met a movie star.

Andy and Ryan exchanged a look. "Yes, *the* Andy," Ryan said with a grin.

"I don't know what Ryan has been telling you about me." He beckoned the two of them into the dining area. "I hope you guys are hungry. Dinner's almost on. Nothing special, just tacos."

"I love tacos." Justin mostly lived off of Mac 'n Cheese, peanut butter and jelly, and dry cereal at home. "Can I help?"

"Sure. Grab the spatula there."

Justin picked it up.

"Okay, I need you to stir the ground turkey. I like it better than ground beef... it has a cleaner taste."

"Got it." Justin used the spatula to turn over the meat, settling it back into the pan with a sizzle and filling his nose with its spicy aroma.

Andy pulled out a cutting board and started chopping lettuce and tomatoes. He glanced over at Justin. "Kid's a pro at this, Ryan," he said with a grin.

Justin grinned back.

Ryan pulled out a long ceramic dish. "My sister made this for us. It's got ridges, see? You put the tacos in here like this." He demonstrated, dropping in eight shells. "That meat about ready?"

"I think so?" Justin tried a bite, almost burning his tongue. "It's good."

"Okay, drain the grease and bring that over here."

Justin did as he was told, caught up in the moment.

"Do we have any more cheese?" Ryan called.

"In the freezer, bottom shelf on the door."

Ryan kissed Andy on the cheek as he brought the cheese back to the counter. "Okay, fill each of those shelves about halfway with meat, then I'll top them with cheese and pop them in the oven."

As he scooped the meat into each shell with the spatula, he saw the look Ryan gave Andy, somewhere between admiration and love.

How do they do that? It was simple. Basic. Something he'd never experienced at home.

He wanted it so much that it hurt.

Once the tacos came out of the oven, they topped them with lettuce and tomatoes, and sat down together at the couple's small table in the dining area next to the kitchen.

What followed was something that Justin had never known before. A real family dinner. Andy brought over the tacos, some baked peppers, a bowlful of tortilla chips, and some of the most delicious looking salsa he'd ever seen.

While they ate, Ryan and Andy talked about work, and Justin just sat back to watch, enjoying the byplay between the two men. It had an ease and comfort that spoke to him of family, stability, and shared time, something like the old "Leave it to Beaver" show he used to watch in re-runs. Or maybe "The Cosby Show." It had always seemed like an impossible dream and here it was, right in front of him.

He wanted to reach out and grasp it.

"I talked to CPS. Justin, they're going to visit your mother's house on Wednesday. Are you sure that's what you want?"

"Yes," he said without hesitation. "She's not my mother. Not really. I don't want to go back there." If he never saw her again, he'd consider himself lucky.

"We have the okay to keep you here for a few days. We've had foster kids before."

Was that what he was now? A foster kid? "Okay." All of a sudden his hunger fled. Then it dawned on him. "You're the social worker friend, too."

Andy grinned.

"Told you he was quick," Ryan said with an admiring smile.

"One more thing." Andy put a warm hand on his. "Ryan and I talked about this on the phone. We'd like to have you stay with us long-term, if the judge okays it. At least through the school year." He addressed Justin as if he were an adult. "Is that something you would like? It's your decision."

Justin looked around the house. It was warm and comfortable, and safe. He'd never imagined living in a place like this. "Yes, please." It came out as a squeak.

"What's that?"

"Yes, I'd like that." He had no idea how much he'd wanted it until it was right there in front of him.

Ryan jumped up. "Hey, I have a little gift for you. Wait here." He disappeared down the hall, and returned with something in his hand—it was a brightly colored braid. He held it out to Justin.

Justin took it. It was a woven, rainbow-colored leather wristband. "Is this—?" He held it out reverently, like a sacred object.

"Yes, the one Andy gave me, that day when he saved my life." He reached over to squeeze Andy's hand. "I *want* you to have it. It says you are proud of who you are. That no one else can take that away from you."

"I can't take this from you—"

"Give it to me."

Justin handed it back, a little hurt that Ryan had taken it away so easily. His protests aside, he really *did* want it.

"Now hold out your wrist."

Justin did as he was told. Ryan tied the bracelet around his arm and admired his handiwork. "It looks good on you."

"Thanks." He marveled at the band around his wrist, and at the kind man who had given it to him.

"I can't save you, Justin." Ryan's unvarnished honesty and his willingness to treat someone half his age—or more!—seriously was shocking. "Only you can do that for yourself. But I'm here to help, if I can."

And just like that, the world shifted under Justin's feet.

I have a home.

Ryan tucked Justin in. "Sleep well, fair prince."

"Thanks." Justin sounded exhausted.

He stopped at the door and turned to watch. The boy was asleep in less than a minute—the day had taken a lot out of him.

He turned off the light and closed the door to the guest room, then returned to the kitchen with Andy, who was just drying and putting away the last of the dishes. "He's a good kid."

"I can tell. That was a nice thing you did today." He hung up the dish towel and followed Ryan back to their bedroom, then closed the door behind him.

Ryan frowned. "Are you sure you're okay with this?" he asked. They had been burned before by some of the foster kids they'd taken in.

Andy nodded. "I have a good feeling about this one. He's a lot like you."

"I hope you don't mind that I gave it to him. I think he needs it."

"Not at all. You have a generous heart. It's something I've always loved about you." He pulled Ryan close, unbuttoning his shirt to expose the man beneath.

Ryan kissed him, savoring the moment after a long, exhausting day.

"No funny business tonight," Andy teased, pushing him away playfully. "We have a guest, remember."

"Fair enough." Thirty years they'd been together, and Andy was still his perfect guy.

Well, maybe not perfect. He often left the toilet seat up, insisted the TP go on the roll upside down, and never managed to remember to get the clothes out of the drier before they wrinkled.

Oh, and he couldn't sing without making the dogs next door howl, and maybe he was a little heavier than he used to be.

To Ryan, Andy was still perfection when he undressed to take a shower. He whistled appreciatively.

Andy wiggled his ass, and Ryan applauded. Then Andy beckoned him inside, where the sound of the water would cover any noise.

Ryan didn't hesitate.

Justin waited until the door was closed and he heard Ryan pad away down the hall.

Then he sat up in bed and looked at the rainbow band again in wonder. It was woven from six colors of leather, a little faded with the passage of time.

A promise. Maybe, just maybe, he had stumbled across a place where he fit in. Where he could just be Justin.

He looked around the guest room. Moonlight streamed in across the white bedspread, and on the far wall, a tall bookshelf was filled with books of various shapes and sizes. A wise-looking Native American woman gazed down at him serenely from a painting on the wall.

Maybe, just maybe, this could be home.

Epilogue

Justin went back to school a week later.

By then, things were all but settled. He had a place to stay at the Hicks-Marks household for as long as he needed it, and his mother, more concerned about where her next drink was coming from than she was about her only child, had agreed not to contest the decision.

He stepped off the bus and onto campus, his head held high, the woven rainbow wristband wrapped around his arm.

There were whispers among the other students and pointed fingers. Zane, the football player, glared at him as he passed by. But no one assaulted him.

"Justin!" someone called, and suddenly he was wrapped up in Marina's arms. "I was so worried about you! What happened?"

He shrugged, "I had a bad week. But now I'm back."

"Nice swag," she said, looking at his bracelet appreciatively.

"Thanks. It's new. A lot of things are new." So much change in just a week.

"Tell me all about it at lunch, okay? I'm late for class." She squeezed his hand and then ran off toward class.

"Hey, Justin."

Justin turned to find Noah standing there. "Hi." His stomach churned, but he forced himself to stay calm.

They faced each other, like gunslingers in an old western. Noah gave him a lopsided smile. "I'm so sorry I freaked out like that."

So am I. "It's okay." Justin turned to walk away.

Noah grabbed his hand. "Look... I said I'm sorry. I mean it."

Justin turned back to stare at him. He was still cute. "Thanks. That means a lot." And it did. Just not *enough*.

"So... maybe we could... start over? Try again?"

Justin leaned forward and kissed Noah on the cheek. "I don't think so."

He turned away, leaving the drummer red-faced and stammering.

He closed his eyes. Noah was trying. For him. Just like Ryan had tried.

"Maybe..."

"Yes?"

He turned back to Noah. "Maybe we can try just being friends."

Noah nodded. "I'd like that." He held out his hand. "Friends?"

Justin took his hand, ignoring the tingle Ryan's touch inspired. For now, friends was good. "Gotta run to class."

"See you after school?"

"Sure. See you then."

He could do this. He would find his way in the world, make new friends, and figure out this whole *life* thing, with the help of his friends and his new family.

I am exceptional, after all.

The Boy in the Band has a bit of history too. I initially wrote it as one of my first attempts to craft a trans character, and drew heavily on my own experience at Canyon del Oro High School in Tucson, where I was a gay kid deep in the closet. I later rewrote it for a submission call for another publisher's Young Adult line. They ultimately rejected it, but it's one I am proud of, especially for the connection of the trials and tribulations of a gay kid in one generation with a trans kid in another. I hope you enjoyed it.

TRANSLATION

"*VADO A LETTO.*"

Dominic stared dreamily out the window at the vibrant ivy climbing the brownstone across the street and at nothing at all. His desk was littered with paper, half-empty cans of Wild Cherry Pepsi, and his iPhone, attached to his ears via a long white cord.

It was another Monday morning in the office.

The sexy male Italian voice on the instructional podcast repeated itself. "*Vado a letto.* I am going to bed."

In the window's reflection, he could just make out his boss, Dante, in the office behind him. Dante was behind his desk, his handsome Italian features drawn tight in concentration. "I'd like to *vado a letto* with him," Dominic whispered.

"What?" Kristen was at the desk next to his. She looked vaguely annoyed at the interruption, frowning at him.

He pulled out the earbuds. "Nothing," he said, smiling privately. "Just a little Italian study time."

She grinned. "Still doing that, huh?" She glanced over her shoulder. "He's out of your league, you know."

"Shut up. At least he plays for my team."

"If he's even single." She stuck her tongue out at him and went back to work.

Break time was over. He stared at his screen, where the layout for page seventeen waited.

It was easy money, writing copy for a home decorating magazine. *In Habit* paid the rent, so he could spend his nights writing the great gay American novel. He'd finished one already and had sent it off to a dozen publishers in the hopes of getting his big break.

Sometimes he wondered if he spent his most creative hours and energy on the magazine at the expense of his true passion. Maybe cranking out copy dulled his writing muscles.

Five years out of college, and he'd been published in two prestigious writing journals (which paid next-to-nothing) and had his first novel rejected by ten of twelve publishers. "We're sorry, it's just not what we're looking for" was the universal refrain. Add in his short story and poetry rejections, and he was closing in on seventy. If that old rule of thumb was right, he was only thirty rejections away from getting published. Really published, with a paycheck.

If only it were that simple.

He finished page seventeen's layout, and the next three, and then took a bathroom break. He needed to be away from his desk for five layout-free minutes.

The bathroom was gloriously empty. Remodeled last year for the DIY issue, it was lined with earth-tone tiles, sparkling steel urinals, and one of those sinks with the wide ceramic bowl that sat above the granite countertop.

It was Dominic's sanctuary. As he relieved himself, he stretched his arms out overhead and rested his head against the wall, letting his mind go blank.

The door swung open, and he pulled his arms down in a rush, embarrassed.

"Ciao," his boss said, standing at the urinal next to Dominic.

"Ciao," he replied. "*Come stai?*" He tried not to let his nervousness show. Dante always affected him that way. With his curly dark hair, olive skin, and smoldering Italian good looks, he was *exactly* Dom's type. But the man's effect on his nerves was especially bad here, when his pants were *literally* down. Dante's cologne was almost overpowering.

"You are becoming good," Dante said, clapping him on the back.

"What? Oh, the Italian." Dominic smiled in spite of himself. "*Grazie*," he said, blushing. "My friend Enrico is helping me learn a few new phrases."

Dante had transferred to *In Habit* three months earlier from the company's fashion division, and Dominic had been enthralled by him immediately. He'd restarted the Italian lessons shortly after.

"We are... how do you say it? Working up a new feature on modern Italian designers for October," Dante said casually. He was not pee-shy, clearly. "I thought you might want to take a part..."

His English was good, but not perfect. That was one of the things Dominic found most attractive about him. Dante buttoned up his fly and went to wash up.

"Take part?" Dominic shook his head. "I'm not that good with the language yet." Truth was, Dante was a hell of a lot better with English than Dominic would ever be with Italian.

Next to each other in the mirror, they were about the same height, but where Dominic was thin and blond, Dante was... substantial. Not heavy. Just solid, a real man—that old tall, dark, and handsome thing.

"Dominic?"

"What?" He realized his boss had been talking to him. "Sorry, just a little distracted. What did you say?"

Dante smiled slyly. He clearly knew the power of his good looks. "I said that all these guys speak their English really well. And you could practice some of your Italian with them. It would be a win-win."

Sitting in on the meeting would be a promotion, at least in responsibility. He wasn't sure he should take it. Was this really what he wanted to be doing for the rest of his life?

But if it meant getting closer to Dante...

"I guess I could give it a try."

Dante sank down into his seat, eyeing the uninviting stack of earnings reports and projections on his desk warily. He felt like he was sleepwalking through this job—what should have been fresh and creative was instead dull, repetitive, mind-numbing.

He glanced out his door. Dominic sat at his desk by the window, the natural late-morning sunlight filtered by the trees giving him an almost supernatural glow.

Since his breakup with Robert six months before, Dante had buried himself in work, ignoring all the handsome guys here in New York City. He hadn't been ready to dive back into that pool yet.

But now maybe he was. And he could do worse than the hand-some copywriter. Dominic was talented, really cute, and he was even starting to learn *la bella lingua*.

Dante laughed at himself. Back home in Italy, he would have just walked up to Dominic to ask him out. But this was *gli Stati Uniti*—they did things differently at work here. And he was different now too, since Robert. Still... Dominic was blond, slender, and sweet. And that kind of sweetness in a man was an aphrodisiac for him.

Then again, he was Dominic's boss. Getting involved with an employee was a dangerous game.

Maybe this whole article thing was a bad idea after all. But he'd already committed himself. He'd have to wait and see what the next few days would bring.

He sighed and grabbed a pile of reports from the top of the stack.

⁂

It was a gorgeous spring day, so Dominic grabbed a slice of pepperoni at Peace of Pizza and climbed the stairs to the rooftop terrace of the four-story walk-up that housed *In Habit* to enjoy his lunch.

He ate half the meal and then sank back into the chair, his eyes closed, listening to a little vintage eighties pop—it soothed his jangled nerves. The sun on his face felt good, and he drifted into a state of bliss, forgetting about the magazine and Dante and his writer's block for a few precious moments.

Someone cleared his throat. Dominic's eyes flickered open. *Speak of the devil*—Dante stood there, his lips moving, but Dominic couldn't hear what he was saying. He popped the earbuds out and caught the tail end of the sentence.

"...if I sit here?"

He grinned. "Sure. Sorry, I was a little lost in the music."

"What do you listen to?" His boss brushed the seat clean and sat down, putting a brown paper bag on the table.

"A little modern synth music, some eighties stuff, sometimes some old-school R&B. Calms me down when I get a little manic." He pointed at Dante's lunch. "I wouldn't have pegged you for the brown-bag type."

Dante laughed ruefully. "I have to be careful with my moneys. My condo is *molto caro*... very expensive. I have to pay for it myself now." He pulled out a sourdough panino stuffed with prosciutto, a Pellegrino, and a hardboiled egg.

God, he's gorgeous, Dominic thought, *with his pressed white shirt, thin black tie, his piercing hazel eyes*. Even his laugh. Dominic tried to keep his cool—this guy was his boss, after all. "It's just you?" he said, taking another bite of his now-cold slice of pizza. "What happened?"

Dante looked thoughtful as he chewed on his sandwich. A cool breeze stirred the leaves on the rooftop, and as he watched Dante, Dominic felt goosebumps rising on his arms. *It's just the wind*, he told himself. But he'd always been a lousy liar.

"My boyfriend Robert left me," Dante said at last, staring off into the past. "We were with each other for five years. He's the reason I came here to the United States."

"Seriously? I always thought you came here just to work for the magazine." *Play it cool, Dominic.*

Dante shook his head. "Maybe I would have come here eventually anyhow, but I met Robert in Venice, at Campo San Giacomo one summer day, and fell in love." He smiled wistfully. "Have you ever felt that... *amore*... that instant reaction to someone? They make you shake all over with anticipation? You want to be close with him, but it makes you crazy?"

Dominic nodded, shivering a little inside himself. *If you only knew.*

"It was like that with Robert. He comes to Venice on a student visa. We are together there for four months, and then he leaves." He took a sip of his Pellegrino. "Have you ever stayed there?"

"In Venice? I wish. Not on my salary." He laughed. "*Magari!*"

"If only, indeed." Dante smiled, and the temperature on the rooftop seemed to warm up five degrees.

"So you came here after him? Robert?"

Dante nodded. "Yes, basically. I was working for the company in Italy; when the job at *Live Style* was open, I took it."

"So what happened?" *If I had a boyfriend like you, I'd never let you go.*

Dante shook his head. "I don't know." He finished his sandwich and salted his hardboiled egg. "No, I do know. He slept around behind me... behind my back. Apparently a lot. But he never did tell me why. We wanted different things."

Dominic laughed, forgetting to be nervous. "We have that in common, then. I had an Italian boyfriend once. He slept around on me too. We were going in different directions."

"Exactly! He wanted to be with someone new all the time. The excitement." Dante shook his head. "I wanted something different. I wanted *him.*" He paused. "I'm sorry, I shouldn't be talking to you about all of this."

"It's okay." Dominic suddenly hated this Robert whom he'd never met. "You didn't deserve it," he said, putting his hand out to touch Dante's. A little spark of electricity passed between them, and they pulled their hands away from each other, laughing.

"You didn't deserve it either," Dante said. "You're a good guy."

"Thanks," he said awkwardly.

"So what happened to yours?"

"My what?"

"Your boyfriend who cheated on you?"

Dominic grinned. "He's my roommate."

They met later in the afternoon to go over the interview plans. Dominic was waiting for him as he entered the conference room. Dante took a seat across the table and slid a packet over to him.

In response to Dominic's raised eyebrow, he said, "That's a prospectus of the four designers we're working with. I'd like you to read it and come up with a few questions of your own."

"In Italian?" Dominic looked worried.

Dante laughed. "No, in English is fine."

"When do we start?"

"Villanova arrives tomorrow morning—can you be ready by that time? If not, we can stop this..." Dominic stared up at him across the table. A part of Dante wanted to grab him and kiss him. Hard. *It might be for the best to call this off.*

"I'll be ready." Dominic looked back down, concentrating on the photo of Mario Villanova.

Dante sighed under his breath. There was no doubt about it. He was enchanted.

He stood abruptly, holding a folder in front of him to cover his interest. "That's fantastic. I've got to get back to my desk—much things to do. Tomorrow morning, *a presto?*"

Dominic nodded. "I'll be ready."

Dominic shut down his computer, threw his backpack over his shoulder, gulped down the last few drops of soda, and bounded down the stairs to the street, breathing in the fresh, cool spring air.

God, I wish I could afford to live here in Chelsea, he thought, walking down to the 34th Street subway entrance to catch a train back home. He lived in Brooklyn—just forty-five minutes away, but a whole different world.

He couldn't get Dante out of his head. The man was perfect—gorgeous, intelligent, Italian—three of his favorite things. And he wanted a real relationship, not just a fuck buddy. *If only he saw me as an equal.*

Enrico would be waiting for him at home. His roommate turned-lover turned-roommate worked at the flat on his own little Internet start-up website that never seemed to start up enough to pay his share of the rent on time, but always enough to allow him to go out to the clubs on a Saturday night.

Dominic found a spot to stand close to the train doors and pumped up the volume, blocking out the outside world and letting his mind drift. This was his downtime—the demands of his writing were still a couple hours away, on the other side of the commute and a bite to eat. The songs flowed one into another, blending decades and styles into a crazy musical salad that somehow worked inside his head.

Eventually the train arrived at his stop, and he climbed up the stairs to the street and walked the four blocks to the second-floor flat on St. John's that he shared with Enrico.

"Hey, stranger," his roommate called from the window of their second-floor walk-up. "Get up here. I made dinner."

Dominic grinned. Despite his many faults, Enrico was an excellent cook.

He grabbed the mail on the way up—there was another rejection for his novel, eleven of twelve. Twenty-nine rejections to go to a hundred.

He stuffed it into his backpack and put it out of his mind.

Enrico tasted the sauce, dropping in a little more fresh basil, hand-crushed—Dominic *loved* basil.

He heard his roommate's key in the door as Dominic let himself in, throwing his pack down on the floor and shrugging off his jacket. As Dominic slid into the chair at the small breakfast table in their tiny apartment, Enrico turned off the gas to the stove top. The timing was perfect.

"Hmmm, lasagna?" Dominic asked, sniffing the air.

"Close," Enrico called back. "*Ti ho preparato dei ravioli*," he said, straining the water. He fished out a serving bowl from under the counter, topped the ravioli off with the sauce he'd prepared and some fresh parmesan, and dropped the whole thing onto the table, along with their old, half-melted serving spoon.

"You made me your mamma's ravioli?" Dominic laughed. "So what's the occasion?" Enrico put down a plate in front of him, along with a napkin and some silverware.

"Beer?" he asked.

"Sure." Dominic grabbed the spoon and served himself a generous portion of the steaming pasta. "Now come on, you never make me your mom's special recipe. *Che è successo?*"

It was Enrico's turn to laugh. "You're getting better. Practice, practice, practice!"

"You're a good teacher." Dominic grinned. "Well, most of the time." He took a bite of the ravioli. Enrico sat down across from him and watched him in anticipation.

"*Delizioso*," Dominic said approvingly. "What's up?"

"I have some news," Enrico said, bringing him a Brooklyn Brown Ale. He dished himself out some ravioli. "I sold the site."

"Holy crap," Dominic said, dropping his fork. "That's fantastic. To whom?"

Enrico shrugged. "Some VC from California. Wants me to run the whole thing while they scale it up." He couldn't stop grinning.

"How much?"

"$2 million to start, plus salary."

Dominic jumped up and embraced his roommate. They danced around the living room in each other's arms for a full minute.

"Sorry you let me go now?" Enrico said at last, out of breath. *He didn't want the hug to end.*

"Not at all. You were a lousy fuck. But seriously, Enrico, that's amazing!"

"I know, right?" He sank down on the couch. "There's just one thing."

"What?"

"They want me to move to SF. That's where all the Internet action is."

Dominic sat down beside him, looking overwhelmed. "When?"

Enrico sighed. "Next week. Don't worry—I'll pay my share of the rent for a few months. Until you find another roommate."

Dominic laughed ruefully. "That'll be a first—you paying the rent in advance?" He looked back at the table. "Hence the ravioli?"

"*Sì, è così.*" Dominic grinned back at him, that rakish smile he couldn't resist. "You're not mad at me?"

"How could I be?" He stood and pulled Enrico up with him. "Come on, let's eat. It's getting cold, and I don't like to waste good pasta."

Enrico followed him. *Why did I ever let you go?*

Later that night, Dominic sat in his bedroom on his old leather office chair.

The laptop screen in front of him was blank. Not the friendly, "come play with me" kind of blank. No, the mocking, soul-crushing, "you'll never write another interesting sentence again" kind.

It was after eleven, and a wind was blowing through the branches outside the window.

Frustrated, he slammed the screen down.

Life wasn't fair. He knew he was a damned good writer. So why didn't anyone else see it?

Even Enrico, his layabout ex-boyfriend, was suddenly moving on. *In a week and a half, he'll be gone and I'll still be stuck here.*

He stared out the window at the moonlit street. Cars passed by occasionally below, the headlights playing across the brick building across the street, Moore's Automotive. How many times had he looked at the same sign on sleepless nights? *It's time for a change.*

Though it was almost midnight, he went to find Enrico. He needed someone to talk to, and the man owed him.

"Rico," someone said, shaking his shoulder. "Rico, wake up."

"What?" Enrico said, turning over. He always slept naked, and as his eyes flickered open, he was surprised to see Dominic. He pulled the sheets up over himself, strangely self-conscious. *It's not like he hasn't seen it before.*

"I'm sorry," Dominic said. "I just needed to talk to someone."

Enrico sat up, his back against the headboard. "What's wrong?" He rubbed his eyes sleepily.

Dominic shook his head. "I'm sorry. Never mind, it's late." He turned to go, but Enrico caught his hand.

"Sit." He pulled Dominic down onto the bed. "Come on, out with it."

Dominic settled down next to him on the bed. "I feel like I'm wasting my life, Rico." He sighed. "I got another rejection letter today."

"From whom?"

"Putnam. It's my eleventh. Just one more to go." He squeezed his hands together in his lap. "What if they all hate it? What if I'm not any good?"

Enrico laughed. "That's the last thing you have to worry about, Dom. I've read your book. It's brilliant."

Dominic laughed too. "You *have* to say that."

Enrico shook his head. "No, I don't. Listen, I've read the other stuff you've written, most of it, and there's some real crap in there for sure. But you've grown as a writer these last five years. If they can't see that, fuck 'em. You can always self-publish."

"I guess. It's just that..."

"You feel a little left behind?" Enrico put an arm around his ex's shoulder, well aware of his proximity. He missed these late-night talks together. Missed being Dom and Rico. He'd been a fool to let Dom get away.

They were nose to nose, and Enrico thought there was a spark.

But Dominic turned away. "Yeah. A little. I need to make some changes."

Enrico was silent for a moment. At last, he said. "You could come with me to San Francisco."

Dominic stared at him. "Really?" He looked surprised. "I don't think so. It's sweet of you to offer, but I need to be here. New York is where writers get published."

Enrico nodded, disappointed, and whatever had been in the air between them slipped away. "I guess. But there's one other thing I can help you with that will truly change your life for the better," he said, masking his disappointment with a wicked grin.

"What's that?"

"I can help you get that boss of yours in bed."

"How?"

"I have a five-point plan."

Step one: Know your prey.

The next morning, Dominic got to work early, opening the office door with the keys Dante had entrusted him with. It was a clear, crisp Tuesday morning, and the breeze worked its cold fingers under his scarf and jacket as he struggled with the balky lock, making him shiver.

He slipped inside and climbed up to the second-floor office. It was warmer upstairs, and quiet too. The fluorescent lights were off, leaving the room lit only by the slanted sunlight. He put down his things and powered up his computer.

Then he set about his exploration of Dante's private office.

There was very little of a personal nature in the room, just a photo of his boss with an older woman in front of an old stone house. His mother? She had the same hazel eyes.

There was also one of those page-a-day calendars with English words—ha!

And Dante's laptop. Dominic considered firing it up, but his time was limited and he didn't want to get caught.

He checked the desk drawers. They were unlocked. One held hanging file folders, records, forms, letterhead—nothing of interest.

The next drawer was full of office supplies and, weirdly, an old horseshoe.

In the last drawer, he hit the jackpot. There was a CD of the Italian boy band Il Divo. A ticket stub for the Guggenheim in Venice. Menus for five Chinese restaurants. A stash of PowerBars. And a signed copy of *Debito d'onore*, a Tom Clancy book, translated into Italian.

The door downstairs creaked open on its hinges. He had company. Quietly, he closed the drawer and tiptoed back to his desk, avoiding the squeaky floorboard in the middle of the floor, before whoever it was could reach the top of the stairs.

By the time Dante entered his office, Dominic was hard at work.

"You're in early," his boss called.

"I had a little research to do."

Step two: *Body language.*

They met with the first designer at 10:00 a.m. in the glassed-in conference room. His name was Marco Villanova, and he was quite possibly the gayest man Dominic had ever met. He wore skin-tight orange pants from Abercrombie and Fitch, a floral-print shirt, and a golden silk scarf around his neck. His nails were painted matte black.

"Ciao," Dominic said.

"*Ciao bello,*" Marco said, giving him an air kiss on each cheek. "*Come ti chiami?*"

"Um... Dominic." His Italian failed him. "And you're Marco?"

"Yes, darling," he said with a broad smile, but it felt like he'd failed a test.

Dante came in behind him and gave Marco a big hug. "*Ciao amico... come stai? Per quanti anni non ci abbiamo visti?*"

"Too long, amico. Too long."

They settled in around the table and talked design. Dominic wore a tight V-neck shirt that showed off his chest, and he sat next to

Dante, his body language open and relaxed. At least, he hoped so—he felt more closed and stiff.

It felt so unnatural to keep his arms at his sides all the time instead of crossing them, and he was pretty sure he was giving Marco an excellent view of his crotch from across the glass table. But Enrico swore by this stuff—an open body posture was essential to show his interest in Dante.

"So how do you think of Marco's designs?" Dante asked him, handing over the man's portfolio.

"I think they're great," he said, looking Dante right in the eyes. Enrico said that eye contact was important too—get him all hot and bothered for you. "They remind me of that boy band... Il Divo, is it?"

Dante frowned. "But you haven't looked at them even."

They stared at each other for a long moment. But it didn't *feel* sexy. It just felt weird.

Dante looked away first. Dominic had won the staring contest. So why did he feel like he'd just lost?

"Are you feeling okay?" Dante asked.

"I'm fine," he said. "I like Chinese food," he blurted out. *God, I'm such an idiot.*

Dante shot him a strange look. "Well, look at the portfolio later and tell me how you think of it. I want to feature Marco in the article, and I want your thoughts." His tone was noticeably cooler.

They wrapped up the meeting, and on the way out the door, Marco pinched his ass. "I'm staying at the Travel Inn," he said with a wink. "If you're free later." Then he literally glided out the door.

Dominic shook his head. He sure hadn't meant to hook *that* fish.

Step three: Laugh at his jokes.

Dante called him into his office just after lunch.

His boss was on the phone with the printer. Dante motioned for him to take a seat.

He waited, staring at the framed covers of past issues of the magazine on the wall behind Dante's head. Then he counted the stripes in the carpet under his boss's desk.

As Dante took the printer to task for errors in last month's issue, Dominic stared at his fingernails, noticing for the first time that his right pinkie finger had no "moon" under the nail. *How weird is that?*

The phone slammed down in its cradle, startling Dominic out of his reverie. Dante ignored him for a moment longer, typing something into his laptop.

"You called me in?" he ventured at last, wanting to get back to his work.

"Just a moment..." Dante shuffled some papers, apparently looking for something, and then set the pile back on his desk. "Done. Yes, I wanted to talk to you of the meeting."

"Okay... what about it? I thought it went well." He tried laughing, although Dante hadn't made a joke. It sounded forced, even to him.

Dante glared at him. "It should have been better. Seriously? The way you are flirting with the client? Maybe you're not ready for this responsibility."

"I-I'm sorry," Dominic stammered. "I *am* ready. It was just..."

"Just what?"

"It was just an off day. I'll do better tomorrow." He was mortified and eager to get out of the room before his boss noticed.

"I hope so. Just fix it. Dominic..."

"What, sir?"

"I want that you will succeed here. Don't lose this opportunity."

He tried laughing again and got a black look from his boss.

Dante watched Dominic go, kicking himself for being such an ass. He'd meant to give Dominic a polite, professional warning. But something about him, about the way he was acting today, got under Dante's skin.

He glanced up and saw Dominic sneaking a look at him in the window reflection, and hurriedly got up and closed his office door.

He really needed to release some tension—he felt all worked up —but that was never a good idea *here*. Even with his door locked.

So he threw himself into his work, spending the next several hours wrapping up his budget projections for next quarter, ignoring the persistent tightness in his jeans.

After he finished, he decided he needed to apologize to Dominic —he'd treated him too harshly and it wasn't good for their work relationship, let alone the possibility of something more. But when Dante opened the office door, he was gone. "Where's Dominic?" He glanced at the clock—it was only a quarter after four.

"He said he had something urgent to do," Kristen said without turning around.

Dante frowned. It wasn't like him to leave early, especially without saying a word. Ah well, it could wait until tomorrow.

He sighed and closed the door.

———

Dominic slumped down on the train seat with his eyes closed. His head hurt.

After the meeting with Dante, he'd needed to get away from work, from *him*. The whole plan had gone off the rails. He knew it, and now he felt stupid for even trying. *Why did I listen to Rico?* Good things happened to other people, not him.

He turned up the volume and flipped through his music until he found some old-school hard rock, letting it overwhelm him and push away the dark thoughts in his head.

The train passed from station to station, darkness alternating with light outside the windows. He breathed in deeply, his temple resting against the cool glass, trying to calm his angry and scattered thoughts.

At least Enrico should be home when he got there. He needed someone to talk to.

At last, he reached his own station and made his way home. He climbed the steps two at a time and burst through the door, letting it slam behind him. "Rico, I've had a shitstorm of a day…" he started, but all the lights were off. No one was home.

He flicked on some lights and went through the mail. Nothing—not even a rejection.

He grabbed a Wild Cherry Pepsi and a bag of Oreos and threw himself down in front of his laptop.

He opened a blank page, and this time something happened. He started to pour everything he was feeling onto the page—the copywriter and his boss, the back and forth, the desire and missteps and foiled plans.

It flowed from him in a rush, like the strong, steady pressure of a tsunami, clearing everything out before it with an unimaginable force.

His main characters sparked and laughed and shouted and intertwined, and the whole story was just *there*, as if a door inside him had been thrown wide open.

The sun set outside, and the commute traffic drifted by below as the words continued to rush from his brain through his fingers and onto the page. He stopped only to take a brief sip of his Pepsi and snatch a cookie or two, intent on the process.

Only it wasn't a process, not tonight. It was a state of being, a high—like being inside the story. He was a conduit.

Headlights threw crazy shadows across his dark bedroom ceiling. He pushed opened the window to let in some fresh air with one hand while still typing with the other, and the sounds of the street drifted up into the flat. Car brakes squeaking, passersby laughing, the sizzle of the hotdog vendor's cart at the corner.

He sucked it all in, the sounds, the smells, the thick New York atmosphere, and it flowed through his fingers with everything else.

This was what it felt like when the dam of writer's block finally broke, these precious moments when the writing wasn't work but pure joy. Immersed in something greater than himself, tapped into another world that was writing itself through him.

Evening passed into night and the moon rose above, casting its pale silver light into Dominic's room.

Still he wrote. He could see the whole story laid out before him now, a plot line in his head like a glowing golden roadmap. His lovers split, traveled separate paths through the City, their ultimate reunion preordained. Lives twisted and melted down and were recast, and the ending drew ever closer. It just felt *right*.

Somewhere around three in the morning, he finished, the final scene flowing out of him just as readily as the first. He typed the last few words, capping it off with an exclamatory THE END. Then he exhaled the breath he hadn't known he was holding.

Exhausted, he slumped down in his chair, too tired to make it to bed, and fell asleep.

Across town in a condo overlooking the East River, Dante stared out at the same bright moon. Thin clouds wrapped it in silver, and the light sparkled off the river below.

He sighed, remembering how he and Robert used to enjoy walking in the City in the winter under the moonlight, bundled from head to toe.

It was time to let him go. Not the memories—he would always treasure those. But the man was long gone and he wasn't coming back.

He had packed up the last of Robert's things, the little bits and pieces of a life together that his lover hadn't taken with him. Hair products. Photos of the two of them. Trinkets they'd bought together in Venice. All into a cardboard box, sealed with packing tape.

Then he'd gone to bed, but something had woken him up. Some sense of unfinished business that tickled his mind in the middle of the night.

So now he stared at the moon and wondered what the next chapter of his life would bring.

Tomorrow he would say something to Dominic. Tell him that he was ready for a new life or something. That he was ready to move on.

So they worked together—who cared? He could always take another position.

He was ready to take a chance on life again.

Dante left his home early. He wanted to catch Dominic before the rest of the office showed up, and he often came in before work to get some things done.

As he walked up 10th Avenue, his heart beat a little faster. He was actually excited about this. He thought about getting a coffee at the Everyday Grind, but decided he was too worked up already.

The world looked a little brighter, even if it was a brisk Wednesday morning—he could see his breath and he rubbed his hands together for warmth before shoving them back into the pockets of his long wool coat.

He unlocked the door to the office and climbed the stairs, framing in his mind just what he wanted to say. He paused before taking the last step, took a deep breath, and plunged ahead.

There was no one there.

It's still early, he told himself. Disappointed, he settled his brief-case on the floor behind his desk and turned on his computer, determined to get something done to take his mind off the butterflies in his stomach.

Surely Dominic would come through the door at any moment.

Fifteen minutes stretched into a half hour, and then an hour. He made himself coffee just to have something to do, but his earlier instincts had been right—it just made him jittery. An hour and a half, and others began to arrive, filing into the office one by one.

Still no Dominic.

Finally it was a quarter after nine. He was forty-five minutes late and Dante was getting worried, and then angry. *First he leaves early without a word, and now he's running late without a call?*

He looked up Dominic's number and called him. There was no answer.

He slammed down the receiver, getting startled looks from some of his officemates. At the moment, he didn't care.

———

Enrico sat in Dominic's chair at the end of the bed, watching his ex sleep. It was early afternoon—he'd found Dom slouched in this same chair in front of the keyboard at half-past four and had dragged him into bed.

Dominic started to wake, stretching out his arms above his head and yawning. He opened his eyes and pushed himself up.

"Hey, lazybones," Enrico said. "Sleep well?" It must have been some night.

"Hey," Dominic said, rubbing his eyes. "What time is it?"

"About 1:00 p.m. You have a bit of a bender last night?" He was so cute when he first woke up, his hair sticking up in a fauxhawk.

"Yeah... wait, 1:00 p.m.? Shit!" He jumped out of bed, throwing the covers off. "Shit, shit, shit! Dante's gonna kill me."

"Hey, slow down. It's covered. I called in sick for you. Said you came down with that bird flu thing."

"You didn't!"

Enrico laughed. "I said you had a fever and you couldn't come in today."

"Asshole." Dominic threw a pillow at him. "But thanks. I had a writing epiphany last night, I think." He sank back down onto the bed.

"What happened?"

Dominic related his run-in with Dante and how he'd screwed things up.

Enrico sat with him, nodding and listening, being a friend. He wished they could go back to what they'd had and forget all the baggage between them.

Maybe someday soon, if he played his cards right. When Dominic finished, he grinned.

"What? I basically just screwed up both my potential love life *and* my relationship with my boss."

"It's not so bad," Enrico said. "And I know how to fix it."

Dominic shook his head. "The last time I listened to you, I ruined things."

"Not this time. This one can't fail." *At least I hope not.*

Dante turned off all the lights except the one in the stairwell and locked the building door behind him for the night. Dominic had missed two meetings today and hadn't even bothered to call.

His earlier ardor for the copywriter was all but gone.

If Dominic didn't show up tomorrow, he'd be fired. Even if he did, the man better have a damned good excuse—like he'd been run over by a bus and they'd had to amputate both his legs.

Dante walked home in a foul mood.

Dominic woke slowly on Thursday morning, sunlight streaming in through his window. He felt great. Today was the day things would finally start to change for him. His writing orgy had produced something pretty good—he hadn't been so sure when he'd first woken up the previous afternoon, but when he sat down to read it after lunch, he was pleasantly surprised.

It was good. Maybe not Great American Novel good, but it was something. With a bit of work and filling out, he had the bones of a decent novel to follow up his first one, if it ever got published.

Time enough to worry about that later. He stretched, enjoying the sheer luxury of being in bed, and relaxed for just a moment longer.

At last he climbed out of the covers to get ready for the new day. Everything felt just a little better than usual this morning—the hot shower on his naked form, the sharp tang of Irish Spring invigorating him.

Even the long ride to the office didn't seem so bad, as he planned his entrance. He knew there was something happening between the two of them, him and Dante. And he thought Dante felt it too. He felt emboldened by his writing success, and Enrico had helped him with a little Italian to sweep his boss off his feet.

He would ask Dante out, consequences be damned.

He arrived half an hour early and was delighted to see that Dante was already there, alone, working in his office. He dropped his pack on his chair and knocked on the doorframe. Dante didn't look up.

"Come in," was all he said.

Dominic did, and before Dante could interrupt him, before he could lose his newfound courage, he said *"Dante, ti voglio scopare. E spero che mi voglia scopare anche."*

Dante looked up, and his features visibly hardened. "Where were you yesterday?" he said, his voice dangerously low.

"I was at home, sick..."

Dante stood and leaned forward, hands clenched on the edge of his desk. "Then why didn't you call?"

Dominic was at a loss. He did call. Well, Enrico called. *Oh God, he did call, didn't he?* "I... I'm sorry, Dante..."

"Mr. Giordano."

"I'm sorry, Mr. Giordano." How had things gone so far downhill, so quickly? Outside Dante's office, he heard some of his coworkers start to arrive. "I meant to call. It's just..."

"You leave early without telling on Tuesday. You do not arrive at work at all on Wednesday, and do not even telephone to tell me why." Dante's voice was slowly rising. Now he was almost shouting. "Now you come here and tell me you want to fuck me?" He pounded the desk, and Dominic jumped back a step.

He'd never seen Dante like this before. *What the hell did I say?*

"Take your backpack and leave. I have to let you go, Mr. Ryan." He wiped his hands together like he was brushing off something dirty. "You'll find your final paycheck in the post next week."

Dominic ran from Dante's office to his desk to gather his belongings, his cheeks hot with anger and embarrassment for the second time that week, not wanting to talk to anyone.

Kristen grabbed his arm. "Dominic, what happened?" she said, frowning, but he shook her off.

"Leave me alone." He snatched up his backpack and ran down the stairs and out to the street, not caring where he was going, only needing to be as far from that place as possible.

* * *

Dante watched him go and closed the door of his office, ignoring the startled looks of the employees who'd witnessed the scene. He should have handled that better.

But he hadn't expected the copywriter to openly proposition him here in the office—that was way out of bounds, and given that Dominic also skipped out of work without an explanation or call the day before, what choice did he have?

He sank down into his chair, resting his head in his hands. "*Cazzo*," he cursed and brushed all the paperwork off his desk and onto the floor.

* * *

Dominic spent the rest of morning in Times Square, watching the tourists go by, berating himself for screwing things up. And in record time.

It was a cold, blustery day, and a little after noon it started to rain. Dominic cursed his luck and hurried to the subway station to catch a train home. So much for his Chelsea dreams.

He rode the train in silence for once—it was almost empty since most everyone else was still at work. He didn't know what to do next. He had enough saved up for a month or two, but how would he pay for the apartment after that? And how would he get another job? They weren't exactly growing on trees these days, especially for someone who had just been fired.

On the way up to his apartment, he picked up the mail out of habit, stuffing it into his bag without bothering to look at it.

Enrico was gone again, and the apartment was empty.

He'd started to realize that something wasn't right on his way home. Even *he* shouldn't have been able to run his life into a ditch so quickly, not without help.

When he got back to his computer, he pulled out the scribbled notes he'd made, the plan Enrico had helped him put together. He typed it into Google translate: "Dante, ti voglio scopare. E spero che mi voglia scopare anche."

"Crap," he said, reading the result. *Dante, I want to fuck you. And I hope that you want to fuck me too.*

He googled the word *scopare*. Literally it meant to sweep, but there was that other, more explicit meaning, too. And it was often confused with *scappare*, to escape, or get out of here. That's what he'd meant to say. It was supposed to be *scappare*.

Enrico had written it down for him. Enrico had laid out the whole plan to "get" Dante.

Enrico said he had called in sick for me. Enrico wanted him to move to California.

Dominic sank back into his chair, stunned. He'd blown it with Dante, for sure, but he'd had help. Enrico had wanted to get him fired.

He sat there for a long time, just staring at the table in front of him, waiting for Enrico to come home from wherever the fuck he was.

At last, he spied a letter sticking out of his half-opened backpack. He snatched it up and glanced at the return address—it was from the last publisher he'd sent his novel to nine months before. The gestation period, Enrico had called it. It had sounded funnier then.

He ripped open the envelope, forgetting the horrible events of the day for just a minute. This one thing could wipe away the miasma of this moment, could put him on a road to something better, if only...

"We're sorry to inform you..." was all he read before he crumpled up the letter in a little ball and hurled it across the room. "Shit, shit, shit."

It was at that moment that Enrico came home.

Enrico climbed the stairs toward their apartment, humming. He'd spent the day shopping, buying some new clothes at Neiman's to take with him to California.

He juggled the bags and his keys, finally managing to open the door, and saw his roommate sitting on the couch. "Hey, Dom…" he said, dropping his bags by the entrance, and stopped short.

Dominic stood slowly, his face dark like a thundercloud, all purple rage and thunder. Enrico frowned. "You don't look so good."

"I got fired this morning." Dominic's voice sounded strange, low and strangled.

"_Cazzo_!" Enrico said. "What happened?"

"You didn't call in sick for me, that's what happened." He poked Enrico in the shoulder. "You told me to tell my boss I wanted to fuck him. That's what happened."

The blood drained from Enrico's face. He'd never seen Dominic like this. He backed away.

"Why the fuck did you do that to me?" Dominic asked. He grabbed Enrico's shirt and pushed him up against the door. "What the hell were you thinking?"

Enrico squirmed in his grasp. "It's not what you think," he said, his eyes wide. "I just… I just wanted…"

Dominic was way into Enrico's personal space. "You just wanted what?"

Enrico tried to shrink away. "I just wanted you to move with me," he stuttered. "I wanted things to be the way they used to. I never thought they would fire you."

Dominic let him go, his disgust palpable. "I had a good job there. It wasn't perfect, but it was a job. And I _really_ liked Dante." He turned away.

Enrico put his hand on Dominic's shoulder. "I'm so sorry—let me fix this..."

Dominic shook him off. "You've done enough." He grabbed his jacket and his keys, and pushed past Enrico to the door. "I'll be out for four hours. When I get back, I want you gone. Maybe your new sugar daddy VC can put you up in a hotel somewhere until it's time for you to leave."

It wasn't supposed to go down like this. "Dom, I'm sorry. Come on, don't let things end this way." Desperate, he played his last card. "I think I'm still in love with you."

"Don't." Dominic shook his head without turning back. "Be gone when I get home." Then he was out the door.

Enrico stared at the door for a long time, but Dominic wasn't coming back for him.

When Dominic returned later that evening, there was no sign of Enrico, although some of his stuff was still there. Time enough to deal with that tomorrow.

That night, he tossed and turned for hours before finally settling into a decent sleep.

In the morning, he awoke to the sound of a heavy rain outside. For a moment, he forgot about the previous day—the firing, the fight with Enrico, the final rejection of his novel.

He lay in bed at perfect peace, listening to the rain beating down outside, occasional thunder playing like background music across the sky. But then it all came crashing back.

He groaned, pushed himself up out of bed, and took a long shower. It was after eleven by the time he made it out to the living room. *One thing about getting your ass fired—the sleep-late benefits are killer.*

He ate breakfast alone—a stale danish and a glass of milk—and then sat down on the couch, not sure what to do next. His life had collapsed all around him, and he had no idea where to start putting it together again. It was Friday, at the end of one helluva week.

Start with something small, he thought and spied his half-opened backpack still lying on the floor by the couch.

He pulled it up onto the coffee table, made from a couple milk crates and a scavenged board. He pulled out the contents—his paperback copy of Tolkien's *Lost Tales,* his phone, and the rest of the mail from the day before.

He leafed through it. There was the electric bill (who knew how he'd pay for *that* now), two credit card offers, that envelope of coupons no one ever uses, and a letter from some place called Scrivner and Associates. Curious, he ripped it open and read it.

Dear Mr. Ryan,

I hope this letter finds you well. My name is Toby Scrivner, and I'm a literary agent representing a number of up-and-coming authors.

John Davidson at Prometheus forwarded your manuscript to me, and I have to tell you, it's one of the best things I've seen in quite a while. Frankly, I'm not sure why they passed on it, but one man's loss...

Anyhow, I hope you don't mind, but I ran it by a friend at Random and he loved it. He's willing to offer you a handsome advance to publish it in the Fall season. Print, eBook, audio - the whole thing.

If this interests you, I'd love to hear from you. I didn't have a phone number for you, so I'm hoping this reaches you. If it doesn't, I may have to resort to more desperate measures to find you.

Sincerely,

Tobias Scrivner

Hands shaking, Dominic grabbed his phone and called.

"Tobias Scrivner," a male voice answered.

"Mr. Scrivner, this is Dominic Ryan, and I'd very much like to meet with you."

"Ryan, Ryan…" The sound of keys clicking. "Ah, Mr. Ryan. Yes, can you come by tomorrow at 9:00 a.m.?" he said.

"Sure, I'll be there." He took down the address and hung up the phone, grinning from ear to ear. His luck was finally starting to change.

Dante locked up the office, juggling his umbrella and the keys and his leather briefcase, losing his grip on his umbrella. It left him drenched by the water flowing off the small awning above the door from the falling rain. "*Porco cane*," he said, thrusting the keys into the pocket of his slacks.

"Here," someone said, and Dante looked up to find another man standing there holding out his umbrella. The poor soul was soaked to the bone.

"Thanks," he said awkwardly and turned to walk away.

"Dante? Dante Giordano?"

He spun around, surprised this guy knew his name. "Yes?"

The man held his hand out. "I'm Enrico. Dominic's roommate. Sorry I'm such a mess, but I've been out here for a while waiting for you, and I left home in a bit of a hurry this afternoon without an umbrella. Can we talk?"

"It's wet out here…"

Enrico smiled, and Dante saw a flash of the charm that surely had attracted Dominic to this man in the first place. "There's a coffee shop on the corner. Believe me, you're going to want to hear what I have to say."

Dominic walked down Flatbush, whistling. Saturday morning had dawned clear and cool, the rain gone. The meeting with Mr. Scrivner had gone very well, and he marveled at how things in his life had turned around in the space of twenty-four hours. At this time yesterday, he'd been unemployed, alone, and thoroughly dejected.

Now he had a $10,000 advance and the promise of a good deal more if his first book sold well.

Okay, so he was still alone. One thing at a time.

Morning was shading into afternoon, the sun was shining, and it was actually warm out. The hotdog vendor was at the corner, and Dominic decided to treat himself. "Hey, Joe, give me a dog with the works." The vendor stacked up his hotdog with sauerkraut, mustard, and onions, and he took it down to Prospect Park, finding a bench by the lake to people watch.

The young men of Brooklyn were out in force today, jogging or roller blading through the park, many without shirts. *Maybe this whole unemployed thing isn't so bad after all.*

Although he'd have to get back to his writing tomorrow—Toby wanted a draft of his second novel in less than a month. But today he had no worries.

After a leisurely hour in the park, he made his way back home, ready to do an initial run-through of the manuscript he'd written two nights before.

Someone was waiting for him on the steps of his building. Dominic was astonished to see that it was Dante. He looked miserable.

They stood in front of each other for a moment, neither speaking. Dominic felt the familiar tightness in his throat, the nervousness Dante always inspired in him, but he pushed it down.

"Why are you here?" he said at last, trying not to let the exasperation slip into his tone. His old life had shown up on his doorstep just as his new one was beginning.

Dante met his gaze, and Dominic saw regret there. And maybe something else. "I'm sorry, Dominic."

"Sorry for firing me?"

"Sorry for very many things. I didn't know."

Dominic was confused. "You didn't know what?"

"Your... roommate, Enrico, came to me last night after work. We talked for a couple hours." He looked away, measuring his words. "He told me what he did. Why you didn't come in the other day. Why you didn't call. Why you said that which you said."

Dominic needed to sit down.

He'd made peace with the whole thing—well, the book deal had helped. But he'd decided he would be happy to never see Dante again. And now here he was.

He sank down onto the stairs, and Dante sat next to him. "You'll get your fancy Italian pants dirty," he protested.

Dante laughed ruefully. "Too late for that."

They sat in silence for a moment watching the cars go by. Spring was finally here—the wind blew past them, cool but with a promise of warmth.

Finally, Dominic said, "Thanks for coming. But you really didn't have to."

Dante shook his head. "I needed to say I was in error. I don't say it often."

Dominic laughed. "Tell me about it."

"Obviously, your job is yours again if you want it."

Dominic shook his head. "I appreciate it. I really do. But I just got a book offer. A good one."

Dante grinned. "*Santo cielo*, Dominic, that's great! I didn't know you were writing!"

He nodded. "I'd almost given up. I was rejected by twelve publishers... and then this." He fished out the agent's letter and handed it to his ex-boss.

Dante took it and read it eagerly. "You have no idea how happy this makes me!"

Dominic smiled a little. "I'm sorry, too, for the games I played. I made a fool of myself."

"Maybe *un po'*."

"A little my ass. All I wanted to do was to ask you out for coffee. I hoped... well, I guess we'll never know, now." He stood and took the letter back, stuffing it into his backpack. "Like I said, I'm glad you came by. I'm sure you'll find someone else." He started to climb the stairs.

Dante grabbed his hand, pulling him back down, his gaze intense. "I guess I didn't make myself clear. I want you back. And I usually get what I want." And with that, he pulled Dominic to him and kissed him.

Dominic's face flushed. It felt good. So good.

But then Dominic pushed him away, surprising even himself. "It's too fast," he said, looking down at the beautiful Italian man before him who *wanted* him, who had come to his doorstep to tell him. "I need a little time."

Dante frowned, marring his beautiful features. But he nodded. "I understand. It's been a week of crazy for you. Call me, then? Next week?"

"Sure." He could still feel Dante's lips on his. "Hey, I really am glad you came."

They stared at each other for a moment more, neither saying a word, and then Dante turned and walked away.

Dominic watched him go until he disappeared around the corner. *He came all the way to Brooklyn for me.*

He shook his head. *Dominic, what the hell is wrong with you?*

Dominic woke up, breathing in deeply, inhaling the welcome smell of coffee coming from the kitchen. Today was the day.

It had been six long months since he'd sold his novel with the help of his new agent. Today it would hit the bookstores and, more importantly, Amazon.

He resisted the urge to jump up and see if it was available on the site yet. He wanted to savor the moment.

He marveled at how his life had changed in just six months. No longer did he commute every day to an office job that sapped his creativity. No longer did he struggle just to get a short story published. His publisher had booked him on a six-city West Coast tour, and his second novel was already slated for publication next year. *It's a start.*

And he was no longer alone. He had the sexy, handsome Italian boyfriend he'd always wanted. Not just a boyfriend, but his fiancé. He wondered at the white gold ring on his finger.

He glanced at the clock—surely they could manage a little together time before he had to pack for the tour.

He stood and strode across the hardwood floor, cold on his bare feet, to the floor-to-ceiling window to take in the view. He never tired of it—it was all that he had ever dreamed of.

The fog was slowly pulling back from the Golden Gate Bridge, and the rooftops of the city below glimmered in the sunlight. The view from their thirty-seventh-floor apartment was nothing less than stunning.

"Hey, sleepyhead," his lover said, coming up behind him and putting his arms around Dominic's shoulders. He could feel his fiancé's desire beneath the 501's as they pressed up against his ass.

"Hey, lover," he said, turning to kiss Rico, who pulled him down onto the bed, where they collapsed in a nest of blankets and sheets.

"Big day today," Enrico said, running his hands through Dominic's hair and bringing them to rest at the back of his neck.

Dominic said nothing, just staring at his handsome fiancé, remembering that fateful day when he'd realized just how much Rico still loved him. That he'd been willing to risk losing everything to set things right. That this was the man he really wanted.

He kissed Rico again hungrily, and they rolled over across the bed together, lips and bodies locked together.

"Don't you have to get ready for your tour?" Enrico said when they came up for air.

Dominic grinned, unbuttoning Rico's jeans. "Not just yet. I have something more important to attend to first."

He was half an hour late to his first book signing downtown. But he was too happy to care.

I haven't been to New York City since the late Eighties, so this one required a lot of legwork on Apple Maps and Google to try to get the details right. I do speak Italian, so it was a lot of fun to work a bit of the language into this three-way love triangle, and my husband is Hispanic, so I leaned on him and my own childhood in Tucson to inform Enrico's character. I also want to be that writer who can write an entire (fantastic) novel in a night. Hasn't happened yet! This one was another Mischief Corner Books submission.

SLOW THAW

Bettencourt Station

IT WAS the start of the end of the world, but Col Steele didn't know it yet.

The rhythmic *whomp whomp whomp* of the helicopter's rotary blades matched the beating of his heart.

I'm here. I'm really here.

He pressed his face to the glass, eagerly taking in the landscape below, capturing the view in his phone. There was no cellular network here, of course, and he had his Sony A73 packed away for the real work, but his phone was good enough to record his own personal memories.

The sparkling blue and white of the Ross Ice Shelf spread out before him, almost indescribable in its frozen beauty. The ice seemed to stretch on forever here in the South, as they called it. On the ice.

The copter had left the Southern Explorer a few minutes earlier, taking off from the grey deck and passing over a span of cold ocean water, where a waddle of penguins played in the Ross Sea.

The cliffs of the Ice were white enough—and tall enough—to put the cliffs of Dover to shame with their splendor.

Col checked the temperature gauge on the console. It was a relatively balmy Antarctic day, with the temperature hovering just below zero Fahrenheit.

"First time?" His pilot, Joseph, steered the copter over the ice field with practiced ease.

"Yes. Not yours, I assume?"

"Nope, I've done the run to Amundsen–Scott more than a dozen times, people and cargo. Been out to Bettencourt three times now."

Col nodded. Tad Bettencourt was his benefactor—a billionaire who was keenly interested in the science and effects of global climate change.

He picked me. Out of more than two hundred research scientists, the man had chosen Col to be the next fellowship scientist to join Javier Fernandez at Bettencourt Station for a six-month internship.

It was still sinking in.

The timing couldn't have been better. Col had no desire to be home for the holidays this year. After a bad breakup with David, he was nursing a broken heart and was in no mood for Christmas trees and candy canes. Far better the frozen tundra of Antarctica to match his frozen heart.

The Ross Ice Shelf was much more varied a landscape than he'd expected. The smooth, white ice near the shore gave way to a variety of landforms, the result of the ice being pushed and pulled around by gravity and shaped by wind and snow and rain for millennia.

There were mountains and valleys, the peaks white and the shadows a beautiful blue.

In other places, the windblown snow created long scalloped shapes along the ice.

In at least one spot, a wide, shallow pool of melted water almost glowed turquoise in the sunlight. *Not a good sign.*

"You see a lot of melting out here?"

Joseph nodded. "More every year. It's been a slow thaw, but every summer season it goes a bit faster. Lots more icebergs too.

Seeing one of those calve off the main shelf is something else. *Crack! Thunder!* And a great splash of water as it hits the ocean."

Col grinned. "I've seen it in the Arctic. I spent a year based out of Whitehorse, studying the ice sheets up north."

"Never been. Though I hear the girls in the Yukon are wild."

Col snorted. "I wouldn't know." What he didn't say was that he'd been one of them, once. On the outside, at least.

That was a lifetime ago.

Now this new life was laid out before him, and he just wanted to move forward.

He captured as much of the landscape as he could manage with his phone, awed that he was finally here. Then he tucked it away to just take in the experience.

"Might wanna get your phone ready," Joseph said at last. "We're almost there." The pilot pointed off to starboard, and a small speck appeared in the distance, alongside a long line in the ice.

"It's bigger than I imagined."

Joseph's eyebrow went up. "Bettencourt?"

"No. The Giant Crack."

Joseph laughed. "You scientists suffer from a severe lack of imagination."

Col grinned. "It's true." He stared at the Crack. It stretched from one edge of the horizon to the other, a sign of things to come. He'd seen many pictures of it, of course, but seeing it in person was awe inspiring and a little frightening. It had happened two years before, but since then, the shelf seemed to have stabilized again.

It was the reason he was here, as much as his breakup with David.

He snapped a few pics, then looked down at Bettencourt Station.

It was a modest place, maybe the size of a couple RVs hooked together. It was two modules built by Northrop-Grumman to Bettencourt's specs, brought in by military copter and hooked together. One served as the laboratory and the other as living quarters for the scientific team.

Fernandez was there now. His last lab partner, Astrid Danvers, had departed a few days earlier. It had all been in the briefing email.

Col whistled. It was going to be a tight space for his six-month rotation down there.

Still, it would be worth it. Careers were made by postings like this, and he'd have a chance to put his education and experience to work at something that might actually help the planet.

Fuck you, David.

He took a couple more shots, and then settled in for the landing.

Javier Fernandez scratched his neatly trimmed beard absently. He stared at the results from his latest ice core test, frowning. He'd run it through the Osterberg melter, testing it for traces of minerals, dust, and pollution.

After two years down on the ice, he was part of the five hundred club—the elite group of scientists who had spent more than five hundred days down South. Not that he ever spent any time with the others.

Tad Bettencourt, that crazy billionaire of Silicon Valley fame who had funded the station, wanted him to find out the true age and history of the Ross Ice Shelf. He also hoped to discover if it was likely to break apart in the near future. If it did, it would have potentially catastrophic results for the whole planet.

The Great Crack, not far from the station, was evidence that it likely *would*. It was just a matter of time.

Unlike other temporary installations, Bettencourt Station was designed to do everything on-site. Other mobile labs had to send their cores off the Ice, taking time and risking contamination as they were shipped from the remote southern location to labs in the northern hemisphere.

She was loaded with all the climate science and research Javier could cram into her, and her satellite connection allowed him to access any new research in scientific journals.

Plus, she was mobile.

The steady *thwump thwump thwump* of a helicopter's rotors distracted Javier from whatever he'd been thinking.

He glanced at his Penguin Babes of the Antarctic calendar—a gag gift from his brother the last Christmas. His new assistant was due in. Not that *they* called them that. Fellowship scientist or some other hogwash.

To Javier, they were pot cleaners and meal makers.

Five days until the next Nativity. Not that he really cared much about that anymore. He'd long since given up his Catholic roots, much to his mother's consternation. One more reason he was glad to be so far away from the madness of the rest of humanity. There would be no Christmas at Bettencourt Station if he had anything to do with it.

You're a mean one, Mr. Grinch...

He growled. It had been nice to have a couple days to himself after that Swedish Ice Queen had departed. Her heart was as frozen as his own.

The station was small enough when just one person lived there, let alone two. She'd taken to second-guessing everything he asked of her, almost as a matter of sport, and her shrill voice... He grated his teeth at just the thought of it.

At least his new roommate was a guy. Trans guy, but he didn't give a shit about that, one way or another.

He'd thumbed through Col Steele's files the day before. He was qualified enough—a couple years of experience up north in Greenland and the Yukon. Probably spent half his time dodging the poor starving polar bears.

At least they only had penguins and seals to contend with down here, and both mostly stayed near the coastline.

Javier slipped on his heavy parka and gloves and put on his Gor-Tex jacket. Dressing in Antarctica was tricky. You didn't want to put on so many layers that you started to sweat, because your sweat might actually start to freeze in the bitterly cold winters.

December down here was one of the summer months, and it was an almost-balmy two degrees Fahrenheit outside.

He pulled on his dirty Mukluks and opened the pressure-sealed door, then closed it quickly behind him. Solar panels on the station roof gathered sunlight for power when it was available, and a couple portable pop-up wind turbines helped as well, but the station was still reliant on diesel fuel for the main part of its power.

The boys down in Mac-Town had three beautiful turbines to help provide energy there, but they still used diesel too. He was well aware of the irony of a climate scientist using diesel fuel.

The copter came down onto a flat patch of ice thirty meters from the station, blowing up loose bits of ice and snow from the surface into the deep blue sky.

Javier waited for the blades to slow before he made his way across the ice, his Mukluks giving him secure purchase on the slick surface.

He growled again. *Why do they make me babysit these children?* Not that Steele was so much younger than he was. At forty, the man was about a decade younger. Still... much of his next week would be wasted teaching the man the basics of how Bettencourt Station operated.

Nothing to do about it now.

Col Steele climbed down from the helicopter, his bunny boots catching firmly on the Antarctic ice. Cute, a bit nerdy with his glasses. At least he had good footwear.

Steele waved, and Javier nodded. "Doctor Fernandez?" Steele held his hand out.

"The same." Javier pushed past the man to hail the pilot. "Joseph! What have you brought me today?"

Col stared at Javier's retreating back. *That was rude.*

To be fair, the *great* Javier Fernandez *did* have a bit of a reputation. He brooked no nonsense, and when he'd been teaching at the University of Alaska, Anchorage, rumor was that half his students hadn't made it past the first week.

Still, the man was brilliant at what he did. Col had read some of his papers on climate change and ice cores taken from Greenland

and had been impressed with Fernandez's acumen and powerful language.

He followed Professor Fernandez back to the helicopter, where the Professor was engaging in a cheerful conversation with the helicopter pilot.

"... couple crates of freeze-dry. Oh, and I brought you this." The pilot reached behind his seat and pulled out a golden-colored bottle.

The Professor held it up and grinned. "Herradura Añejo. You remembered."

"Is alcohol allowed?" Col wasn't naive, or at least he didn't like to think so, but he hadn't pictured Professor Fernandez as a lush.

Col himself hadn't had a drop of alcohol since he was seventeen, scared to death he might out himself. Not that it mattered now, but old habits died hard.

The Professor glanced at him and frowned. "Brought me a fingy, huh?"

Joseph chuckled. "He'll pick things up fast. Seems like a smart guy."

Col liked Joseph. "Fingy?"

"Fucking new guy." Joseph slapped his back. "Don't worry, he'll get sick of picking on you in a couple days. And yes, alcohol is allowed."

"Believe me, I'm gonna need that bottle after a *couple days*."

Col rolled his eyes.

"Take these crates back into the Bettencourt. There's a storage closet in the kitchen area where you can put the packets away." Fernandez dismissed him with a wave and turned back to his discussion with the pilot. "How's Felicia and the kids?"

Col sighed under his breath. Reduced to grunt work the minute he landed. He didn't deserve this. He was a damned good scientist in his own right, even if he had yet to scale the heights *Professor Javier Fernandez* had reached.

Then again, the man *was* stuck out here, far away from any of his colleagues and almost any human contact. Maybe he'd pissed off the wrong person at UAA and was bitter about his placement on the Ice.

Or maybe he's just an asshole sonofabitch.

In any case, there were only two of them to do everything on station, and there was bound to be a lot of scutwork on an assignment like this.

Col sighed under his breath and went to grab the first of the plastic crates.

It was cold out, bitterly cold, but he was warm enough in his arctic gear. He'd bundled up in five layers of clothing. He was even sweating a bit under all that cloth.

He hefted the crate in the air and carried it back toward the station.

Bettencourt Station was a strange-looking thing, black as night, probably to help it absorb whatever heat it could. It also made it stand out against the snow, an alien in this pristine world. It was about the length of two trailers, festooned with solar panels, small wind turbines, and a couple satellite dishes on the sloped roof.

The base of the station, by contrast, was a mess of white skids and armored treads like those on a tank.

The Bettencourt could move across the ice on those treads, which could also be retracted to allow for downhill motion on the skids.

He'd read up on the mission, scouring the net for every bit of information he could find before coming south for this post.

Tad Bettencourt himself was a bit of an eccentric genius who'd made his money building electric charging stations across the US. He was always getting himself in trouble for his crazy statements on Q, or whatever the social media site was called now, and was richer than God.

Col climbed the steps of the station, putting one hand on the palm pad to open the door while balancing the crate in the other.

"Access denied." The voice was sexy, Australian.

Col frowned and tried again.

"Access denied."

"Um, little help here?"

Fernandez looked back at him and shook his head. "Tell it access code alpha beta alpha."

"Could we maybe get me added to the system soon?"

Fernandez laughed. "We'll see if we have time." He turned back to his conversation with the handsome pilot.

Col shook his head and palmed the door pad again.

"Access denied."

He wanted to throttle the cheery Australian. "Access code alpha beta alpha."

"Access granted." The door slid open, just as the crate slipped out of his grasp, dumping food packets everywhere.

"You okay over there?"

"Just fine." Col set the crate down on the steps and gathered up the fallen packets.

The door slid closed.

"Access code alpha beta alpha." This time he managed to get through without losing anything.

He pushed his way through to the warm interior, and the door slammed closed behind him, nearly catching him on the ass.

Why in the hell is there an access code? What was the man afraid of? Killer penguins? He sighed again. It was going to be a long six months.

The entryway was in the middle of the station.

He wrinkled his nose. It was a bit... ripe inside. Not unusual for such a small space, where people were enclosed for a long time. Things had been worse up in Greenland, where he'd shared a space with five guys and four women.

To his left, blinking lights and consoles indicated the research part of the station.

He went into the module on the right.

The wide space through the doorway was a living area, complete with seating and a television on the right and a small kitchen on the left. There were four doors. The two at the back were probably bedrooms. He checked the others. One was a small clothing closet.

The other was the storage closet.

He set the crate down and went out to get the others.

"Little help might be nice," he muttered to his new mentor, picking up the second one.

"You seem to be doing just fine." The man patted him on the shoulder.

Bastard.

Four trips later and Col was definitely sweating. The last of the crates was his own meager personal belongings, which he set aside. He'd been assured everything else he would need would be provided at the station.

He peeled off a couple layers of clothing, laying them over the couch. Then he started putting away the food supplies.

The storage area was neatly organized and clearly labeled. It was easy to figure out the system.

He was halfway through the first crate when the Professor popped his head in from outside. "Where did you go?"

"Putting away the supplies, like you asked."

"Ordered."

"What?"

"Ordered, not asked. Come on, *fingy*. I have some things for you to carry that I need to send back with Joseph. Don't want to keep him waiting." He disappeared into the research part of the station.

"Don't want to keep him waiting," he muttered under his breath sarcastically.

Then he laughed. *What am I, ten?*

He shook his head, looking around at the tiny station. *This is my life.*

Then he followed the Professor into the research module.

―――――

Javier watched the newbie carry the last of the crates to the helicopter.

Most of it was gash—trash to be carted back to civilization. *Carry in, carry out.*

The rest consisted of lab samples he was sending back to Bettencourt's labs in Los Angeles for further analysis.

So far, Steele had done everything Javier had asked with little more than a muttering complaint, so he was already a better fit for the job than the Ice Queen.

Astrid had made a point about arguing with him about every little request, claiming such scutwork was beneath her as a research scientist. She seemed to expect magical elves to appear out of the snow to take care of such mundane tasks for her.

Col, on the other hand, at least seemed to recognize that somebody had to do the work. There might be hope for him yet.

The pilot and Steele finished loading the copter, securing everything with bungie cords.

Javier waved as it took off into the clear blue sky.

It was warm out. Way too warm, even for the height of the summer season in December. Javier had been down South for a couple years, and the temperature had never stayed so high for so long. It worried him.

So far, the Ross Ice Shelf had been mostly stable, the Great Crack notwithstanding, but rapid changes to the Earth's climate threatened to undo the delicate balance between land and sea and ice, and no one knew for sure when the tipping point would come.

Steele trudged across the snow to the station.

"Good work." Javier grudgingly palmed open the door to the station. "But you're wearing too many clothes. You don't want to sweat under all those layers. Your sweat will freeze and give you hypothermia."

"Got it." Steele pushed past him into the station like a surly teenager, though the man had to be at least forty.

Javier closed the door behind them and sealed it against the cold, and peeled off his Gore-Tex jacket. "Why don't you take a little bit to get settled? Your bedroom is through the door on the right."

He hoped Steele wasn't a serial masturbator. The walls inside the station were thin to keep down the weight, and he didn't need to hear that. Astrid's own nocturnal activities had been enough to keep him up at night.

Javier sighed. *I always have my headphones.*

"Will do." Steele pulled out his phone and slipped a pair of earbuds of his own into his ears.

"You realize there's no cell phone service in Antarctica, right?"

Steele didn't hear him.

The man disappeared into his room with his crates and slammed the door behind him.

Javier sighed. Maybe it was going to be a long six months, after all.

He turned and headed back into the research module, determined to finish his interrupted analysis of the latest slice of ice core.

Settling In

Col slammed the door, ignoring the Professor's snide remark. Music cut off the last few words, a rough-pop cut of The Homely Boys' "I Wanna Be a Virgin."

Of course he knew there was no cell service in Antarctica. He was a respected scientist in his own right, and he'd fought for every scrap of that respect. As a trans man in a cis male-dominated profession, he'd had it doubly hard, and he wasn't going to let some exiled two-bit professor bring him down.

Col sighed.

Professor Fernandez was a lot more than that, and Col's own academic future might depend on what happened during his six months down in this frozen wasteland. He'd just have to grit his teeth and bear it.

He sat on the firm bed, staring out the small port window. A thin film of ice formed a crescent along the edge, creating a rainbow where the sun struck it.

In the distance, the Transantarctics poked their heads above the snow and ice, and the wind kicked up a dusting of snow. It was such a beautiful place, really, empty and serene, about as far away as you could get from the hustle and bustle of the world.

From David.

With a sigh, he set about unpacking his meager belongings.

It was mostly clothing. The room itself was spare, with a twin bed on one side and a writing desk and chair on the other.

One of the previous occupants had scratched "Fuck you, Javier" into the desktop in capital letters. It made Col smile.

There was a small closet built into the back of the room on one side, and a small, functional bathroom on the other. He found hangers for his clothes and hung them up to air out.

The station was a reasonable sixty-five degrees, give or take, so he stripped down to jeans and a T-shirt. He pulled out a picture of his mom, smiling in front of Half Dome in Yosemite a couple years back when he'd taken her there on a weekend camping trip.

She'd had a hard time with his transition the first few years, but of late she'd come around, proudly telling her friends about how "My son the scientist is going to save the world."

He wasn't so sure about that. *This world might be beyond saving.*

He set the photo frame on the desk and turned off the music.

Pulling out one of his notebooks, he sat back on the bed and pulled his feet up. He made a new diary entry, his observations scientific and personal of the journey here from the ship and the events after his arrival. He had a thing for paper, especially when he was in the field. Paper couldn't be hacked. It was never lost in the cloud, and it didn't run out of power at the most inopportune moment.

When he was done, he sat back and stared at the bare white walls for a few moments.

I have to assert myself. If he let Professor Fernandez walk all over him now, it would set the pattern for his whole time here.

His mom smiled at him from the desktop. *Be yourself. Everyone else is already taken.* It was one his mom's favorite sayings. She'd become quite the Oscar Wilde aficionado since his double coming out.

"Love you, Mom." He kissed the photo and set it back down gently.

Then he put his diary away in one of the desk drawers and went to confront the Professor.

He found the man in the research module, staring at a curved computer screen.

"Oh good, you're here." Fernandez waved him around to his side to look at what he was working on. "What do you think?"

Col stared at him for a moment, his anger dissipated by the Professor's sudden change of mood. "What?"

Fernandez pointed at the screen in front of him.

Col leaned in. It was a spectral analysis. "From one of the cores?"

Fernandez nodded. "The last one. Pulled it up yesterday."

Col whistled. "That can't be right."

"That's what I thought. But take a look at these others." He pulled out a folder from one of the under-counter drawers and handed it to Col. "These are the last five samples. We're at the edge of the shelf here, getting down into the shallows below the ice."

Col thumbed through the file. "These carbon dioxide and methane levels are at least three times higher than I've seen elsewhere."

Fernandez took the folder back. "Exactly. I thought the first one was an outlier. Maybe a contaminated sample, or we tapped an abnormal pocket beneath the ice. But the amount of trapped carbon we're looking at..."

Col sank down into the other chair, his face white, his anger forgotten. "Runaway heating. The tipping point."

Fernandez nodded. "You're good at this shit, right?"

Col gulped. "I... I think so."

"Great. I need you to run the same tests and cross-check my results. This has to be absolutely ironclad before we send the information off to Bettencourt."

"Just to Bettencourt?"

"He's the one who pays the bills."

"The world needs to know." Colin stared at the screen. "This... this could change everything." Not that the politicians would listen. They'd become adept over the years at diverting attention whenever the climate alarm was raised. Even with the new, progressive government, it might be too late. Still... this was too important to let slip by.

The Professor studied him. "Ready to get to work?"

"I... sure. What do you want me to do?" He hoped he didn't come up lacking.

Fernandez put a folder down in front of him. "Start with these. There are more samples in cold storage over there." He pointed to a metal door. "Use standard decontamination procedures—we don't want to futz up the samples."

His hairy arm grazed Col's, and Col suppressed a shiver of excitement. *Not now. Not him.* This was too important to let himself get sidetracked.

He took the reports. "How do I access the system?"

"Have you used a Mac before?"

Col nodded.

"It's the same GUI. Look for the app called Core-Results. Bettencourt had some of his tech geeks whip it up just for us."

"Thanks." He sat silently for a minute, wondering if he should say anything about how Fernandez had treated him when he arrived. Or how he was treating Col now. "I'm sorry if we got off on the wrong foot—"

Fernandez turned to stare at him, his brown eyes boring into Col's skull. "Look, we're *not* friends. You're here to do a job and do it competently. Manage that, and we'll have no problems." He turned back to his own work.

Col did the same, though it stung. Here he was holding out an olive branch only to have it viciously thrown back in his face.

He sighed quietly. He'd wanted the Professor to treat him as an equal, and he'd gotten his wish.

So why did he feel so annoyed?

Javier put away his notes and equipment, returning his workstation to its pristine state. It was a discipline born of years in the US Army, serving stateside and in Iraq for three years.

The kid had a point. What if Bettencourt decided to bury the information for his own personal or business reasons? He knew little about the man beyond what he'd been able to find out on the web and during their brief personal meeting.

Tad Bettencourt was a billionaire and an altruist who gave to Democratic causes, spent millions on renewable energy projects, and who often said he wanted to "leave a better world for his grandchildren." That last bit had been emblazoned across an ad for Bettencourt Energy, his father's former oil company that had completely transformed itself into a clean energy conglomerate under the younger Bettencourt's leadership.

What if the news of a huge carbon sink under the Ross Ice Shelf conflicted with one of those business ventures?

What if their benefactor found reason to bury the whole thing deeper than the carbon itself?

It would come out eventually, just like the trapped carbon, but by then it might be too late.

"You about done?"

Steele had been quiet the whole afternoon, working diligently through the core data. "Ten minutes."

Maybe I'm an asshole. It wasn't the first time he'd considered the idea. Or been told it to his face. He tried to be practical and professional, and he wanted everyone else to be the same. Was that so much to ask? At fifty years of age, he had little time or patience left for other peoples' bullshit. "Got it. I'm going to get some dinner going."

A grunt was all he got in reply.

He made his way back to the kitchen, checking on the supplies Joseph had brought in. "Oooh, freshies!" In addition to the tequila, there was a crate of fresh fruit and vegetables that Steele had stored in the refrigerator. Javier salivated at the sight of not-dried cilantro and onions. He'd whip up a batch of his famous tortilla soup with some of the dried stores and a few choice fresh ingredients from the closet. It wouldn't be as good as what he used to make with Terrence back home.

Nothing had been the same since Terry had passed away, five years before.

He found the ingredients he needed and went outside to scoop up some snow to use to rehydrate the packets of dried food. It was a lot cheaper to use snow for water—it was one thing Antarctica had in abundance.

He dumped some dried tomatoes in the water, and set about chopping onions. They filled the kitchen with the most wonderful smell, transporting him back home.

"Smells wonderful, Javi." Terry's arms slid around his waist.

"Hey, watch it. I'm chopping here."

"I can smell the onions. Tortilla soup?"

"Yup." He kissed Terry's cheek and went back to work.

"How long are you home for this time?"

"Six months. They're putting together an expedition up in Alaska next month, but I told Sampson I needed some time at home."

"Six months! That's an eternity."

"Go clean up. Then set the table?"

"You got it. Welcome home."

Javier blinked, tears in his eyes.

It was the onions.

He was about halfway through preparing the meal when Steele arrived.

"All done?" He shook the pan, sautéing the onions. They smelled even better cooked.

"Yeah. Your results so far look dead-on." Steele looked around the room. "Can I help?"

"Sure. Pull down the tabletop." He pointed at the wall next to the kitchen. "Dishes are in the cupboard over there."

"Got it. You can call me Col, by the way. It doesn't mean we have to *be friends*."

Javier set the pan down and turned off the burner. "Look, I've been down here for a long time, and I'm not so good at the basics of human interaction anymore." He rubbed the back of his neck. "I'm sorry I said it." Saying it was like chewing glass.

"Sure, okay." Steele was still trying to figure out the table release.

Javier shook his head. He crossed the room to help Col with the task. "*Scientific genius*, huh?"

Col laughed. "*Human being*, huh?"

Javier snorted. "Touché. You just reach around here, and push like so..." His cheek grazed Col's arm. "And voilà." The table extended from the wall, and two small suspended stools unfolded underneath it.

They stood face to face for a moment. Col looked so handsome in his geeky way.

"Easy as that," Javier said gruffly and turned back to his cooking, trying to ignore the effect the man had on him. "Dinner will be ready in about ten, if you want to wash up."

"What about the dishes?"

"Go. I'll take care of them." He did *not* want to turn around. To face Col again. Not for a couple minutes, at least.

He had enough to worry about with his work and the whole being-a-human-being thing without developing a crush on Col.

Col lay naked in bed, the covers thrown off, staring at the ceiling. Here he was in the coldest place on Earth, and he was too warm to sleep. *Some fucking irony*.

The Bettencourt modules were efficient at gathering energy and storing heat. Maybe too efficient.

Of course, that wasn't the only reason he couldn't sleep. It was his first night in a strange new place, and his mind was still working through all of the new stimuli.

He hardly ever slept well anymore, in any case.

There had been a time when he could just lay down and be asleep almost instantly. When he would sleep the whole night without waking to go to the bathroom, without tossing and turning, thoughts about the day past and the day still to come running rampant through his brain.

A time when Christmas had meant *something*, too.

Col turned on his side, staring at the circle of light that surrounded the window hatch. There would be no darkness outside that night.

He got up and pulled the window cover down, blocking out the sunlight.

He could still feel where the Professor—where Javier—had brushed against him when he'd helped Col pull down the table.

Col lay back down on the bed, closing his eyes and willing sleep to claim him.

His left hand brushed one of the scars under his pecs, feeling the slightly raised ridge of skin that ran across his chest.

What would Javier think of them? They were a part of his journey, and he wouldn't wish them away, even if they did mark him for what he was. They didn't define him.

Javier was rugged, handsome, exactly Col's type. *Just like David.*

Col pushed away the blankets, sitting up in bed, feeling aroused. Agitated.

He needed a cold shower.

He padded to the small bathroom cubicle. It was efficient, like a bathroom on a cruise ship, but Col was thankful to have his own inside his room.

He opened the shower stall and turned on the water. It heated up surprisingly quickly.

Col slipped inside the narrow space and turned down the heat until the water ran lukewarm over his slender form.

He would never be stocky like David—or Javier—he'd given up on that vision of masculinity a long time ago. Genetics was what it was, and he'd learned to be happy in his own skin.

He turned his face up, feeling the shower splash across his cheeks.

His ardor diminished under the cold water.

After a few minutes, he turned off the water and got out to dry off.

Javier was his boss, even if there had been a spark between them at dinner.

He hung his towel and picked up the picture of his mother. "Mamma, what would you do?"

Her warm eyes stared back at him, but she didn't say a word.

He went back to bed, pulling the covers over his chest, and fell asleep almost immediately.

Javier sat at his desk, the window cover open just enough to provide light to see by, and wrote in his personal journal.

It was his daily habit to take notes about the events of the day and his own feelings about them.

It was something he'd started when Terry was killed. A friend had suggested it as a way to get the emotions out that were poisoning him from the inside.

After Terry, it had been easier to withdraw from the world, first emotionally and later almost entirely. After a series of meaningless affairs, he'd given up on men entirely, and within two years had taken a job at a remote scientific outpost in South America, studying the retreating glaciers in the Andes.

Now he was here, about as far as he could get from the rest of humanity, only having to deal with one or two others of his species at a time.

Col wasn't the worst of them. At least there was that.

They'd had a mostly pleasant dinner together, sharing where they were from and some nice small talk.

A nagging *something* scratched at him whenever he looked at the man.

He'd never fallen for a trans guy before. His dating history, pre-

Terry, had been fairly brief, as he'd only come out a couple months before they'd met. His guys had been strictly cisgender, though he had nothing against trans guys.

But something about Col made his skin tingle.

It didn't matter. He had no intention of dating anyone, not ever again.

He finished his notes and put the journal away on the bookshelf next to his bed, the fourth one he'd filled since he'd arrived here in what many scientists called Terra Nova.

He padded into his bathroom and splashed some water on his face.

Water was running in the station's pipes.

Strange. Col must still be up.

He almost went to knock on the man's door to see if he was settling in okay. Only for that reason.

Somehow he restrained himself.

The man needed his privacy.

The water ran for a few long moments. *Hollywood shower.* He'd have to mention water conservation to Col in the morning.

Javier sighed. He dried his face off, and pulled off his underwear, dropping it into the hamper in his closet. He'd have to organize a load of laundry the next day.

He dropped into bed and was asleep in seconds.

Expedition

Someone was pounding on his bedroom door. Col stared at it through half-closed eyes and then dropped his face back down onto his pillow. "Leave me alone, David!"

"It's not David. It's Javier."

Col's eyes sprung open, and he sat bolt-upright in bed. "Javier?"

"Yeah. Your new boss, remember? Get dressed. You drink coffee?"

"Um... yeah. Black." Col rubbed his eyes. He'd been dreaming of David. David doing the most amazing things to him in bed.

He growled. David had left him for a guy twenty years younger than him—Jules or something like that? *Goddamned bastard.*

"See you in five."

"Got it." He wondered what Javier was so excited about.

He got up and pulled out a clean pair of underwear. He stretched his thin frame, almost touching the ceiling.

Things were a bit tight. That made sense. Less air, less need for energy to warm it up. He'd gotten used to similar situations before. Still, he missed having space over his head.

He pulled on a pair of long johns, a thermal shirt, and his socks and shoes. If he needed more, he could come back for them.

Vanity was one of the first things to go when you were trapped inside a tin can at the ass end of the world.

He opened the door to the welcome smell of coffee.

"Hey, welcome back to the land of the living. How'd you sleep?" Javier offered him a cup and leaned back against the kitchen counter.

"So-so. Bad dreams. You?" He sat down on the table.

"Like a baby." Javier took a sip of his own cup. "David?"

"What?" Col drank half his coffee, his brain slowly shifting back to *awake*. "Sorry. He's my ex. I must have been dreaming about him."

"Ah." Javier set down his cup, pulling out a box of cereal and setting it in front of Col. "We're going out on the ice today. You'll want to eat a lot, bulk up. You burn a shit-ton of calories out there."

Col nodded. "Heard that." He poured cereal into the waiting bowl.

Javier topped it off with a heaping of raisins.

"Milk?"

"Of course. I mixed it up earlier. I like my milk cold."

"Nonfat?"

Javier shook his head. "Full fat. You'll need it here." He handed Col the pitcher.

Col grimaced. He'd worked his way down from whole milk to two percent, then to one percent. It had taken a year, but he'd finally gotten himself used to nonfat. Now whole milk tasted like cream. "I'll manage. What's out on the ice?"

Javier sat across from him and picked up his own spoon and napkin, his short-sleeved shirt showing off his hairy, muscular arms.

Col looked away.

"Nothing in particular. I like to take new recruits out for a night, and it's good to get a feel for the ice and the conditions now and then. Plus, it's summer out there. It's practically bikini weather."

Col stared at him for a moment, then realized the man wasn't joking about his gender. He was sensitive to things like that, but he tried to give folks a pass if it was unintentional. "Yeah, what, almost zero Fahrenheit?"

"Something like that."

They plowed through breakfast, and Col helped himself to seconds.

When they were done, Javier showed him what to pack.

The station had two Ski-Doos—"doos" in the local lingo. The pyramid tent came in two parts, and they split the weight among the two snowmobiles.

Food went into each of their backpacks—some of the fresh things Joseph had brought with him and some ration packs.

Javier called them "rat packs."

Next, they packed a cook stove and several canisters of gas.

A couple changes of clothing and some tools filled out the rest of their packs.

"Have you ever ridden a doo before?"

Col nodded. "A few times, in Greenland."

"Good. They're pretty standard. Go finished getting dressed. We'll leave in about ten minutes."

Col grunted assent. The coffee and food were taking effect, but he was still half asleep. He returned to his room and splashed some cold water on his face.

Then he suited up, being careful to wear fewer layers than he had on his arrival.

He slathered sunblock on his face. He'd been burned once—quite literally—in Greenland from the intense reflection of sun on the ice, and with the hole in the ozone layer over the South Pole that now returned every summer, he'd heard it was much worse down here.

"Okay, ready to go." He was excited to get out onto the ice. He'd figured he'd be stuck indoors for the first week or two, but he'd been dying to see more of Antarctica. How many people ever got to come here, the last frontier in the world?

They left the station and mounted the snowmobiles. In no time, they were making their way across the ice.

———

Javier led the way, forging a path across the ice. It was warm, warmer than it should have been, capping off a veritable heat wave across the southern continent.

Pools of standing water had appeared here and there, a deep arctic blue, something that worried him deeply.

Col, behind him, seemed oblivious to the change. "It's really beautiful out here," he called, sounding like a cat in a cage of canaries.

"It is, but you have to be careful. The ice can hide deep slots."

"Slots?"

"Crevasses. You don't wanna get slotted."

Col looked around, his forehead creased.

Occasional gusts of wind picked up snow from the ground and threw it through the air in flurries, but it was calmer than usual.

They followed the Great Crack eastward, reaching its end in about an hour.

Javier turned to make a run for the base of the Transantarctic Mountains, one of the most easily recognizable features of the southern continent. The mountains were a series of individual ranges.

The peaks of the Queen Elizabeth range loomed ahead, stark against the white snow. The Ski-Doos bounced along the open terrain, and they made good time, though they had to skirt a few fissures along the way.

The snow was white, blinding in the sunlight.

They decided to stop at one of the fissures in the ice and stared down into its variegated blue depths.

"Some of the ice down there is hundreds of thousands of years old." Col peered down into the slot.

"Don't get too close. This time of year, the ice can go soft underfoot, especially on the edges."

Col backed up carefully, but even so, he set off a mini-avalanche, ice and snow crashing into the depths. "I see what you mean. Stupid of me. I've been off the ice for too long."

Javier patted him on the back. "Don't worry. You'll get your ice legs back. Come on. I want to make it to the edge of the range by mid-afternoon. Maybe we'll run into some country mice."

"Country mice?"

"Some of the Mac-Town folks, out here on the ice. City mice stay at McMurdo, and country mice—"

Col laughed. "Yeah, got it."

They remounted and rode on in silence, accompanied only by the ice and the sound of the katabatic winds, the flows of cold, dense air that moved down the slopes toward the sea.

Javier had checked the forecast, and the winds were supposed to be mild for the next several days—they were almost always gentler in the summer months than during the wintertime.

With Antarctic weather, you never knew.

There was a slight chance of a storm late the next day, but they'd be back to Bettencourt before it happened.

At last, they reached their destination at the base of the Queen Elizabeth range. This time of year, some of the mountain rock was visible through the snow, creating a stark black-and-white patchwork.

"It's beautiful!" Col stared up at the imposing peak. "I always thought of Antarctica as one big sheet of ice. It's hard to remember there's a whole continent under the snow."

Javier nodded. "They say there were palm trees on its shores at one time."

Col laughed. "So this would be some kind of tropical resort, then?"

"Yeah. Something like that." He turned away. Col couldn't have known. No one knew about it. Just a random comment that cut Javier to the quick.

"The mountain looks like a Bev Doolittle painting."

"Who?" He tried to shake the pain that squeezed his heart.

"You know... she does those snow-and-rock paintings with the double images? Like a Native American's face, or a pinto horse hidden in the rocks. I wonder what these ones hide."

Javier had no idea what the man was talking about. "The history of the world? Come on. Let's have a bite to eat and then set up camp."

"I brought a sandwich." Col dug into his bag.

"Nutties are better." He pulled out a chocolate bar and took a bite.

"Maybe later. I want something healthy first." He pulled out his sandwich, wrapped in plastic. "Hmmm, that's strange."

Javier chucked. "Frozen solid?"

"Yeah. Like a bread-and-lettuce popsicle."

"Happens every time. Here, eat one of these." He handed Col a chocolate bar. "Keep up your energy."

"Fair enough. I can eat the sandwich later."

They finished their meal and got out the parts of the tent. Javier showed Col how to set it up. "You want to put the entrance down-wind, not facing it, or you'll be up in the air if you get a strong katabatic blow. You also want to face a corner into the wind, not a flat face."

Col nodded. "Makes sense."

The tent was big enough for the two of them and their gear. They worked together to put it up, starting with an ice pick on the windward side to hold it in place. Then they drove the tent pegs deep into the snow.

Javier watched Col as they worked. He was cautious and methodical, just the kind of level-headed partner you wanted out on the ice.

When they'd finished, Javier inspected the work. "Not bad, for your first time. "

"First time in *Antarctica*."

Javier snorted. "That *is* your *first* time." Col was still green, likely to make mistakes. Careful or no, one mistake out here could get you killed. "Let's have lunch."

Col was surprisingly hungry. Javier had been right—you burned a lot of calories out here on the ice. He'd ridden with a dog team up north and had been exhausted at the end of the day. This wasn't that bad, but still, he was sapped.

His friend Andreas had been the dogsledder in the Yukon. Col had always loved his dogs, though they were more rough and aggressive than your typical pet dog.

He and Javier climbed into the tent together. Col was uncomfortably aware of Javier's close proximity, especially after the man removed his ski hat, scarf, and jacket and rolled up his long sleeves, exposing the dark hair on his arms.

Col looked away, taking off his own outer layers, freeing his feet from his heavy rabbit fur-lined boots. *Bunny boots.* He grinned.

The tent was warming up, the little cook stove doing its job inside the well-insulated fabric layers. The open vents carried away the carbon monoxide.

Javier handed him a small metal pot. "Grab some clean snow."

The man seemed to have reverted to his old taciturn self after a few hours of congeniality. Maybe he only had so much of it in him each day.

That was a cheery thought.

Col took the pot and unzipped the tent flaps, reaching outside. The cold air chilled him, especially without his extra layers, but he was able to scoop up enough to fill the pot from a clean patch that hadn't been beaten down by their own boot prints.

He ducked back inside into the warmth of the tent.

Javier put the pot on the little stove to heat. It quickly melted down to water.

"Tea or coffee?"

"Um... tea, please." He'd gotten bitten by the tea bug in Greenland, when he'd bunked with an Englishman named Harrold Grimsby. Harrold had been particular about his tea, having it brought in from a specific shop in London on Piccadilly Circus. *We British never let our tea steep more than the allotted time, unlike you Americans, who leave the bag in the water the whole bloody time.*

Col grinned at the memory of the large, affable, black-bearded scientist.

Quite a contrast to his current company.

He tried to draw Javier out. "How long have you been down here?"

"Three years." Javier handed him a couple biscuits and something else, flat and dark.

"What's this?"

"Pemmican."

"Ah." He'd had the mix of pounded meat, fat, and spices before. It was a staple out in icy locales—easy to transport and high in carbs and protein. It tasted like beef jerky gone bad, in his experience.

He took a bite. It was cold but was thawed enough to be edible.

"Hey, it's not bad!" The compound had a bit of a sweet taste.

"I make my own, and I add a bit of honey and some dried fruit and nuts to make it taste a bit better." Javier put the tea strainer into the pot of hot water, and the leaves released their flavor, filling the tent with a wonderful cinnamon smell.

After a couple minutes, he removed the strainer and poured them a couple mugs of tea.

Col lifted the tin mug in salute. "To our own little tropical resort."

Javier's face went white. He closed his eyes and set down his tea, hugging himself tightly.

"Hey... did I say something wrong?" Col reached out to touch his arm, but he jerked away.

"No. I'm sorry. It's not you." Javier picked up his tea and his own piece of pemmican and turned away, hiding his face from Col.

The rest of the meal passed in silence.

In the afternoon, Javier took a short hike up the mountainside, leaving Col behind to write in his journal. He needed some fresh air. Needed some time to think.

It was an almost balmy afternoon on the southern continent, the sun warming the icy plain and lighting up the mountain peaks before him.

He climbed through the snow to reach the closest naked outcropping of rock. An algal bloom had colored much of the rock green—not uncommon in the warmer summertime.

Javier pulled off one of his gloves and touched the rock. It was almost warm under the sun's rays. He pried a piece off and slipped it into his pocket for his collection.

There was something about actually *touching* the land, connecting with it, something primal that spoke to him in a way that the endless miles of snow and ice didn't. Frozen water was ephemeral. Eventually, in the length of time, it would all melt away.

Rock was hard, durable, real. The bones of the earth.

He turned around and looked back the way he had come. In the distance, he could see the tent, a small, red dot against the great blue-whiteness of the world.

Our own little tropical resort.

Javier hadn't told Col how much he'd resembled Terry in that awkward moment inside the tent. Or how the pain had welled up in him once more, fresh as the day Terry had died.

"Hey, I have a surprise for you." Terry bounced into the room like Tigger, his face alight with excitement."

"Oh yeah? What's that?" Javier was sitting on the couch, sorting through the mail that Terry had saved up for him from his latest three-month jaunt up to the Arctic.

Terry dropped down onto the cushion next to him, jostling Javier's carefully laid-out piles.

"Hey, watch it!" He picked up a catalog that had fallen under their coffee table.

"Sorry. But you'll forgive me. You know Deanna at work?"

"Sure." How did he ever get on so many email lists?

"She and her wife Julie have a time-share in Kauai, and they can't use it this year."

"We are *not* buying their time-share." He used his antique letter opener—the one that had been his mother's and had a mermaid on top carved out of whale ivory—to open his royalty statement from Hot Climate Press. "Woo hoo! Seven dollars and thirty-two cents."

"You're *not* listening."

Javier sighed. "You're right." He set aside the pile he'd been sorting through and turned to face Terry. "You have my full attention." At forty-five, Terry was still as handsome—and cute—as he'd been when they met in grad school.

"We have a week in Kauai, and all we have to do is pay the airfare."

"Seriously? Let me see that."

Terry handed over the reservation. "And I already got us a flight —economy, but still. Hawaii. We've always wanted to go."

After three months spent in the Arctic, albeit in the arctic summertime, Javier had to admit that Hawaii did sound pretty damned good. "White sand beaches, palm trees, gorgeous Hawaiian guys..."

Terry nodded. "I thought we could get a couple of them in for a massage the first night. Really relax us and set the stage for the rest of the trip."

Javier looked at the dates. "This is next week!"

"I know! You... you *can* go, right?"

"I'm supposed to give a lecture at UCLA next Wednesday." They'd asked him months earlier.

Terry looked crestfallen.

"I can change it."

"Could you?"

"Yeah. Let me call Mark and see if I can do it next month instead." It would mean shuffling some things around, but he could see how much this meant to Terry.

These long absences were hard on them. If they'd been one of those couples with an open relationship, things might have been easier.

Coming home was always a week-long re-entry process, as they learned to live with each other again. It was something he always looked forward to immensely.

"It's going to be so much fun. Like having our own little tropical resort."

"It sounds amazing." Javier hugged him, holding him tight. "I'm so glad I'm home. I missed you."

"I missed you too."

———

Three days later, Terry was dead. Javier's life went from bright tropical colors to Antarctic black and white, his flesh and bones trapped under a smothering curtain of ice that would never thaw.

Col couldn't have known, but his offhand comment had ripped open an old wound.

With a heavy sigh, he started back down the hillside toward the waiting tent, and Col.

Col set down his journal and took a sip of his now-cold tea. He'd left the flap of the tent open just enough to let in a little air. The winds from the morning had calmed, and now it looked to be about as nice a day as he was likely to see in this cold clime.

He put his journal back in his pack and suited up, pulling on his insulated trousers and bunny boots, and pulled on his windbreaker. Mindful of the snow glow, he applied some fresh sun block, and put on a balaclava, scarf, and sunglasses.

Mom would be proud.

He pushed his way out of the tent to stand on the snowy verge.

The sun was dipping toward the horizon but would never quite drop below it. They were at the winter solstice, the longest day of the year in the southern hemisphere, and the time of eternal daylight near the south pole.

Christmas was coming, but all the commercial craziness of the holiday was so far away that it seemed nonexistent. Here it was just sky and snow.

The whole world was still around him. It was a perfect, peaceful, quiet moment. The Antarctic air was crisp in his lungs, but the sun was warm on his shoulders. He liked doing nothing, just for a minute or two. To have no responsibilities and no cares.

"Hey, fingy!"

Col turned to find Javier making his way down a frozen slope. "Hey, old timer. You feeling better?"

"What do you mean?" Javier crossed the remaining distance between them and held up something dark.

"You seemed preoccupied over lunch." Col took the thing from him. It was a bit of rock. "Ooooh. Nice. I think? What is it?"

"Just a souvenir for when you head home. A real piece of the continent that won't melt when you leave it out."

Col's heart thumped. "Thanks."

Javier looked back the way he had come, shielding his eyes. "And thanks for asking. Yeah, I feel a little better. Helped to have some alone time."

Col snorted.

"What?"

"Alone time? I'd think that's all you'd have in a place like this. Don't you ever miss home? Crowds? Frappuccinos?"

"Not really." They stood there together quietly for a moment, staring out at the mountains. "Though I would really love a fresh, juicy rib-eye steak, hot off the grill."

Col grinned. "There you go. I always miss Oreos and chocolate milk when I'm posted at the ends of the Earth."

"And IMAX Theaters."

"And Grindr."

Javier exploded in laughter. "Yeah, not too fucking useful down here. 'There's one other user in your area.'"

"Seen him. Next."

They dissolved into laughter together.

For the first time since he'd arrived, Col decided he didn't *hate* Javier.

"You know, we may not have IMAX down here, but this is still a pretty fucking awesome show."

Col nodded as they watched the wind pick up flurries of snow, spinning them around in the air like fairy dust.

Some day in the not-too-far-distant future, as surely as he stood there, this would all be gone. *Some future human, if we survive, might stand right here with a mai tai and toast to the tropical climate.*

He held up an imaginary glass to the mountain that had been here long before humankind and would probably survive long after.

"What's that?"

"Just a flight of fancy." *You're such a dork.* "Hey, you hungry? This whole Antarctic thing really does take it out of you...."

Cracked

Javier lay on his sleeping bag, willing himself to go to sleep. Some nights it was harder than others.

It wasn't so long ago that he'd been able to go to sleep the instant his head hit the pillow. Now, as often as not, he lay awake for hours, tossing and turning.

He missed his youth.

He glanced over at Col, laying in his sleeping bag on the far side of the tent. The man had taken off his shirt, and his chest was visible above the folds of his own bag. His transition scars were evident under each nipple.

It must take a hell of a lot of courage to go through that. To take a body everyone around you told you was female and remake it to match what was inside you.

It made his own coming out pale by comparison, though his mother might have disagreed. She had screamed holy hell when he'd come home for Christmas and told her he liked guys and had threatened to disown him. That had been almost thirty years before.

How he'd escaped an exorcism, he'd never know.

He grinned to himself. She'd come around eventually and had so loved Terry she'd threatened to disown her own son instead if they ever broke up. "*This* is a good son. Look how dutifully he calls his own mother, every day, to see if she's okay."

He really *should* call her.

He glanced at Col again. Wondering.

With a grunt, he turned over on his side, staring at the white of the tent fabric.

After what seemed like a long time but could have been just minutes, he drifted off into a troubled sleep.

Terry lay still in his coffin.

Somehow, that seemed so wrong to Javier.

Terry was *never* still.

Even when he sat on the couch to watch TV, his knee bounced up and down, releasing the constant stream of energy inside him.

He shouldn't be still.

It was a stupid thought. Terry was dead. He would never move or bounce or twitch again. Yet it wouldn't let him go.

Javier's mother came up beside him, putting an arm around his waist. "He was a good man."

"He shouldn't be still."

She nodded. "You're so right. He was always on the move. Never tired. He was like your father."

"Really?"

She reached up to touch his face. "Oh yes. You *look* like my Jose, but you were always calm. Focused. Your father was always in motion, looking for the next thing to do."

Javier closed his eyes, trying to picture his dad. Jose Fernandez had died when he was fifteen, an accident at work. Mostly now, when Javier thought of him, he pictured the photo of his father in his military uniform. So young and handsome.

So still.

He wiped his eyes and knelt to kiss Terry on the lips. "Te amo."

He wouldn't cry. Not yet.

Not until this was over.

***

Javier's eyes flickered open. Something had awoken him.

He sat up, looking around the tent. The tent was still illuminated by the midnight light from outside, and nothing seemed amiss.

Col still slept, now turned away from him.

All was peaceful, quiet. Still, Javier's sense of unease deepened. His stomach clenched.

He reached over, shaking Col gently. "Col, wake up."

"Let me sleep."

"Something's happening—"

Then he *felt* it. The ground underneath shook, like an earthquake.

Antarctica had quakes, but they were rarely large enough to register on the surface without special detection equipment.

Unless it was an avalanche.

"Col, get up!" Javier shook the man hard. "Avalanche!"

He quickly pulled on his clothes.

The rumbling grew louder.

He'd chosen the site carefully. There were no visible snow over-hangs, no slopes full of ice to come crashing down on them.

His ears didn't lie. Something was happening out there.

He laced up his boots and threw on his jacket and hat. His stomach was churning.

Col did the same, moving with practiced efficiency. The man's experience showed.

He pushed out into the open air and looked around.

The mountain above them was stable, and there was no sign of an avalanche bearing down on them.

What the hell?

Col had emerged from the tent behind him. "Javier."

"What?" Javier turned around to look back toward the ice shelf.

The rumbling had become a roar, accompanied by a sharp, cracking sound.

"Holy shit."

The Ross Ice Shelf was breaking in two a few hundred meters below them, the Great Crack spreading across the ice.

The crack widened and extended, the rumbling now grown to a roar as parts of the ice subsided and the shelf itself dropped ten meters. The activity shook the ground like an earthquake as it drew closer, and Col dove back into the tent, coming back out with his camera and crouching down instinctively to keep his balance, to record as much as he could of the spectacle.

The event sent up a cascade of ice and snow.

Thank the stars the winds are blowing away from us.

"Is this... normal?"

Javier shook his head. "Not for at least a hundred thousand years."

Col couldn't look away. *We did this.* It was a sobering thought. Humankind had unleashed changes on the Earth they were only now starting to understand.

Somewhere out there was Bettencourt Station, now separated from them by a divide that was who knew how deep. "How are we going to get back to the station?"

"I don't know." Javier crawled into the tent and returned with the sat phone. He dialed a number, frowning at the crack as if it were a personal affront against him.

"Yeah, this is Fernandez, out at Bettencourt Station."

The crack had now moved past their position and was being met by one from the other side.

"Yeah, we're in the field. It's the *whole goddamned shelf.* I thought you boys had decided it was good for another decade, at least."

The ice shelf was huge, spanning a prehistoric bay hundreds of miles wide. Even if it had started to disintegrate, it would take time. Years, probably decades, but the end was in the air.

"Yes, the whole shelf. We're up here by the range, watching it. We're gonna need a lift."

The noise ended as suddenly as it had begun, and Col sank back into the snow. "Holy fuck."

"Yeah, you do that." Javier hung up the phone angrily.

"What happened?"

"They're scared shitless down there. Said they'd have to get back to me."

Col shivered. All at once, it hit him how far out they were, how remote this place was from almost everything else. How dependent they were on others for their very survival. "So we wait."

"No." Javier spat the word out.

"What?"

"Out here, you make your own luck, or fate makes you." He glared at the new divide in the ice. "Come on. Help me get things packed up."

"Isn't it better if we just wait for them here?"

Javier turned on him. "Listen. We're out here in an unpredictable place, where the weather can change on a dime. We've just witnessed an unprecedented event, which means we have absolutely no fucking idea what might happen next. We have a limited amount of fuel and a finite amount of food. Every minute we waste standing here arguing is another minute we could be making our way toward Mac-Town."

Col gulped. "Mac-Town? How far is it from here?" He tried to remember his Antarctic geography. They were near the top of the Ross Ice Shelf, and McMurdo Station sat near the bottom, not far from water.

"About three hundred miles across the ice, with a glacier in-between."

"But the helicopter..."

"Can pick us up anywhere along the route." He climbed back into the tent, and Col followed him. "If you want to stay here, that's up to you. But I'm taking the tent."

Col sighed. Javier had been down here a lot longer than he had, and while this event might be unprecedented in human times, the Professor had more years of experience here than Col. "Okay."

"Good. Go through your pack and take out everything you don't need. We'll wrap it up in a tarp and leave it here by the mountain. They can come back for it later." He started emptying his own pack, moving with practiced efficiency.

Col tackled his own with considerably less certainty.

He pared down his clothing, keeping only the set he had on and an extra shirt and pair of socks.

Javier added a couple pieces of cookware to the pile but kept one pot, all the heating fuel, and food.

When they were done, they had slimmed down their two packs' worth of gear to one.

Javier wrapped the remaining gear in a tarp and tied it off. He handed it to Col. "Take this and find a secure place for it up by the mountain face."

Col nodded and took the pack out into the cold. He'd been

looking forward to a full night's rest in his sleeping bag, but fate was busy rearranging his options. He sighed and trudged up the hillside. He found a crevice in the rock to wedge the gear into, where it would be reasonably safe from the weather.

When he got back, Javier had the tent half-collapsed.

They worked together, pointedly ignoring the new Antarctic feature that had precipitated their unplanned flight.

Javier was a model of efficiency and strength, while Col felt like someone had just pulled the world out from under him. "You're not scared?"

Javier stopped what he was doing and looked up, fear evident on his features. "Honestly? I'm scared shitless. But scared doesn't get us out of here." He closed his eyes, and when they reopened, his look of determination had returned. "Just take a deep breath and tell yourself you're gonna make it home okay." He went back to folding up the tent.

Col did as he was told and let out his breath in a puff of white. Somehow he felt better knowing Javier was scared too. "Do we have enough fuel to get there?"

Javier carried the tent to one of the snowmobiles and tied it down. "Honestly, I'm not sure. It's going to be a near thing. Here, take this and tie it to the front of your doo." He tossed one end of a rope to Col.

Col knelt and secured the rope as directed. "We're gonna pull it?"

Javier nodded. "It'll use a little less fuel. We can tie down the pack on yours and ride tandem on mine."

"Got it." Col shivered at the prospect of being pressed up against Javier's back. *It's just the cold.*

In a couple more minutes, they were on their way.

Javier growled under his breath.

He was exhausted. Waking up in the middle of the night had done him no favors, regardless of the fact that it still looked like day out. He wished he was back in bed at the Station, with the prospect of a warm breakfast and a good day's work in his immediate future.

Instead, they were stuck out here, separated from the comforts of "home" by the massive new crack in the ice.

Now they had run into an unexpected obstacle, a lateral crack that split the ice and snow in their path.

He'd filled the skidoos with fuel before they'd left the station, but the range of each was less than half the distance down to Mac-Town.

He gritted his teeth and turned to follow the new crack, heading up toward the mountains.

"Everything okay?"

Javier was intensely aware of Col, attached to his back, the man's arms wrapped around his waist. "Just a detour."

The satellite phone rang.

Javier brought the skidoo to a halt and pulled the bulky device out of his pocket. "Fernandez here."

"Hey, Javier." It was Jim Haft, the communications officer for McMurdo Station.

"When can you come get us?"

Jim sighed. "Not for a while, I'm afraid. Can you guys make it down here on your own?"

"Negative. We don't have enough fuel. What's happening down there?"

"This is a major event. The powers that be have decided to evacuate Mac-Town as a precaution, but we're grounded until they figure things out. All our resources have been pressed into getting things sorted here. You guys are okay out there for the moment, right?"

"For now, yes."

"What's going on?" Col had gotten up to stretch his legs.

Javier covered the mouthpiece. "They can't come for us yet."

"There's more." Jim sounded worried. "You've got a storm coming in."

"In December?"

"Yeah, I know. But it happens. It's a warm one, so it's gonna make traveling over the ice difficult. Want my advice?"

"Do I have a choice?"

"Hey, just the messenger here. You're a vet at this stuff. Get as close as you can, and then hunker down when the storm comes. When it's over, we'll come get you."

"Got it."

"Javier?"

"What?"

"Good luck." Jim hung up.

Javier restrained himself from throwing the phone into the crack in the ice. "Goddamned mother-fucking turd-eating sons of bitches."

Col's mouth dropped open. "What's going on?"

"The copters are grounded—things are a mess down there. They can't come get us, not yet, anyhow. Come on, we have to get going."

Col climbed onto the skidoo behind him. "What are we going to do?"

"There's a storm coming."

Col glanced out toward the distant sea, filming the ice crack.

Javier followed his gaze. There were clouds in the distance.

"Can we get there before it hits?"

"I don't think so. Even if we had more gas.... But we have to get as far as we can." He started forward, following the crack toward the mountains a couple hundred meters in the distance. "The storm's a warm one. Our friend El Niño coming out to play."

"That's good, right?"

Javier shook his head. "It means the surface will turn to slush, and it could worsen the condition of the ice shelf."

"Holy shit."

"Yeah, my thoughts exactly. Look, as long as we keep our heads and use our resources wisely, we should get through this. Okay?"

"Okay."

Col didn't sound entirely convinced.

Col wasn't convinced.

He closed his eyes, doing what he'd done since he was a kid when faced with something bigger than he could deal with.

He pretended it didn't exist.

With his eyes closed, he could pretend he was back in San Francisco, in his college days, when he'd still been Colleen, his arms wrapped around Charlie's waist as they zoomed across the Bay Bridge from Berkeley on Charlie's Harley for a day in the city.

He could still smell the salt water of the Bay and feel the warm September air, could still feel the cracked black leather of the bike's seat between his legs.

The skidoo shifted, and he opened his eyes to find himself back in Antarctica as Javier navigated the far end of the slot that had blocked their way.

He picked his way along the edge, finding the smoothest path he could, and then they turned back toward the sea. Javier urged the little craft along, nursing as much as he could out of it with a steady pace.

Faster, faster! Col knew it was counterproductive, but he wished they could move more quickly.

Speed could be deadly on the ice.

He glanced behind them. The second skidoo bounced along after them like a duckling after its mother.

The phone rang again.

"Can you grab it?"

"Sure." Col reached into Javier's pants pocket and fished out the phone, trying not to think about where his hand was. "Col Steele here."

"Steele?"

"Yes?"

"This is Tad Bettencourt."

"Mr. Bettencourt! What can I do for you?"

Javier's muscles tensed up under Col's grasp.

"You can tell me what the hell is going on down there! I can't get a straight word out of the USAP. You two all right?"

"Yeah. The shelf has cracked. Pretty badly. We were out on the ice when it happened."

"God damn. Is the station okay?"

"We don't know, sir. We can't reach it."

There was silence on the other end of the line.

"Mr. Bettencourt?"

"Sorry, was talking with one of my weather guys. You need to get back to the station and lock it down."

"I'm sorry, sir. we can't—"

"Get your asses back to the station. That's an order. It's worth more than both of your careers. Call me when you get there." The line went dead.

"What did he say?" Javier's voice was dangerously low.

"He ordered us back to the station."

Javier shook his head. "Not gonna happen."

"I told him. He..."

"He what?"

"He said the station was worth more than either of us."

Javier snorted. "Typical rich asshole. 'Future of the planet' my ass. When it comes down to it, all he fucking cares about is the bottom line."

"So... what do we do?" Col's stomach rumbled.

"We just keep going. There's no way to get there from here."

"But Bettencourt—"

"Is nine thousand miles away."

Col sighted. "This isn't what I signed up for."

"You and me both." He reached back to squeeze Col's leg. "We'll get through this. *Then* we'll deal with Bettencourt."

<hr>

Javier glanced up at the sky. The storm was coming in fast, dark clouds blowing over the ice from the Ross Sea. They'd have to find shelter before it hit.

He'd been steering them steadily southward. The trip should have taken three hours with backup fuel on the more open ice of the shelf. He'd been sticking close to the Transantarctic Range because he didn't trust the open ice, and that meant he had to make constant detours around ice formations and natural rock outcrops.

True, it was an ethereal, beautiful landscape of faery castles and ridges whose colors ran from white at their base to turquoise blue at their peaks. At another time, he might have enjoyed the other-worldly beauty of it all.

Col continued to take pictures and footage of the newly formed crack in the ice shelf as they went.

Javier had moved beyond exhaustion to a white numbness that blanketed his mind like the snow that covered his heart. Too little sleep and too much exertion had worn him down, and he was starting to see things—flashes of light, movement in the corners of his eyes. He blinked rapidly, rubbing the back of his head to keep himself awake.

The engine started to sputter. He glanced down, coming fully awake.

The fuel gauge was below zero.

"Damn it."

"Running out of gas?"

He nodded. "I'll nurse it along for as far as I can, but we're going to have to dump it and switch to the other doo."

A chill but wet wind was blowing up from the sea now. The katabatic wind had reversed course with the storm.

They had to have covered at least a third of the distance to Mac-Town, and yet, when they caught glimpses of the sea as they crossed over hillsides and higher ground, it didn't seem any closer.

The engine sputtered again, and this time it didn't stop.

Javier pushed the skidoo as far as he could manage before it died entirely. The snowmobile coasted downhill a little farther, ending its run in a snowbank.

"Come on. Let's do this quickly." He slid off the snowmobile onto the ice, and patted the machine. "You served us well."

He didn't miss Col's grin.

"Sweet."

"Shut up." He untied the tent from the back of the skidoo and tried to loosen the rope that connected the two snowmobiles.

It took him longer than he would have liked. Despite the gloves, his hands were cold, and the weight of the other skidoo had pulled the knot tight.

In the end, he got his knife out and just cut the rope.

Doing the same at the other end, he then wrapped the rope up and stuck it in his pack. "You want to drive?"

"Sure." Col rubbed his hands together and blew into them. "I managed to catch a few z's while I was in the passenger seat." He winked, and Javier couldn't decide if he was serious or not.

In five minutes, they were on their way again. Javier wrapped his arms around Col's slender form, grateful to have the break. "We need to find someplace high and level, away from large accumulations of snow."

Col nodded.

Saving his energy, most likely. Javier approved.

They continued on as the wind grew, and the sky clouded over, becoming lead gray.

After about twenty minutes, Col turned the skidoo up toward the mountains and pointed ahead.

A series of low hills ran along the base of the range, covered in ice and snow.

"That should work."

Storm

Col guided the skidoo across the frozen landscape, intensely aware of the touch of Javier's strong arms through his layers of clothing. He imagined he could feel their warmth, their strength. He felt strangely safe with Javier holding him, and some of his fear dissipated.

His career was likely over. With an enemy like Bettencourt, who would hire him after this?

They had much more immediate concerns. If they somehow got off the ice alive, he could worry about his academic success then.

The wind pried at his clothing, blowing up gusts of snow that temporarily blocked his view.

He had never realized how big Antarctica actually was. He knew it intellectually—from one end to the other, it was about the same width as the continental United States. Still, to travel across it by snowmobile—to actually see it like this in person—so much ice and snow and barren rock—made him feel small and insignificant.

What would the world care if one Col Steele froze to death amongst such immensity? If he fell into a slot and was never seen or heard from again?

He shoved those thoughts aside. Right now, *this moment* needed his attention.

"How about here?" He slowed the skidoo down along the top of one of the hills that was relatively wide and flat.

"Looks good to me!" Javier had to shout over the sound of the wind. "We need to build a wind break!"

Col's stomach rumbled. He must be burning calories crazy fast. His stomach practically begged for food.

One more thing he needed to ignore. The list was getting long.

They dismounted and took out their folding shovels from the remaining pack.

"Along here." Javier drew out a line in the snow.

"Got it."

Together they piled up snow in a wide but unstable wall, working out from the middle.

Col's arms were sore already from the exertion of managing the snowmobile's path over the uneven ground, but he pushed himself hard, consoling himself with the thought of a long, warm shower—or bath—when he got back to civilization.

"We *will* get back." Javier shouted it over the wind.

Col stared at him for a moment. *Can you read my mind?*

Javier had already gone back to his work.

In half an hour, they had built up a decent berm to protect the tent from the worst of the storm and wind. They used the shovels to compact the snow for the tent as much as they could and then set about erecting it.

Col checked his phone. It was just after noon on the twenty second.

This time the setup went faster, their practice the day before paying dividends.

In another fifteen minutes, they had the tent erected and filled with their remaining belongings, just as the first of the storm began to pelt the hillside with slushy snow.

Col crawled into the tent with Javier right behind him, and they zipped up the entryway, sealing the storm outside.

<hr>

Now that he was no longer exerting himself, the cold crept into Javier's body. His teeth chattering, he lit the little camp stove, placing it in the middle of the tent.

The small space slowly warmed up.

They stared at each other across the light of the flame as the snow battered the tent from the outside and grinned like two schoolboys who'd just pulled off a prank on the teacher.

"We fucking made it."

Col nodded. "Barely. We're still a long way from Mac-Town."

"Maybe so. But we made it *here*." Javier stretched his sore arms.

Col yawned. "I am so fucking tired."

"Don't sleep yet. We need to warm it up in here and then turn off the heat. We don't want to risk carbon monoxide poisoning."

"But the vents—"

"—can get covered with snow."

"Ah." Col started rummaging through the pack.

"I'm going to call Mac-Town and see how things are down there." Javier took out the phone and dialed the base.

"McMurdo Station." The man sounded tired.

"Hey, Jim, it's Javier."

"Hey!" Jim's voice perked up. "You guys are still alive!"

Javier grunted. "Don't sound so surprised."

"I'm not. Just happy to hear from you. Where are you?"

"About a third of the way there. How's the evacuation going?"

"Rough. This storm blew in fast. We've battened things down here to wait it out."

Javier nodded. "Makes sense. We just got the front end of it up here."

"You guys okay for food and heat?"

"I think so. We're hunkered down too. Gonna get some rest while the storm blows out. How long you think that will be?"

"Not... probably a day.... Should be able to weather it."

Javier pressed the phone closer to his ear. "Sorry, what was that? You're cutting in and out."

"Storm's messing... communications."

"Got it. I'll call you later."

"...firmative."

Javier cut the connection and checked the phone's battery. It was down to about fifty percent.

He tucked it away where it would be safe. It was their only lifeline back to civilization. They had to save all the rest of its power.

"Jim says they're hunkered down at McMurdo—"

Col was already asleep, tucked into his sleeping bag.

The man looked ten years younger than his forty years, his face slack in relaxation. He was beautiful. *Poor guy must be exhausted.*

Javier turned off the heater, closed the vents, and crawled into his own sleeping bag.

In less than a minute, he was fast asleep.

Col woke with a splitting headache. His head was thick, and his stomach twisted in his gut.

He pushed himself up, swaying and barely able to keep his balance, and looked around.

The tent was blurry. A dim light glowed in its center.

Poisoned.

His training forced that thought through his sluggish brain.

Must get fresh air.

Col struggled toward the tent flaps in the dim light.

He missed the zipper tab the first try, falling on his face against the cold floor of the tent.

He reached for it again and this time managed to grab it with his fumbling fingers.

Col pulled down the inner flap, cursing his weakness.

Javier must have left the cook stove on, just a little.

In another minute, he had the second flap open, and bitterly cold, clean air and some wet slush blew into the tent.

He took a deep breath. It was the sweetest thing he'd ever smelled.

Col padded back across the small space on his hands and knees to where Javier lay, apparently fast asleep. He shook the man's shoulder, trying to rouse him. "Javier, come on. Wake up!"

His own headache was lessening, though it would be a while before it went away entirely. The slushy rain continued to pound the tent, but Col didn't care.

Javier slept on, oblivious to Col's attempts to wake him.

"Goddamnit."

Carbon monoxide poisoning could lead to serious brain damage, even death. He was lucky as hell he'd awoken in time. Turn off the heat or open the flaps. That was Camping 101.

There was nothing else he could do for Javier at the moment other than make sure the air remained fresh and warm enough to sustain them.

He pulled the flaps closed and opened the vents near the top of the tent, something they must have neglected to do in their exhaustion.

Then he turned the cook stove up a bit to warm up the air inside once again.

He sat on his sleeping bag, watching the flame, and keeping an eye on Javier. "God help us if you're... sick." Col wasn't a religious man, but old habits died hard. His mother had raised him Christian, and when things got rough, you prayed.

When the tent was warm enough, he turned the stove all the way off, double checking it, listening for the hiss of any escaping gas. When he was satisfied that there was none, he closed the vents again and tried once more to wake Javier.

The man mumbled this time—a good sign?—but still didn't wake up.

"You're gonna be okay, Javier." It was as much for himself as for the Professor that he said the words.

Col climbed into the sleeping bag with his companion, determined to use his own body heat to keep both of them warm, and zipped it up.

It might have been erotic in other circumstances, but at the moment all he wanted was to take care of Javier.

He lay there for a few moments against Javier's cold back, warming it with his own chest.

It had been a long time since he'd had someone else in his arms.

Thoughts of David flashed though his head, the happier times, when they'd lived together in London for a year before Col had shipped out to the Yukon.

For the first time, he considered whether—just maybe—the breakup had been his fault too. What had happened between them.

Maybe David had needed more than he'd been able to give. Maybe his being away on the road had been too much for their relationship to handle.

Maybe the moon is made of green cheese.

He sighed.

At last he drifted off into a deep, dreamless sleep.

Javier dreamed about Terry.

Strange, disconnected dreams of times they had spent together.

Terry walking in the snow ahead of him.

Terry disappearing into a blizzard.

Calling for him in the blackest night, without answer.

At one point, Col's voice called his name. The man's voice echoed in his head, bouncing off invisible walls.

Javier tried to reach it, struggling upward through a warm sea filled with bubbles, but he couldn't find the surface.

Am I dying? Is this what death feels like?

"Javi."

He spun around to find Terry, surrounded by bamboo, sunlight filtering down through the poles, yellow and green, to strike the ground in mottled patterns.

The Huntington Gardens was one of their favorite places. Especially the bamboo grove, where you could slip away from the rest of the world and feel safe, enclosed, and protected.

"Terry!" He grabbed his husband and pulled him close, breathing in his scent—Cool Water with a hint of masculine musk. He closed his eyes, feeling warmth spread through his whole body.

They kissed, and then Terry let him go.

"I missed you. Oh holy crap, how I've missed you."

"I know." Terry was just as Javier remembered him, six foot three, red-haired and bearded, wearing a plaid shirt, like a gay version of Paul Bunyan.

"How are you here?" He wanted to rip off Terry's shirt, to rub his furry chest.

"Something's happened. You've come too close to me. Too close to death."

Javier shivered. "I was asleep."

"You have to go back. It's not time for you to be here yet."

Cold seized Javier's heart. "I don't want to leave you." *I can't lose you again.* "Don't make me go."

Terry pulled him close, turning him around and wrapping his

arms around him from behind. He bent down to rest his head on Javier's shoulder. "You have to go. The world needs you. Troubled times are coming." His lips brushed Terry's ear. "I will *always* love you, and I will always be here for you. But you'll find someone else to stand with you back there."

"I... I don't want anyone else."

"It's time. Don't you think five years is long enough to wait?"

Time shifted.

Javier was leaning back in his chair, staring at his laptop screen.

"I'm running to the store. Wanna come?" Terry hovered over his shoulder.

"Nah, go ahead. I'm catching up on the research before our trip. Gotta hit the ground running when we get back from Hawaii."

"Gotcha. I'm getting some steaks for tonight and some of that Kansas City barbecue sauce you love. Do we need anything else?"

"Not that I can think of." Javier was actually just about finished with his research, but he wanted to catch up with his social media posts, and it was cold and rainy out. Snow he could handle. Rain, not so much.

"Text me if you think of anything else."

"I will." It was a regular game between them.

Terry pecked him on the cheek. "Love you."

"Yeah, you too."

As the door to the garage slammed, Javier opened up Facebook and started checking his messages. His friend Ollie had sent over a paper he was working on, and he needed some feedback.

Javier pulled it up and started reading.

A half-hour later, there was a knock at his door.

"Terry, did you leave your house key again?" He sighed. The man was so forgetful. Half the time, he left one of their grocery bags at the store and had to run back to get it.

The rain was pouring down now outside. He could hear it through the fireplace on the roof like a hundred drums.

Javier opened the door to find a police officer there, a trim Hispanic woman whose name tag said "Rodriguez."

"Mr. Fernandez?" She looked serious.

"Yes, is something wrong?"

"I'm sorry to tell you this—"

He screamed.

Time shifted again.

The sunshine through the bamboo seemed like a mockery, a promise of life and light after the deadly rain.

Javier beat Terry's chest with his fists. "It was my fault. I should have gone with you. I didn't want to go out in the rain. I should have told you not to go. I should have been there. I should have—"

"Shhhhh." Terry squeezed him tight. "Nothing you could have done would have changed things. It was my time. I know that now."

"I didn't say I loved you." Of all his regret, of all the things that pained him, that was the one that hurt the most. He had been so preoccupied with his stupid online life that he'd let his real one slip away almost unnoticed. Until it was gone.

"I knew you did." Terry kissed him again from behind and held him tightly.

He could say it now. "I love you."

Terry grinned. "I love you too. I want you to be happy, *mi vida. Mi amor.*" Then he was gone.

Javier woke. The air was cold, but he could still feel Terry's arms around him.

For a moment, he was back at home in his comfortable bed with its starched white sheets, in the Spanish-tiled bungalow in West Hollywood. Terry's arms were around him, and all was right in the world.

His eyes flickered open. The fabric of the tent was inches away, dim in the storm-clouded light. The snow continued to hit the tent, soft slaps that turned to slushy water and rolled down to the ground.

Someone's arms were around him, and they weren't Terry's.

He undid the sleeping bag's zipper and extricated himself from Col's embrace.

Col's eyes flickered open. "You're awake."

"Yeah." He had a headache. He pulled a couple Tylenol out of his pack and downed them with some water from his canteen.

Water was one thing they didn't lack out here.

"How do you feel?" Col was sitting up, his arms wrapped around his knees, staring at Javier curiously.

"Okay."

"How many fingers am I holding up?"

Javier glanced at him. "Four. What the hell are you going on about?" He was grumpy. He needed coffee. He bent over to light the cook stove.

"Aren't you going to ask me why I was in your sleeping bag?"

Javier snorted. "I assumed you'd tell me when you were ready."

"Javier, you almost died last night."

Javier spun around. "What the hell?"

"Carbon monoxide."

Javier's gaze dropped to the cook stove. "Holy crap."

"Yeah, that about sums it up." Col crossed over to his own side, going through his bag. "I woke up with a splitting headache and a sick stomach. We left the cook stove going without the vents open."

Rookie mistake. "Did you... Were you calling my name?" His stomach rumbled.

"Yeah. You were really out of it. I was afraid you were going to end up brain damaged or something."

Javier wanted to kick himself. He could have gotten them both killed. "I'm sorry, Col. Jesus, that was stupid."

Col glanced back at him. "It's not your fault. I was knocked out as soon as I hit the sack." He pulled out a pack of dried ramen. "Saw this in the back of the pantry. Took me back to my college days. What say we relive our too-poor-to-buy-food days?"

Javier grinned. "I always thought all the flavors tasted the same."

"Except for the shrimp."

"Yeah, that one was kinda nasty." He put his arm on Col's. "Thanks for saving me."

"You're welcome."

"Grab some clean snow?"

"On it."

As Col went out to fetch the snow, Javier took out the last of the tea. He'd heat the water and make the tea first, then use the rest for the ramen.

He was starving, but they had to stretch out their food a little longer.

"Here you go." Col handed him the pot and turned to close the tent flaps behind him.

"What was he like?" He set the pot over the burner, and the snow began to liquify, melting down into water.

"Who?" Col sat down cross-legged on his sleeping bag, pulling off his glasses to wipe them on his shirt.

"Your ex. Dylan?"

"David." Col sighed. "David was handsome. Rugged. That guy at the bar who everyone wanted. But he came over to me."

Javier grinned. He took out the tea bags and put one in each cup. "Gym rat?"

"Not really. Just... sure of himself. Happy in his own skin."

"What happened?"

Col ran his hand through his long blond hair. "I don't know. One minute he loved me, and the next—"

"Oh, come on."

"What?"

"It's never just like that."

Col laughed bitterly. "Yeah. You're probably right. He left me, but I was never home."

"A climate scientist's life." He poured some of the hot water in each cup and handed one to Col.

"Something like that." Col took the cup and held it up to his face. The steam rose off the water past his face. "He slept with someone else."

"Now that's fucked up."

Col laughed. "Yeah, it really was."

Javier cracked open the ramen packet and crumbled the noodles into the boiling water, followed by the packet of dried sauce.

"What about you?" Col sipped his tea, watching Javier over the rim.

"What do you mean?" The smell of the ramen brought back so many memories. College. Late nights cramming for chemistry and physics. Coors beer.

"You had someone, once. You still wear the ring."

Javier glanced down at his hand. Truth be told, he hardly even thought about it anymore. It was just another part of him now. "His name was Terry. He was the love of my life." He stirred the ramen.

"What happened?"

"The ramen is about ready. I forgot how quickly this stuff cooks. I used to eat it raw." He took the pot off the burner and turned off the flame. He set it down on a hot pad and handed Col a fork.

"What happened to Terry?" Col was staring at him, his brow furrowed.

Javier sat back, returning the stare. "He went out for groceries and never came back."

"Holy shit."

Javier closed his eyes. "He spun out in a rainstorm and slammed into a power pole. They said it was instant."

Col set down his tea and put a hand on Javier's knee. "How long ago was that?"

"Five years." Suddenly he wasn't hungry anymore, but he forced himself to eat.

"What was he like?"

Javier smiled. "He was full of energy. Boundless energy. He never met a problem he couldn't solve."

"I like him already." Col took a forkful of ramen. "Oh God, that's just as awful as I remember."

"It really is." Javier grinned.

Col leaned forward to grab another forkful.

Their eyes met across the pot.

Something passed between them.

Col kissed him. The man's lips were rough from the cold.

Javier fell back on his hands, dropping his fork. "Whoa, back up a bit there."

Col looked hurt. "I'm sorry. I thought..."

"You thought wrong." Javier turned away. He wasn't ready for *that*. Not yet. Despite what Terry said.

I want you to be happy.

He had more important things to worry about at the moment. Being happy would have to take a back seat.

Col pulled on some clothes and grabbed his camera. He needed some fresh air. He pushed through the tent flaps into the cold outside.

He should have been used to the never-ending sunshine by now, but on this long, unplanned run toward the coast, it was starting to wear on him.

He wanted stars.

The storm had let up for the moment, though the sky was still leaden. The frozen ground underfoot was slushy, almost sticking to his boots.

He pulled out his phone and took another video of the area, narrating softly as he scanned the ice shelf far below. "The world is so much larger than we are. We think we control it, but it's times like this that you realize just how small and unimportant you really are." Antarctica was a whole, still mostly unexplored world after all these years. Who knew what lay hidden under its massive ice sheets?

We may be about to find out.

Massive amounts of carbon and methane lurked beneath the ice at both poles. Enough to warm the world far more than the hoped-for maximum of two degrees.

What kind of world will our kids inherit?

He knelt and scooped up some snow from the berm, which had been partially eroded by the wind and the storm.

Maybe it wasn't too late. Maybe one of those kids would be a scientific genius who would figure out a way to scrub the greenhouse gasses from the atmosphere.

Maybe we won't make it home. Maybe I'll never know.

He shivered as the cold penetrated his single layer of clothing.

The snowfall began again, closing off the view. He hurried back toward the tent entrance.

He had things he wanted to do. Worlds to save.

People to love.

I'm not ready to die.

So what if it wasn't Javier?

There would be someone. Not *everyone* was an asshole.

Col re-entered the warmth of the tent, shivering with more than just the cold. He put away his camera and pulled out his journal from the pack.

"Still snowing out there?"

"Looks like it." He sat down in the far corner of the tent, determined to get his thoughts down before they fled.

"I'll call Mac-Town for a forecast update from the weather guessers—"

"Great." Col's face was burning. He *really* didn't want to talk with Javier right now.

Javier frowned.

He'd reacted badly to Col's kiss. He knew it. It wasn't his fault. The whole thing had taken him by surprise.

I ought to apologize. He grunted under his breath. He wasn't good at *sorry*.

Instead, he pulled out the sat phone and dialed up Mac-Town.

Nothing happened.

He frowned at the phone. Either the storm was scrambling the signal, or maybe the McMurdo antenna had blown down.

As if in response to his thought, the wind gusted, shaking the walls of the tent.

He put the phone away.

Col was writing furiously in his journal. Javier wondered what was so important. If it was about him or about the predicament they were in.

Probably both.

"Look, I'm sorry." It came out before he had time to think about it.

Col looked up at him. His blue eyes narrowed. "Don't worry about it."

He returned to his writing.

In for an inch, in for a mile...

"Since I lost Terry..."

Col looked up again, his lip twitching as their eyes met. "I'm sorry." He put down the journal and pencil. "Was he a scientist?"

"No. He was a sports agent."

Col raised an eyebrow.

"I know. We were apart a lot of the time. He was planning to take me to Hawaii the next week so we could reconnect..." His voice hitched, and he turned away. He hadn't meant to open up this whole emotional can of worms again. "Anyway, I just... when you... it just surprised me. That's all."

"You're not ready."

"I—"

"No, it's okay. I get it." He picked up his pencil and went back to journaling.

That's not what I meant...

It was too late. The door Col had tried to open was firmly closed once again.

Javier sighed. He went back to cleaning up after the meal, collecting the waste to be carried out with them, if and when rescue finally came.

Then he took out his own phone and opened his email. He couldn't send it here, but he could leave a message... just in case.

Dear Mom... Sometimes life doesn't go the way we want. But I wanted you to know I was loved. I had a good life. And you taught me everything I needed to know....

Except how to apologize.

Crash

Col lay in his sleeping bag, drifting in and out of consciousness. They had decided to preserve their strength to make a final run toward Mac-Town, whenever the storm finally let up.

Javier was dozing in his own bag, snoring loudly.

Col almost laughed at that.

The storm had ramped up again, and the wind howled over the ice like a banshee.

It was clear to him now. He'd made a fool of himself when he'd tried to kiss Javier. It had stung to be so roundly rejected, but he'd been a bit of an ass in turn.

Truth was, the rejection still stung him to the core.

When he'd first transitioned, he'd gotten it all the time.

"Not interested."

"You're not my type."

And the worst of all: "I don't date *girls*."

Transphobia was still rampant in the community, especially on the dating apps.

Col had all but given up.

Then he'd met David at a conference in Sweden. The man had been handsome, charming, and completely unconcerned with Col's birth sex.

"What's a handsome bloke like you doing in a dive like this?"

Col had looked up from his cranberry and soda to find a tall, dark-haired angel. "I'm here for the climate change conference."

The man slid onto the barstool next to him. "I know. I heard your speech. It was brilliant."

Col grinned. "Col Steele." He held out his hand.

"David Orway."

Col flagged down the bartender. "Drink for my friend here?"

"Pimm's Cup, please." David returned his smoldering gaze to Col. "Do you really think we can stop it?"

Col was lost in the man's eyes. "Stop what?"

"Climate change."

Col frowned. "I don't know. If we really wanted to, maybe. But there are so many people whose jobs and money depend on the status quo." He sipped his drink nervously and wished, just for a second, that he was a drinker. A little alcohol would be a shot in the arm right about now. He wasn't used to being hit on by guys as handsome as David. "Are you a scientist?"

"Nope." He pulled out his wallet and handed Col a card. "Reporter for the Guardian."

"Ah. There must be a lot of stories here for you to chase down."

"Stories, yes. Really cute guys, no. You scientists are a pretty stodgy bunch."

"Some guys like that kind of thing."

David snorted. "Daddies, yes. Professors, not so much."

"Touché."

"You have any plans tonight?"

Col sighed. "I was going to look over the agenda for the rest of the weekend. There are so many sessions I want to attend...." Then it struck him. The man was hitting on him. *Jesus, I'm dense sometimes.* "I mean... nothing I couldn't put off."

David grinned, the canary's feathers showing between his teeth. "Good. Come on. You have to see the view from the rooftop. Stockholm is amazing at night."

He dragged Col off his stool and into his life. For three happy years.

Then it all came crashing down.

Something woke him up.

Col blinked, looking around the tent in confusion.

Javier was already up. "Hello?"

He sat up, rubbing his eyes. "What is it? Bettencourt again?"

Javier shook his head. "That's great news. We'll get moving as fast as we can." He hung up the phone.

"Who was it? What did they say?"

"That was Mac-Town. The storm just passed them by. We should be clear shortly. They want us to pack it up and get as close to the coast as we can."

"They can't pick us up here?"

Javier shook his head. "The evacuation is underway, and there's another storm coming. But they should be able to come get us later today."

Col pulled out his phone. It was December twenty third. "Just in time for Christmas Eve?"

"Yeah, suppose so. Come on, get out the rest of your food. We'll save the chocolate for the road, but we should eat everything else. We'll travel light, and we'll need all the calories we can get."

They pulled out all of their stores, which in the end amounted to a few packets of dried green beans and corn, a pouch of dried beef stroganoff, some frozen and thawed berries that had been fresh when they'd left Bettencourt Station, and a packet of Funyuns mostly crushed to dust that made a nice seasoning for the vegetables.

They cooked the whole mess together, making a bit of a beef and veggie stew. "Not exactly four-star cuisine."

Col laughed. "I must be hungry, because it smells like Heaven."

Javier laughed. "One of these days, I'll make you a real meal."

Col raised an eyebrow. "I'll hold you to that. We'll have lots of time once we're officially unemployed."

They ate directly out of the pot once again.

Col savored the flavor. It was actually pretty damned good. Or maybe that was just his hunger speaking.

It was like one of those cooking shows, where the chefs had to use the crap out of a vending machine to prepare a gourmet meal.

Most likely it *was* a godawful mess and only tasted good because he really was *starving*.

He watched Javier eat. The man took meticulous care with his food, just like he did with everything else, nothing wasted.

The crusty loner he'd met just a few days before was all but gone, replaced by something—someone—much more human and real. It would be nice to go out for a real meal with him.

Col squashed the thought. Javier had made his position very clear on that.

Javier finished his last bite. He cocked his head, staring at the tent roof. "Listen."

"I don't hear anything."

"Exactly!" As he spoke, sunshine hit the tent, lighting up the little space. "We're going to Mac-Town!"

———

The skidoo bounced over the snowy terrain, almost like it was eager to reach the end of its journey. It had taken them longer than anticipated to get going, as the skids had frozen to the ground when the ice had melted and hardened again in the relatively warm storm.

Javier had to take a pickax to it to free them.

Now they were on their way, and the weather was fair for the moment.

The land out here was weird and beautiful. Javier kept them on flat ice as much as he was able, but they passed many beautiful ice formations sculpted by the hands of Mother Nature and time. The flat ice was white, but the sculptures were filled with subtle gradients of blue and turquoise that were as detailed and beautiful as any man-made art.

There were walls of ice as finely layered as any rocky bluff up north, created by year after year, eon after eon of accumulated snowfall, each layer filled with hidden bits of the past.

There were overhangs that dripped rows of icicles like teeth, sharp enough to kill a man if they were to fall. In other places, the ice had melted and reformed, creating winding caverns of blue light that twisted back into the ice.

They passed under a huge archway formed entirely from frozen water. Above, the sun glinted off the ice, creating rainbow patterns in the arch.

It was quite literally a winter wonderland. It saddened Javier that one day it would all melt away. There would be nothing like it left on the Earth.

He was lucky to be one of the few to see it.

Col held on to him, and it was comforting to know he wasn't out here alone, whatever else was going on between them. The Ice was too big for one person. "Hey, you awake back there?"

"Yeah, I was just admiring the view."

"It's an amazing place."

Col laughed. "Yes. It is. It's also goddamned huge."

"Yeah, I was just thinking that too." He glanced down at the gas gauge. It was at a quarter tank.

"Are we gonna make it?"

"We'll make it." Javier tried to sound more certain than he felt. "Even if we have to walk the last couple miles."

"Right. Hey, do you hear that?"

Javier cocked his head. "Just the doo."

"No, it's... deeper. Like a rumbling."

Javier pulled the snowmobile to a halt. They were riding along a high patch of ground with a decent view downhill toward the sea.

Out over the water, another storm was gathering, but by the look of it, they still had a few clear hours.

"Look!" Col pointed toward where the land met the sea.

Another crack was forming where the shelf met the land. It raced toward them, the ice falling into the almost frozen sea below, opening up a seam of the most beautiful turquoise blue.

The gigantic ice shelf was collapsing far faster than anyone had thought was possible.

They'd been following along the margin, using the relatively flat ice of the shelf to make better progress.

Now that looked like a deadly mistake.

"Hold on!"

They fled across the ice, heading back toward the mountains as the new crevasse behind them deepened and spread. The sound was almost deafening now, a guttural noise like the crashing of a thousand cars.

Col gritted his teeth and pressed himself against Javier's back, holding on for dear life. He glanced back over his shoulder to see the ongoing destruction.

Clouds of snow and ice hid most of it, but they also marked its advance. "Go right!"

Javier veered to the right and gunned the engine, and the skidoo lurched across the last hundred meters of relatively flat space on the ice sheet.

A cloud of snow overtook them, reducing visibility to almost zero.

Col put his head next to Javier's ear. "I'm sorry for... for whatever I said. Or might have done."

"Not now!" It came out as a growl, barely audible over the crash of ice.

Col shut his mouth.

The skidoo bounced over the snow, rapidly using up the last of their fuel.

At least they were headed in the right direction.

They burst out of the snow cloud back into the bright sunshine, leaving the rumbling behind.

"Holy crap, that was close."

Javier turned back toward him with a wild grin. "Told you we'd be okay."

"No you didn't—Javier!" The ice—"

Javier turned back. Too late.

The skidoo slammed into a low wall of ice, just tall enough to bring her forward progress to a crashing halt.

Col flew through the air and hit the snow with a bone-breaking crunch.

Javier blinked.

He was lying face up in the snow, the sun beating down on him.

The world was silent.

He pushed himself up, shivering in the cold.

Where am I?

He looked around. The snow was littered with colored bits and pieces of things.

A chocolate bar. The backpack. The tent.

Col. The man was sprawled out on the snow, not moving.

Javier scrambled across the snow to his companion.

Col lay on his side. Still. Like Terry.

"No, no, no, no, no..." Javier felt for his pulse.

There was one, but it was weak. His leg was twisted at an awkward angle, and his skin was tinged blue.

Javier eased him over onto his back, careful to move his leg only as much as he had to. Col needed warmth. Then they could figure out the rest.

Col moaned.

That's a good sign.

The man looked so young. So innocent.

He left Col there and went to retrieve the tent. Thankfully they had wrapped it well, and he had all the parts.

He set it up quickly, efficiently, keeping his emotions in check. *It's all my fault.*

Col was not going to die.

I'm not going to lose you again, Terry. Col.

The two men were nothing alike. Somehow that didn't matter.

When the tent was set up, Javier retrieved the sleeping bags from where they had landed and shook off as much of the snow as he was able. He put one inside and opened it up to hold Col.

He used the other one as a travois, carefully lifting Col's body onto the blue nylon.

He pulled Col across the ice as gently as he was able, getting the man into the tent with a minimum jostling of his injured leg. He laid Col on the other sleeping bag. He took off Col's goggles. One of the lenses of his glasses was cracked.

He took those off too and set them aside, and then pulled the sleeping bag over him for warmth.

He'd look at the injured leg later.

Next, Javier pulled the pack inside and got out the cook stove.

He lit it, and warmth started to fill the tent. Then he went out to check the skidoo.

It was a total loss, a broken wreck. They were lucky their injuries weren't worse, but the poor little doo wouldn't be taking them any farther.

He climbed up the slope to see what damage had been wrought by the latest event.

Storm clouds loomed over the water in the distance, and now that some of the snow kicked up by the latest crack had subsided, he could see a new inlet where the ocean had flooded a few miles inland.

The destruction of the Ross Ice Sheet, an Antarctic fixture older than human civilization, was well underway.

Javier stomped back to the tent, climbing inside the warming space gratefully.

He unpacked his backpack and found the sat phone.

It was crushed.

Holy shit. This is all my fault. He'd gotten cocky, high on an adrenaline surge at having escaped the snow cloud kicked up by the collapse of the ice behind them. He'd forgotten to be careful, just for an instant, and it had almost killed Col.

There must be more he could do to make up for his error. They had to be less than fifty miles from Mac-Town. *There must be another way to get their attention.* If only he could make a fire. *The doo!*

He took the pot and went outside to scoop up some clean ice and brought it back into the tent to boil. He'd make some tea to help warm Col up when the man awoke.

He shoved the matches into his jacket pocket. Then he gathered up everything they had left that might be flammable—backpack, wrappers, even most of their clothes—and hauled it outside. He carried it the twenty feet to the snowmobile, piling it all on top.

Normally he wouldn't think of defiling the pristine environment like this, but the skidoo was already a wreck, and their circumstances certainly weren't *normal.*

He unscrewed the gas cap, praying there was enough gas left in the tank for one last *hurrah*. He used a shirt as a fuse, threading it as far down into the tank as he could manage. He pulled it back out, and it was soaked with gas.

"Perfect." He turned it around and pushed the other end into the tank. Then he took the matches out of his pocket. Taking a deep breath, he struck a match and lit the shirt on fire. Then he turned and hauled ass back toward the tent with a quick prayer to the Holy Mother.

He threw himself down onto the ice, waiting for the explosion.

Nothing happened.

He got up and stared at the half-visible skidoo and its pile of trash. *Maybe the fuse went out.*

He started back toward the snowmobile.

The vehicle exploded, sending up a cloud of black smoke and knocking Javier back on his ass.

Bits of debris showered down once again across the snow around him.

Javier stared at the rapidly rising column of black smoke and laughed. "Fuck you, fate."

He got up and dusted himself off, feeling indestructible, like goddamned Superman.

The feeling would wane. It always did.

For the moment though, he had hope.

Col shivered. He was weak and groggy. Something was wrong with his left leg. It throbbed, sending occasional twinges of pain up to his brain, and burned.

He opened his eyes, and the world was too bright and fuzzy.

He tried to sit up and yelped in pain.

"Hey, you're awake!" Javier's face loomed over his own, recognizable but blurred.

"What happened?" There was definitely something wrong with his leg. "Where are my glasses?"

"We hit an ice wall. You broke your leg, I think. It's okay. Help is coming." Javier handed him something. His glasses.

The "help" part sounded suspect, but Col was too strung out to question it. He slipped his glasses on. One side was a crazy kaleidoscope of shattered images.

"Sorry, one of the lenses broke when you hit the ice. Let me help you sit up. I made you some tea."

Together, they managed to get him into a sitting position. The pain from his leg was jarring, but it calmed down again once he was still.

"It's got some painkillers too. It will warm you up and help with the pain." Javier gently helped lift him up. Holding him with one arm, Javier picked up a cup with the other.

Col took it and sipped it tentatively. "It's awful." *At least it's warm.*

"Drink it. It will help."

Javier, my mother. But he complied. The liquid coursed down his throat into his stomach. He coughed.

Javier pulled away the cup. "You okay?"

Col cleared his throat and nodded. "More."

He managed to get it all down.

Warmth spread through him. He felt safe, almost comfortable, despite his injured leg.

"Javi?" It was the first time he'd used a nickname with the burly man, but he figured he could get away with it, broken leg and all.

"What?"

"Are we going to get out of this alive?"

This time there was no mistaking the flash of doubt that crossed Javier's face.

"Tell me the truth."

Javier closed his eyes. "I think so. I *hope* so. I started a fire. Someone at Mac-Town should see it and come to investigate."

Col nodded, gathering his courage. "Then would you..." The meds were kicking in, and he was feeling almost giddy. "Would you go out with me sometime?"

Javier laughed. "Like I'm supposed to say no to a guy on his deathbed?"

Col grinned. "Exactly."

"Let's just get through this whole rescue thing first."

It wasn't a no.

"I'm going to lay you back down." He eased Col back into the sleeping bag slowly.

Col's leg protested, but soon he was settled, and the warm glow of the painkillers and the hot tea combined to wrap him in a cocoon of contentment.

"I love you," he whispered as he slipped back into sleep.

Javier stared at Col.

It was the meds talking. Surely. They'd only been with each other for a few days, albeit *intense* ones. Col didn't love him.

He was grateful, perhaps. Or *fond*.

Still, there was *something* happening between them. As hard as he'd fought it, something had sparked there.

He'd sworn, after Terry died, that he would never love anyone again. It was too hard. That loss had scarred him deeply. It was easier to be alone, to take care of just oneself. Less chance of such life-rending pain that way.

I want you to be happy.

"Oh, shut up, Terry."

Now that Col was settled and drugged, Javier opened the sleeping bag to take a look at his leg.

He used his knife to gently cut away the layers of clothing.

Col's skin was unbroken, though it was turning purple in one spot. That was good, at least. Better than exposed bone, anyhow.

There was no way to tell the extent of the break without an X-ray.

He could at least stabilize Col's leg for transport.

He went outside and pulled out a couple tent pegs, casting a worried look at the approaching storm.

They were running out of time.

The skidoo continued to burn, and now a line of smoke stretched up into the sky. Someone at McMurdo had to see it, if there was anyone left.

Javier took the tent pegs inside, wiped them as clean as he was able, and used them as makeshift splints.

Col grunted but didn't awaken as Javier lifted the man's leg and used one of the remaining shirts, torn into long strips, to wrap it around the spikes. That should hold his leg mostly immobile.

Then he tied the man's pants back together around it.

He sat back to look at his handiwork. It was a bit of a mess, but it would have to do,

His stomach rumbled.

He made some tea, and when it was ready, he pulled out his final chocolate bar—Hershey's Special Dark. It was a last supper of sorts, and a vigil over the man who'd been a stranger just four days before. Who now was... something else.

He sat back to wait for rescue, chewing thoughtfully on the nutty, wondering if Col was dreaming.

Half an hour later, the steady *thump thump thump* of an approaching copter rebounded across the ice.

Col blinked, the bright light confusing him.

The ground underneath him seemed to be rocking back and forth.

He turned his head to the side, taking in something green.

Everything was blurry.

He felt around and found a plastic tray in front of him. His glasses lay neatly folded there.

He picked them up and slipped them on his face. His vision cleared, though one of the lenses was cracked. He looked at the green thing again.

It was a small artificial Christmas tree.

What the hell?

He sat up, looking around the room.

It was clean, crisp, antiseptic. A hospital room?

Maybe so, but a small one, with no windows.

He lifted the covers to find a temporary cast on his left leg, held in place by ace bandages.

The last thing he remembered was Javier holding him in his arms. And tea? *Maybe it wasn't all a dream.* "Hello?"

Javier's head popped through the doorway. "Hey, you're awake!"

"Yeah, I guess so." After the last few days, it was hard to tell dreams from reality. "Where are we?"

"It's a cruise ship called the Expedition. She was close by and had a surgeon on board." Javier pulled up a chair. "You're lucky. You had a severe fracture in your left leg, but not a full break."

"What happened?" It was starting to come back to him.

"You don't remember?"

"There was a crash. Oh, and some godawful tea."

Javier laughed. "Kinda knocked you on your ass."

"And..." His face got hot. "I... I asked you out, didn't I?"

Javier looked serious. "Yeah. You did. It was totally inappropriate. We work together, after all."

Col hung his head. "Jesus, I'm an idiot." He looked away, not wanting Javier to see him blush.

"I didn't say no."

Col turned back to Javier so quickly he almost gave himself whiplash. "Wait, does that mean... Are you saying yes?"

"Well, it *is* Christmas. It'd be kind of rude for me to say no today of all days, wouldn't it?" He pulled something from behind his back. "I got you something."

"No fair. I didn't get anything for you."

"Well, you were kinda indisposed. And really, it's not much." Javier got up to hand it over, a package no bigger than his hand. He sat down on Col's bed, careful not to jostle his leg.

Col took the present. It was *crunchy.*

He ripped off the wrapping paper—where Javier had gotten that, he had no idea—and laughed when he saw what was inside.

"I know it's not your favorite." Javier grinned.

"*Shrimp* ramen? Seriously? Where the hell did you find this?"

Javier grinned, taking ten years off his age. He shrugged. "I asked around. I hear it's the worst of all the ramens."

Col grabbed his shirt and pulled the maddening, handsome scientist in for a kiss.

This time, Javier didn't pull away.

When it was over, Javier put his hand on Col's furry cheek. "Merry Christmas, Col."

"Merry Christmas, Javi."

Just for a moment, Col thought he saw someone in the doorway. A burly, redheaded, bearded man who was grinning like an idiot.

He shook his head. Those were some damned good meds.

He was alive, and he had his man. It was enough.

At the start of the end of the world, it was the beginning of something bright and beautiful and new.

Epilogue

The helicopter flew over downtown Fargo, and Javier stared down at the city with some trepidation.

Six months after the ice sheet had started to collapse, he'd accepted a new position—the head of the Bettencourt Institute, an organization created to find ways to slow or even halt catastrophic climate change.

With the new regime installed in the White House and the nation still reeling from a series of climate-fueled disasters over the last several years, the time was ripe for change.

"I think I see it!" Col pointed at the white building ahead, on the edge of town.

Javier grinned, squeezing his husband's hand. It had been a slow thaw between them out on the ice, but now things had warmed up between them. Considerably.

He grinned at the thought.

So far, the new facility was just the one building, a huge white geodesic dome straight out of the sixties. That would change. Soon it would be the focal point of a huge campus, combining scientific disciplines from around the world, all built using renewable materials and using renewable forms of energy. "You did this."

"What do you mean?"

"Your videos. Your photos. The article you wrote about finding love at the end of the world."

Col's story, coming at just the right time, combining such graphic evidence of climate change with such a human man-on-the-ground perspective, had captured the public imagination as well as the interest of the new Administration.

Tad Bettencourt had even stepped up publicly to brag about "my scientists," the angry words and demands on the ice all but forgotten.

Now the two of them had been thrust to the forefront of a new movement.

Javier's hands were shaking.

"What's wrong?"

"It's just... people. There are going to be so many people."

Col laughed and squeezed his hand. "You seem to handle new folks pretty easily. I should know."

"Fingy." He kissed Col's cheek.

"Yeah. Just like that. Call them all 'fucking new guys.' Soon you'll have them all eating out of your hand.

"Hey, it worked with you."

"Yeah, *that's* what it was."

"But on the Ice, it was just one or two at a time." He sat back and sighed. "What if I'm not cut out for this? This is too important to fuck up."

Col squeezed his hand. "We're in this together. Look, we made it out of the jaws of the South. How difficult can this be?"

Javier growled, but inside he was content. Happy even.

Terry would have been proud.

"All right. Let's land this thing and get this over with."

Ribbon cutting. Endless speeches. Mind-numbing speeches. Then they would head South to monitor the collapse of the ice shelf.

He couldn't wait until the two of them were back out on the Ice.

When Mischief Corner Books issued a call for stories called Escape From the Holidays, I couldn't resist. And how much farther can you go and still stay on Earth than Antarctica? This story also marked the flowering of my status as a climate activist author—hopefully wrapped in a great story that makes it go down a little easier. This one took extensive research on Antarctica and how scientists survive there... I am indebted to Cool Antarctica's slang page for helping me get the language right.

TEN

December 15th - Bryan

SUNDAYS WERE THE WORST.

Those lazy, quiet mornings, sitting in the big bay window seat across from Ari with our legs entwined.

That happy time was long gone.

Instead, I was waiting out on the sidewalk, leaning up against the railing of the MARRS Building boardwalk. The wind blew chill, going right through my windbreaker, and the sky was slate gray. It never snowed in Sacramento, but it sure seemed to be trying.

I stuffed my hands into my jacket pockets, wishing I had a pair of mittens. As an Arizona boy, I wasn't used to the cold, even *Sacramento* cold.

I stood at the corner of 20th and K in the heart of gay Sacramento, waiting for a guy named Bryan. Spelled with a "Y", of course. We gays are nothing if not predictable.

Christmas music played from speakers in the eaves of the building behind me.

My husband Ari had passed away on New Year's Eve the previous year. He'd been hit by a street-racing Mercedes when we were crossing J Street, and it had been twelve agonizing days in the hospital before he took his last breath.

Three seconds. That's how far behind him I was, checking something on Facebook. I didn't even remember what it was.

Three goddamned seconds.

After a year of being alone, of beating myself up for those three seconds, I'd finally decided that it was time to start dating again. Ari was gone, and nothing would bring him back. He would want me to go on.

Still, my heart wasn't in it.

My mother was sick with worry. Every day I got a call or a text or an email asking if I was okay.

Ari would want me to have someone again.

I was thirty-five, and all alone.

I'd challenged myself to go on ten dates in ten days—maybe I'd find someone new. If not, at least I'd have a reason to be alone.

And so, Bryan.

He was twenty-five, hung, and had no head, at least if his Grindr profile was to be believed.

What was it about gay guys and their abs?

Then again, I'd swiped right when I saw that gorgeous chest, so I guess I'm part of the problem.

Grindr photos never lie, right?

Bryan arrived on time—a point in his favor—and he was young and beautiful. Blond, blue eyed, and yes, all of twenty-five. I laughed under my breath. I had underwear older than he was.

I'm no slouch at 5'11", but he was taller than me.

Ari had been just my height, with black hair and dark brown eyes. Medium, dark, and handsome.

Bryan and I hugged and headed down to Pizzeria Urbano. We grabbed a couple slices and took them outside to the patio. Lavender Heights was quiet today—the cold weather, most likely—and the people-watching was practically non-existent.

"You look just like your photo," Bryan said between bites, flashing me a big white perfectly aligned smile. No one had natural teeth that straight, or that white. "What are you, like forty?"

Ouch. Little shit. "Um, thirty-five," I replied. "And *you* have a head."

"What? Oh yeah, the Grindr thing." He grinned again, and I had to shield my eyes. "I don't want my parents finding me on there."

That surprised me. "You're in the closet? I thought your generation was past all of that."

"Nah, I just don't want them in my business. It's bad enough I have to follow all the 'house rules.' But hey, I like dating *older guys.*"

Ouch again. And he lived at home.

But damn, he was cute.

I tried to get us back on track. "So what do you do?"

"I'm a personal trainer." He eyed his pizza. "I hardly ever eat this shit."

Of course you are. "Yeah? Where?"

"At Lord's Gym in South Sac." He poked me in my less than perfectly flat stomach. "Hey, I can get you back in shape—you eat pizza and carbs like this all the time, right? Come in some time and I'll hook you up." He finished his slice, licking his fingers.

"Suuuuure." I mentally added a new Grindr rule—from now on, any swipe-rights had to have a head.

Bryan was totally wrong for me. Too young, too athletic, not too bright, and he had all the manners of an untrained puppy.

"Wanna go back to my place?" he said, panting.

Oh my God, that tongue.

Ari wouldn't mind.

What the fuck are you waiting for? Ari whispered in my ear. *He's hot.*

I laughed. Of course it wasn't him. But it's exactly what he would have said, given the current situation, and if Ari wanted me to ... "Sure."

Bryan took my hand and led me back to his place, just a couple blocks away.

The next day, I started an Evernote to keep track and rate my dates. I don't usually sleep and tell, but I gave Bryan a four and a half for date-ability, and a ten in bed.

December 16th - David

The next morning, I woke up feeling better than I had in a year. Like spring in the middle of winter—life was opening up for me again.

I had Bryan to thank for that.

I glanced over at Ari's pillow. I kept it on the bed even now, and sometimes I would cuddle up with it at night and imagine him in my arms.

As I made the bed, I picked up the pillow and held it tightly to my chest. "I love you, Ari."

His smell had faded over the last twelve months. That had to mean *something*. It was time.

I put it up into the closet, gently setting it on a pile of blankets and closing the door softly.

After work, I headed down to Sidetrax to see If I could find some better boyfriend material there.

A group from the gay men's chorus was singing as I walked by.

Eight maids a milking,
Seven swans a swimming,
Six geese a laying,
Five golden rings...

I grinned and hurried on.

To be honest, I knew the bars weren't the best places for long-term relationship hook-ups—you were as likely to get an alcoholic or a meth queen as a real prospect. But I sucked at organization and hadn't made any dating plans for the day. If I was going to fit ten dates into ten days, I had to keep to the schedule.

Who knew? Maybe I'd get lucky.

Ari was silent about the whole thing.

Faces was decorated for the holidays as only a gay bar could be.

The lights bouncing off the walls and floors were red and white and green, the shirtless bartender had on a Santa hat and Christmas wreath nipple rings, and the drag queens all wore festive holiday attire, even Jill Frost, who had the whole Ice Queen thing down.

Someone had the good taste to play RuPaul's vintage Christmas album, completing the gay holiday scene.

I tried to flag down the bartender for a little liquid courage. Like I said, the bars were never really my thing.

Of course he ignored me, instead taking the drink order of the gym-toned twenty-year-old who literally *muscled* up to the bar next to me.

I sighed dramatically. *Drama* I was good at.

"Rough night?"

I turned to find the most handsome man I had ever laid eyes on, standing next to me at the bar. He was Cary Grant plus Nick Jonas, with a touch of Rock Hudson. Yes, I *do* know my gay history. He waved at the bartender, and in no time we had a couple of beers.

Funny how that worked.

"I'm David," he said, his eyes twinkling.

"Chris."

"You looked lonely over here." Their drinks came, and David raised his glass. "To Christmas in a gay bar."

"To Christmas." We clinked glasses. My heart was racing. "What do you do?"

"I'm a grad student at Sac State."

"Yeah?" *Just how old are you?*

"I'm interning at Lord, Hall, and Davis as a paralegal too."

Tall, dark, and handsome, and an *almost* lawyer to boot.

And he was interested in *me*.

I grinned. Ari would have approved.

We talked for half an hour, and then he leaned over and whispered in my ear, "Want to get out of here?" His hand was warm on my knee.

We left the bar a little after ten. I was pleasantly buzzed and was feeling better about myself than I had in years. I still *had it*. So what if I was a little older than the average gay bar hopper? This Adonis had chosen *me*.

We got to my car and kissed, deep-throat style.

It was fireworks, car crashes, and peppermint ice cream all in one. *God, I need this.* "Want to come home with me?" I whispered, feeling a little slutty and not really caring.

He leaned in and whispered, "Sure. $100 an hour, yeah?"

I stared at him. "You're a...?"

"Yeah. I thought you knew?" He gave me a lopsided grin. "Gotta pay off my student loans."

It was *almost* worth it. He was that handsome.

In the end, I kicked him out and went home alone to take a long cold shower.

David got a three on my list and an "A" for effort.

Hey, it's not a scientific system.

December 17th - Glenn

I picked up the mail on the way into my apartment from the car. It was the usual junk—a copy of Sacramento Magazine, two Bed Bath and Beyond coupons... and a credit card offer made out to Aristotle Collins.

I closed my eyes, picturing Ari's laugh—"I haven't been Aristotle since I was six!" I smiled and took it inside, grabbed a Sharpie and scribbled "deceased" across the address label. I tossed it in the mailbox and went back inside to get ready for my third date.

Two days, two duds. No matter—with eight dates left to go, I figured I still had a one in five chance at finding marital bliss again.

I always *was* good at math.

Glenn had suggested we meet at some place out in the suburbs called the Melting Pot. He was a little older, conservatively dressed in a tailored suit and tie, his hair cropped short. He looked kind of familiar in that weren't-you-a-character-actor-on-Law-and-Order? sort of way.

I'd found him on Craigslist. I know, I know, it's basically the swap meet of hook-up sites—a lot of the merchandise is a gritty and a little used, but every now and then you found a copy of Action Comics #1. Or a cute bit of flower-based wall art.

His ad had seemed nice:

Mature, middle-aged man seeks younger for fun, possible relations.

I was sure he'd meant "relationship."

The restaurant was dark and smelled like meat and chocolate. It kinda turned me on.

I sat down and smiled. "Nice place."

He nodded. "I like it. It's quiet and out of the way."

"I haven't been to a fondue place in years." The things you do for dating.

Ari had always hated it. Our first two dates had been famously bad—involving a napkin on fire and some classic teeth on lip action

—but we'd given it another try, and somehow the third time had been the charm.

"You're cute." Glenn grinned. He had a nice smile. A point in his favor.

"Thanks." I was pleased. "You're not too bad yourself." I refused to add *for an older guy. I'd* worn that shoe with Bryan, and it was a bad fit, not to mention bad manners. But that tongue...

The waiter stopped by. "My name's Dorothea. Have you two decided what you want?" She gave us her best waitress smile.

Glenn waved her off. "Give us a couple minutes?"

"Sure. I'll check back with you in a little bit."

I felt something between my legs, and looked down to see Glenn's foot, wrapped in a black nylon sock, massaging my crotch. The sock had a little golden cross embroidered on it.

I looked up and Glenn was winking at me.

Nylon socks? Seriously?

I could almost hear Ari laughing.

He was moving a little too fast. I pushed his foot away.

Glenn looked hurt. "I'm sorry. I thought you *liked* me." He tugged at his collar.

His collar.

Boom, I knew where I'd seen him before. "You're Pastor Glenn from All Hallows," I blurted out before I could stop myself. My sister's parish. I'd gone with her once for Christmas Mass and remembered ogling him. Holy shit, maybe I'd *turned* the poor bastard with my gay gaze.

Glenn's face went white. "I... I'm not... I can't..." Without another word, he got up and pulled out his wallet to lay forty bucks on the table. Then he almost ran out the door.

I stared after him. *Why does everyone think I'm a john or a prostitute?*

Then I realized he'd left the money to pay for the meal.

He *was* a decent guy, after all.

I wasn't going to waste the twenty-five-minute drive, so I stayed and treated myself to an awesome chocolate fondue.

I was kind of sad for the guy—I mean, what must it be like to go your whole life lying about who you were? But I didn't date closet cases.

Ari was in total agreement.

I gave Glenn a four on my scale.

Hey, at least he'd paid for dinner.

December 18th - Lourdes

I padded into the kitchen and checked my "Guys of Sacramento" calendar—Christmas was coming quickly, and it was looking more and more like I was going to be serving Santa milk and cookies all alone.

Call me campy, but Ari and I used to do the whole Christmas thing *right*—cranberry and popcorn garland, real noble fir tree, even the plastic reindeer on the front lawn.

You're being too picky. That was an Ari thought.

"Hey, I like what I like."

Suit yourself.

Ari was like that. He'd sulk for a day or two before bringing me an armful of flowers and his best Pretty Woman grin.

Maybe he was right. Maybe I was being too cautious.

In a fit of desperation, I called my sister Beth, who worked at the Music Circus and had been itching to set me up with some of her gay actor friends.

"I have the perfect guy for you." She sounded breathless... either she was really excited to set me up, or she'd just finished her CrossFit class. "He's about your age, cute as a mouse, and limber, if you know what I mean."

Limber.

Beth was an M/M aficionado, and I could just see her picturing her *limber* friend and me together. *Eeeew.* Plus I could almost feel her wink through the phone, all the way from Citrus Heights. "Um, okay."

"Oh, come on. You guys will *love* each other."

I sighed. "What's his name?"

The other end of the line went silent for a moment."Llrrrds." she said at last.

"What?"

"Llrrrds." I could tell she was holding out on me.

"I don't understand what you're saying." This couldn't be good.

"It's Lourdes, all right?"

"Oh, *come on.*" Beth knew I had a hard time with *gay* names. "What, is he French or something?"

"No, he's from Cleveland. I think his name used to be Larry. Look, he's really down-to-earth. You'll like him—I promise."

I could almost hear Ari snicker.

I sighed and took down *Lourdes'* information.

So here I was, once again waiting for a blind date, this time at Cafeteria 15L—his suggestion. That was a good sign. The restaurant was casual and trendy but not *too* hipster.

I got there ten minutes before six and got us a good table by the window, settling in to wait. And wait. And wait.

I ordered a ginger beer, and then another, and checked my Facebook messages, then my feed, then Q and my email. I even played a few rounds of Space Kitty.

I glanced at my phone. It was six thirty and he still wasn't there, and no text or call to explain where he was or why he was late.

I mentally deducted two points off his final score.

At a quarter to seven, after sending the waiter away at least ten times, I was about ready to get up and leave when he swept into the room.

I still don't know how he did it.

It was as if all the light shifted to shine on him when he arrived.

He was dressed all in white, including a snow-white scarf draped around his neck in that European way.

The restaurant went silent, and everyone turned to watch his entrance.

He made a beeline to my table, hair perfectly coiffed. I swear he was wearing eyeliner too. "Chris?"

I nodded, dumbfounded. This was what my sister considered *down to earth?*

He sat down and smiled, and his teeth were whiter than his shirt. *What is it with teeth whitening these days?* "I'm so sorry I am a teensy bit late. I was shopping over at Macy's and the time just got away from me."

The time and whoever was styling your hair, I thought, looking up at the cresting blond wave that appeared poised to crash down his forehead.

No, that wasn't fair. I didn't have to be an asshole just 'cause he was a bit feminine.

"I'm so glad Beth set us up," he said, taking off his oversized white-framed sunglasses to set them on the table. "I *adore* your sister. She's *fabulous*."

So was Lourdes.

Oh don't get me wrong. I have no problem with fem guys. Not that I want to date them, but they are the sparkly part of the rainbow fabric, the queer community that I'm proud to be a part of.

But Lourdes... he was the whole freaking rainbow *and* a fun-sized bag of skittles.

I excused myself to use 15L's bathroom, the really cool one where you can see right through to the women's side wash basin, but because it's identical, you don't realize it until a woman walks in and stares at you. You can see that surprised look—*what the hell are you doing in here?* Until they work it out.

I *love* that.

I took a moment to compose myself, splashing cold water on my face. Just because we weren't going to be dating didn't mean we couldn't have a nice dinner together.

I rubbed my face, and with a deep breath, I headed back to the table.

I managed to get through dinner with Lourdes. He was nice enough, though a bit shallow. I even had a halfway decent time.

Then I went home alone, again.

Lourdes might be a ten for someone, but he was a three for me.

December 19th - Daniel

It was December 19th.

Fuck.

I stayed home from work for the day, calling in sick.

Bill said he understood. They all did. I could hear the pity in his voice. I slammed the phone down angrily.

The nineteenth was the day the light had gone out of Ari's eyes. The day of the accident.

I kept the blinds closed all morning and into the afternoon. I got Ari's pillow down from the closet and hugged it, staying in bed, with a cold cup of coffee on my nightstand and the television on ESPN *something*.

They were playing some sort of golf tournament.

I stared at the television with a weird mix of loathing and longing.

Ari had this weird thing for golf. He said it was the one sport where personal skill truly mattered, where a minute shift of the hand or the leg could result in a completely different outcome.

If only he'd followed that logic and had stepped out onto J Street a moment later.

If only it had been me.

I turned it off and sat there for a while staring at the blank flat screen.

Around four o'clock, something nudged me awake.

I sat up and looked around the gloomy room. There was no one there.

"Oh, shit." I had a date in thirty minutes. I thought about blowing it off. I was in *motherfucking certified mourning*, after all. But *someone* would have wanted me to get on with life, so I went. *Damn you, Ari.*

Daniel was a friend of a friend on Instagram. He mostly posted pictures of himself in various states of dress and undress. He was handsome in that Str8 Acting sort of way.

He met me for coffee at Dunkin' Donuts. That should have been my first clue.

He showed up sharply dressed in a suit and crisp white shirt, along with a bright red tie.

"You're not a priest, are you?" I asked, sipping something called a Dunkaccino. It was no Starbucks.

Daniel laughed. He was handsome in a square-jawed kind of way. "No, not a priest. You?"

It was my turn to laugh. "Hardly. I work as the artistic director for a local theatre."

"Nice. Which one?" He put his hand on mine.

"You've probably never heard of it. It's called the Capitol Street Stage." I was starting to get lost in his green eyes. I had a thing for green.

"Oh." His hand pulled away.

"What?" Damn, what had I done now?

Daniel downed the rest of his coffee in one gulp. "That's the theater that did the terrorist play, right?"

Ari's voice *hissed* in my head.

I shook my head, confused. "The terrorist... you mean the one about the little Muslim girl and the bicycle?" How could someone be upset by a play about a little girl and her first bike?

"She's a Muslim. The whole thing was cover for bringing sharia law to California." He stood abruptly. "You and your *libtard friends* are what's wrong with this country, you know that?" He threw his card down on the table. "Call me when you see the light." He was out the door before I realized what had hit me.

I had found that rarest of beasts—the gay Republican. Who knew they even existed in downtown Sacramento?

And I had my first zero of the week.

Ari would have given him a negative ten.

December 20th - Toby

The twentieth was a crisp winter Central Valley day, so I showed up for my next date with a couple hot apple ciders.

Ari was a little ambivalent about that. *What if he likes coffee?*

"*Everyone* likes cider."

At least the sun was out this morning, something I took as a good sign.

This one was promising. He was a set-up—my friend Jake had gone out with him, but said the guy liked to read too much. Jake was... how can I put this kindly? More of a visual kind of guy. Ari used to say that Jake only liked three things—abs, ass, and about nine inches.

It was kinda weird too, since Jake and I had been having a bit of a fight. But maybe this was his idea of a peace offering.

Anyhow, Toby had agreed to meet me in a neutral location—on a park bench in the Rose Garden, near the Capitol.

"Toby?" I asked.

He looked up from the book he was reading. It was one of Tolkien's—another a point in his favor.

He was cute. Sandy brown hair, hazel eyes. A little shorter than me, but I wasn't a size queen, in either sense.

"Hi," he said shyly.

I liked *shy* in a guy. "Chris?"

I nodded. "Can I sit?"

He slid over to make room.

"I brought this for you. It's hot apple cider from the Everyday Grind... I hope you drink cider?" I held out the cup.

Toby nodded. "Thanks." He took a sip, and his breath came out steaming. "Oooh, that's good." He gave me a big smile, which made him even more appealing.

"Glad you like it." I pointed at the book. "Hey, what part are you at?" I loved that he was reading an *actual* book, not a kindle or nook or kobo. There's just something about paper books... the feel, the smell of the paper and ink.

My dream job was to work in a coffee shop-bookstore, for the heavenly smells alone.

"What?" He laughed. "Oh, the book. I just reached Lothlorien."

I grinned. "I love that part. I first read it when I was ten. I cried like a baby when Boromir died." Try explaining *that* to the other kids on the soccer team.

Ari had hated Tolkien—called him a *misogynist prick*—but hey, you couldn't agree on everything. It had kept things interesting between us.

Toby laughed, a beautiful sound. "This is my ninth time reading them. I liked them before they were cool."

"I know, right?" I still remembered when the first film came out. It was freaking amazing, and it wasn't my own private geek thing anymore. "Hey, I'm getting cold just sitting here. Wanna go for a walk?"

Toby nodded. "What else have you read?"

That started a conversation that went on for hours,. We walked through Capitol Park, past the Vietnam Memorial, the Firefighter's Memorial, through the Civil War Memorial... damn, there are a lot of memorials there.

We talked McCaffrey. Clarke. Asimov. We branched off into Hamilton and Martin and red weddings and a passionate argument on the merits of killing off one of your most popular characters.

I really enjoyed talking with Toby—we had a lot in common, and I must have written down a dozen new authors to look up and read.

I started to wonder—could this be *the guy?*

The afternoon slipped by, and before I knew it, three hours had passed and we'd returned to our starting point.

We like him.

I laughed to myself. Ari was right. I realized I felt *totally* comfortable with him. "So, Toby?" I said.

"Yeah?"

"Do you wanna go out with me? On a real date?"

His smile lit up his face. "I'd love to. Only— "

Oh shit. "What?" Was he an axe murderer? Or worse. a republican? *Been down that road...*

"I have to tell you something."

"What? You're positive?" I'd dated positive guys before. It wasn't necessarily a deal breaker.

"I'm trans."

"Oh." Up to that moment, I hadn't even considered the possibility. Sure, he was a little short, and his voice was a little high, but he was *totally* a guy.

I'd never really thought about dating a trans man. Was he... did he still have... damn, how did you ask *that* question?

Toby turned away. "Does that matter to you?"

"I... I don't know." It came out before I could stop it.

"I see." He got up abruptly and started to walk away.

I grabbed his hand. "Look, I'm sorry. I do *really* like you. It's just... this is so sudden. Can you give me some time to think it over? Can we at least be friends?"

He pulled his hand away. "I have enough friends." He walked away.

I sank down on the bench, pissed off at myself for not handling it better, and pissed off at Jake for not telling me.

Ari was silent in my head.

I really *did* like Chris. But was I ready to date a trans guy?

Apparently not.

I pulled out my phone and gave him a ten. For someone.

Just not for me.

December 21st - Eric

I was starting to despair. Christmas was just four days away, and I was striking out left and right.

Maybe it *was* me.

A dark thought entered my head. Maybe Ari was better off now. Free of me and all my pain-in-the-ass ways.

You asshole. You're not gonna pin this on me.

I laughed. Ari would have said *exactly* that.

I had to keep going, to see this thing through.

I met my next date, Eric, at the ballet. Well, not so much a date as a sudden crush.

He was a dancer, performing in a traveling production called—I kid you not—"Revenge of the Lord of the Dance" at the Memorial Auditorium. It was a spoof on the original show, and I ended up going because Jake had an extra ticket.

Jake had admitted he'd set me up on the date with Toby, knowing that his friend was trans and hoping to surprise the shit out of me.

It was a jerk move, but I *had* handled it badly. Which sucked, because I had really enjoyed spending time with Toby. There could have been something there.

Jake and I were in the fourth row, close enough to have a really good view.

I was entranced by the way Eric slipped across the stage. He *flowed*, each move blending into the next with such grace and beauty that I wondered what he would be like in bed. All that strength and control.

Little did I know.

After the show, I waited for him at the back entrance, hoping to catch him on his way out.

An hour went by, and I was freezing my ass off and just about ready to give up and go home when the door opened and Eric came out.

I almost didn't recognize him in his leather jacket and jeans.

"Um, hi," I managed, and he turned to face me.

"Hello there." In person he was taller than he'd seemed on stage, and he moved with the power and grace of a tiger. His ice-blue eyes gave me a once over, and I could feel him mentally undressing me.

It was like a drug.

"I'm Chris." I shivered. It was the cold. Totally the cold. "I saw you on stage..."

"Did you like what you saw, *boy*?" He moved up close to me, and I could smell his body odor. He hadn't showered. I wasn't sure if the scent was intoxicating or repellant.

"I did." I decided on *intoxicating* and leaned in to kiss him.

He edged back. "Sir," he said, sharply.

"What?"

"You should say 'I did, Sir.'" He put a hand around my neck and spoke softly but forcefully in my ear. "Your Master is going to take you back to his hotel, and..." His voice dropped to a whisper.

My eyes widened as he told me what he wanted to do to me. Things that involved whips and chains and whatever the hell a truncheon was.

I didn't even know some of those things were *possible*.

Where had the sweet, graceful, beautiful ballet dancer gone?

My phone went off in my pocket. *Thank God.* "I have to take this, sorry," I managed, squirming out of his grasp.

It was Jake. "Where the fuck are you? I thought we were going to Mango's."

"Oh, hi honey. I'll be right there." I mouthed an insincere "sorry" to Eric and backed away. "Thank God," I whispered into the phone. "Holy shit. I've never been so glad to hear from you in my entire life."

I walked away from Eric as quickly as I dared. When I glanced back, he was watching me like a hawk watches a rabbit.

When I rounded the corner onto a busier street, I breathed a sigh of relief.

That was close.

And it was my second zero of the week.

December 22nd - Dwight

For my eighth date, I went old school—the personal ads section in OutWord. Hey, that's how the gays used to do it, right? Before the internet and mobile phones?

Dwight's ad sounded nice:

Solid thirty-something looking for the right guy. Loves classical music, fine dining, and the theatre. Lives for the now.

I called his mailbox, and he got back to me within an hour—he had a nice voice too. He said he would pick me up.

I had a good feeling about this one. Me, the eternal optimist.

Ari snorted.

I pulled on my Pump boxers—you never knew where the night would go, after all—and my tightest jeans. A year at the gym had slimmed me down considerably—not that Ari had cared about that sort of thing. But I was back on the market, and I had to show off my wares.

Dwight showed up at my apartment on time—a definite plus. He was a little on the geeky side—thick-framed glasses, his hair parted down the middle—but that wasn't necessarily a bad thing. I was a geek at heart too.

I got into his minivan.

"I'm sorry," he said.

"Sorry for what?" I glanced at my phone. "You're right on time."

He started the car, and as he pulled out onto H Street, he said, "I know I'm not what you expected." He flicked on the music, and Michael Bolton's "How Am I Supposed to Live Without You" flooded the car.

I wanted to rip my ears off, but instead I forced myself to smile, and said, "I think you're cute."

He shook his head. "Kind of you to say that. But I know you don't really like me."

I was quiet for a moment. Bolton warbled on in the background.

I remembered what it had been like to be in the closet. To be ashamed of myself, to think that no one would *ever* love me.

Poor guy.

"Look, you're a perfectly good-looking guy. You just have to believe in yourself."

He looked at me sadly. "You're just saying that because you're stuck in the car with me."

Damn.

I gave up. This guy needed someone to talk to, someone to help him get his head on straight about who and what he was. It was more than I could do for him.

He dropped me back at home after a long, depressing dinner at the Old Spaghetti Factory, and drove off.

His car was covered with bumper stickers, including "My Child is an Honor Student at Caleb Greenwood Elementary" and "Jesus is Lord."

He was either married or a mamma's boy.

Or both.

Ari was right. Probably *both.*

I wondered why I even bothered rating these guys.

December 23rd - Xavier

I spent the better part of the morning of the twenty third shopping for Christmas presents at the Pavilions. A scented candle for Beth, some video games for her kids, and a few gifts for my parents. I loved shopping on the last few days before the holiday, when the malls are swarmed with people and full of life.

Ari had loved it too. Well, he loved it because he loved me.

You know how sometimes guys do nice things for you 'cause they know you love it? But then you find out years later that they hated it all the time?

Ari was like that, with shopping. He used to nod and smile when I'd suggest a trip to the mall, but he never suggested it himself, and he always seemed happy to go back home.

He did it for me.

I decided to follow up the night at the ballet with an afternoon at the theatre. My sister had a comp ticket to a new B Street Theatre production—*Vampire Poet*—recasting George Gordon Byron as one of the vampires he so famously wrote about.

Xavier was in the title role, and he was *amazing*. He was a little older than me—gee, was that my new thing?

His hair was streaked with silver, but he wore it well, like George Clooney. His booming voice captivated me.

I cornered him after the show. "I loved the play."

He grinned, his teeth a reassuringly normal shade of white, "Glad to hear it. You are...?"

"Chris. You're Xavier."

"My fame precedes me." He gestured for me to sit with him in the lobby. "So what brings you to the theater?"

"To be honest, I was looking for a date."

"Lucky for him."

I laughed. "I mean, I was looking for *someone* to date." I explained my plan, and he laughed.

"That seems like quite the undertaking. I'd be happy to..." and he paused for dramatic effect, "fill your slot."

Yeah, it was corny. But he was sweet as hell.

He seemed quite taken with me, too, and agreed to meet me later in the evening for our date. "I have another gig," he said with a wink. "Come by this address at about 9 PM tonight." He scribbled out the location on a piece of paper and handed it over to me.

What the hell.

I stuffed it into my pocket.

I dressed respectably—white shirt, striped tie (not too wide) and a pair of black slacks. My sexy underwear stayed in the drawer. I could always get it out for the second date.

I showed up at the address and had to check it twice. It was a seedy old bar called The Drag out in Rancho Cordova. Maybe the guy was another closet case, and didn't want to be seen in town?

I paid the $2 entry fee and went inside. It was a gay bar, all right, what they called a piano bar, full of older guys and dark wood paneling.

I didn't see Xavier anywhere, so I sat at the bar and ordered a rum and coke.

The place was filling up. I glanced around and saw the usual mix of over fifty suburban gays.

There was a small stage, and a white piano in one corner.

The lights came up, and an announcer hopped onto the stage. "Ladies and Gentlemen, and everyone in-between, welcome to The Drag. I'm thrilled to introduce the marvelous Xsa Xsa Galore!"

"I Will Survive" started playing and the disco ball spun, splattering rainbows of light across the bar. *Oh my God, how cliché can you get?*

Then Xsa Xsa came out from the back, wearing a red sequined ball gown, a green feather boa, and golden glitter ornaments as earrings.

Well, it *was* almost Christmas.

I glanced around. Xavier still wasn't here. At least I got to enjoy a show while I waited. The drag queen was pretty good. She even winked at me a couple times.

Xsa Xsa finished her first song and smiled at the audience. "We have a very special guest tonight," she said, and strolled out into the crowd. She burst into a rousing rendition of "Everything's Coming Up Roses," and made a beeline for me.

I tried to become invisible, but there she was, sitting on my lap and playing with my tie.

Never show a drag queen vulnerability. They'll go straight for your throat.

Then she leaned over and whispered in a deep voice, "I'm glad you came."

"Xavier?" I stiffened.

So *this* was his other gig.

Xsa Xsa winked at me again and sashayed back to the stage.

Don't get me wrong. I love drag queens. I watch "RuPaul's Drag Race" religiously, for God's sake, but I wasn't ready to date one.

Tsk tsk tsk Ari was chuckling in my head..

"Oh, shut up."

The lights went out, and so did I.

I did give him a six. He was a helluva performer, after all.

December 24th – Christian

I stared at myself in the mirror.

There was *something* wrong with me. That had to be it. No one was good enough for me.

Maybe the problem was *me*.

I wasn't doing myself any favors, trying to find someone all by myself to replace Ari. Not that anyone ever could.

So I joined a dating service. I filled out all the forms and waited breathlessly for it to find me a match. Maybe even someone as picky as me could find someone who fit.

And then there he was.

Christian's photo was a bit vague—a soft focus shot that made me curious. And a little angry.

Instagram filters were killing the art of photography.

I pored over his profile:

He liked to read.

Check.

He liked Italian food.

Check.

And he was looking for a long-term relationship.

Check.

I contacted him, asking if he was free for the evening, even though it was Christmas Eve. I suggested a hot chocolate at the ice rink at St. Rose of Lima Park.

Five minutes later, he said yes.

I had a good feeling about this one. Though my good feelings hadn't really panned out.

Still, we had a 99% compatibility score. I figured a computer couldn't be any worse at choosing a man than I was.

When it was time to go, I pulled on a pair of sweats under my jeans, my warmest boots, and my holiday sweater with two amorous reindeer. Hey, he had to have a sense of humor, or this whole thing wouldn't work.

I topped it off with a festive holiday scarf and a white beanie and set out for the skating rink.

We'd decided to meet at the corner of 7th and K, not far from the new arena. I waited on the corner, blowing on my hands and rubbing them together to keep them warm, and wishing I had brought some gloves.

Then there he was.

He looked *just like me*—my height, dark hair, brown eyes. He was even dressed the same, though his reindeer weren't copulating.

It was freaky.

"Chris?" he said.

"Yup. Christian, I assume?"

He nodded. "Well, here we are. Wanna go skate?" We both rubbed our noses with our right hands simultaneously.

I laughed. "Sure." We rented our skates, sizing each other up, and in a couple minutes, we were speeding around the ice rink together.

"I was glad to hear from you," he said at last. "You're my first "over 95%" compatible."

"I just joined the site today—blind luck, I guess. So what do you do?"

"I'm in sales."

"Who do you work for?"

"Lord and Taylor. You?"

I laughed. "I used to do sales for Macy's. Now I'm an artistic director."

Christian smiled. "That's cool. So what's your favorite color?"

"Black," I said without hesitation.

"Me too! Top or bottom?"

I smiled. "Total bottom. You?"

He frowned.

"Seriously?"

He laughed. "Yeah. We *are* kind of similar, aren't we?"

"Kind of?" Like I said, it was *freaky*.

We watched the same shows, loved the same authors, and even our mothers had the same name. Well, mostly. Mine was Emma, his was Emmalou.

We had a great time together, but we both knew it would never work. There was nothing new there.

I like him. Ari sounded plaintive in my head.

I laughed. "You would. You liked *me*. But he's *too much* me and *too little* you."

In the end, Christian and I parted as friends.

I gave him a ten. He was awesome.

He was basically me, after all.

December 25th

It was December 25th.

I had failed completely, and I was all alone on Christmas Day. I called Jake and asked him if he'd meet me for a drink at Faces.

The place was deserted, the sound of classic Christmas tunes filling the air.

I was nursing a spiked eggnog when he showed up, looking all handsome in jeans and a white t-shirt. Handsome, hell. He was fucking *hot*.

I considered the possibility for about two seconds, then discarded it. Jake would never be right for me, or vice versa.

He gave me a quick hug. "So how goes the dating game?"

I shook my head. "It's over. An utter failure." I took a sip.

"Oh, come on. It can't be that bad."

"Let's see." I ticked them off on my hands. "I had Bryan Dumb but Pretty - the Lord's Gym Guy. David the Hustler Intern. At least he worked at a law firm... Lord, Hall, and something? Then there was Glenn the Closeted Priest, Lourdes the Fabulous, Daniel the Republican... need I go on?"

"Sounds like a lot of 'lords.'" Jake chuckled.

"Holy crap." He was right. I pulled out my phone and looked through my Evernote.

"What's that?" Jake asked, peering over my shoulder.

"I kept detailed notes of the experiment. Let's see..." I scrolled to the top. "OK. Here we go. Bryan worked at Lord's Gym."

"That's one."

"David worked for Lord, Hall and Davis."

"Two."

"Glenn was a priest..."

"Servant of the Lord. Totally counts." Jake grinned.

I side-eyed him, then nodded. "Alright, we'll accept it. Lourdes..."

"Four."

I scrolled down. "Daniel?"

"Hmmm. Mr. Republican?"

"Yup."

"Looks like we may have broken the pattern."

"Hold on." I pulled out my wallet. "I think I still have his card. Aha! Daniel *Lord*."

"Five." Jake's eyes twinkled.

"Toby liked 'Lord of the Rings'. Eric the BDSM ballet dancer was in 'Revenge of Lord of the Dance.'"

"Six and Seven."

"Dwight had a bumper sticker that said *Jesus is Lord*. And Xavier was in that play about Lord Byron."

"Eight and nine."

I grinned. "And Christian—my doppelgänger—works for Lord and Taylor."

"And that makes Ten Lords a Leaping!" Jake said, looking triumphant.

"That's so... random." I laughed.

"It really is." Jake was quiet for a minute. Finally, he looked up at me. "You're telling me that not *one* of those guys was dateable?"

I thought about it. The last ten days had been a virtual spectrum of *the gay*. "Well, there was *one*."

Jake nodded. "I figured." He took a sip of his own drink. "So what are you doing sitting here with me?"

I stared at him. What *was* stopping me?

He's right, you know.

Even dead, Ari had an endearing way of making me feel like an absolute idiot.

Five seconds later, Jake was drinking alone.

I climbed the steps of the little house on 25th Street, shivering. I had forgotten to bring a jacket, and it was damned cold out.

The clouds above were low and gray, and they said there might be snow. Snow in Sacramento!

The home was a cute mission-style cottage, decorated with white Christmas lights, with little plastic reindeer out front.

Like me and Ari.

I reached out to knock on the door, but hesitated. *Am I ready?* We were so different...

I closed my eyes. I remembered the first time Ari and I had had a big fight, over the most trivial of things—whether the toilet paper should go over the top or under the bottom.

I was totally a top guy, and he was a bottom.

On top was the *right way*.

When I had made that assertion loudly and with intense finger pointing, he'd laughed his ass off, and we'd ended up debating the proposition in bed for half the night. I'd called in late to work the next day.

We worked because we were different.

That decided it.

I knocked on the door and waited, my stomach churning. I hadn't been this nervous in a long time—not since my third date with Ari.

At last, it swung open.

He looked at me and frowned. "Chris?"

"Hi, Toby." I rubbed my arms, trying to keep warm. "Hope you don't mind me stopping by. Jake gave me your address."

He frowned, but I barreled on. "I just wanted to come by and apologize for reacting the way I did the other day. I was a total jerk." I took a deep breath. "I had a great time with you, and I... I think the rest doesn't matter. You're a great guy. Smart and cute, and—"

"Chris, I don't think this is such a good idea—"

"Oh, fuck it. I *really* like you, Toby. You're funny and cute, and different from me—"

He frowned.

"I don't mean like *that*. I mean, yeah, you probably like golf."

"Um, yeah. Who doesn't?" A small smile slipped past his guard.

"You'd be surprised." I took a breath and then plunged ahead. "Like I was saying, I was an ass, and I want a do over... I was just hoping you'd give me another chance?"

Toby was silent for a moment. The silence stretched awkwardly between us.

This was a bad idea. "I'm sorry," I said at last, turning to go. "I shouldn't have bothered you."

"Wait."

I turned back. "What?"

"Look, I've been hurt too many times. If we're going to do this, I have to know you're *sure*."

Say yes. Say yes!

I nodded. "Absolutely."

A big grin spread across his face. "Wanna come in?"

"I thought you'd never ask. It's fucking cold out here."

The first flakes of snow started falling from the leaden sky. Something shifted, and I knew Ari was gone.

"It's warmer inside." Toby opened the door wide, gesturing for me to come in.

I grinned. I had found my lord. *Thanks Ari.*

I leapt.

What would a December anthology be without a little holiday charm? Ten was written as part of a project on the Twelve Days of Christmas but was never traditionally published. I put it out on its own as a short story in 2018, and am thrilled to once again have it available. It was a joy to write, and includes a lot of my favorite places in my hometown of Sacramento. If you live here, you'll likely recognize more than a few. A suitable end to a collection of stories about love.

THANKS FOR READING!

I'd love it if you would leave a review on all the usual sites. Reviews help us poor starving authors sell more books!

And if you liked *Love & Limitations*, try *The River City Chronicles*, my magical realism circle of friends novel. I'm including the first chapter here... I'm including the first chapter here...

THE RIVER CITY CHRONICLES
CHAPTER ONE: RAGAZZI

MATTEO STARED out the restaurant window into the darkness of Folsom Boulevard. It was getting dark earlier as summer edged into fall. Streetlights flickered on as cars drifted by, looking for parking or making the trip out of Midtown toward home.

The sign on the window read "Ragazzi" (the boys), lettered in a beautiful golden script just two months old. Investing in this little restaurant his uncle had left to them when he'd passed away had been their ticket out of Italy. But now with each passing day, as seats sat empty and tomatoes, pasta, and garlic went uneaten, the worry was gnawing ever deeper into Matteo's gut.

Behind him in the open, modernized kitchen, Diego was busy cooking—his mother's lasagne, some fresh fish from San Francisco, and some of the newer Italian dishes they'd brought with them from Bologna. The smells of boiling sauce and fresh-cooked pasta that emanated from the kitchen were entrancing.

They'd sent the rest of the staff —Max and Justin—home for the evening. The three customers who had shown up so far didn't justify the cost of keeping their waiter and busboy on hand.

Matteo stopped at the couple's table in front of the other window. "*Buona sera*," he said, smiling his brightest Italian smile.

"Hi," the man said, smiling back at him. He was a gentleman in about his mid-fifties, wearing a golf shirt and floppy hat. "Kinda quiet tonight, huh?"

"It always gets busier later," Matteo lied smoothly. "Pleasure to have you here. Can I get you anything else?"

"A little more wine, please?" the woman said, holding out her glass so the charm bracelet on her wrist jangled.

"Of course." He bowed and ducked into the kitchen.

He gave Diego a quick peck on the cheek.

His husband and chef waved him off with a snort. "*Più tardi. Sto preparando la cena.*"

"I can see that. Dinner for a hundred, is it? It's dead out there again tonight."

Diego shot him a dirty look.

Matteo retrieved the bottle of wine from the case and returned to fill up his guests' glasses. "What brings you in tonight?" *Maybe they saw our ad....*

"Just walking by and we were hungry. I miss the old place though.... What was it called, honey?"

Her husband scratched his chin. "Little Italy, I think?"

"That's it! It was the cutest place. Checkered tablecloths, those great Italian bottles with the melted wax... so Italian."

Matteo groaned inside. "So glad you came in" was all he said with another smile.

Four hours later and he'd served a grand total of five customers. At least they'd all been drinkers. Wine was all that was keeping the place open these days.

Diego closed down the kitchen, and they sat together at the big round *famiglia* table in the middle of the place, the blinds on the windows closed, and counted their earnings.

"$203," Matteo announced, tucking the cash and deposit slip into the bank sleeve for deposit. "Another hundred days like that this month and we can pay the rent." He sighed. He'd been sure, when they made their plans to come here, that America would be their land of opportunity.

Some days he longed to return to *Italia*. Sure, the government was corrupt, and the taxes were too high, and the opportunities were rare. But with all her flaws, it was still his home.

He wasn't sure that this place ever would be. The Americans had such strange customs—eating at five in the evening, drinking everything with ice, and going everywhere in their cars instead of on foot.

Diego looked up from his half-finished plate of lasagne. He took a slow sip of his wine and said softly, *"Ho un'idea."*

Matteo looked up. "What kind of idea?" He was doggedly sticking to his plan to become fluent in English by speaking it every chance he got. Diego was less diligent about his practice.

"Una scuola di cucina. Posso insegnare a questi Americani a cuocere meglio."

"A cooking school? Here in the restaurant?" The idea was crazy. They had no experience as teachers. Sure, Diego was a fantastic self-taught chef, but how would they get things started?

They'd already spent a lot of money on advertisements—radio, newspaper, even nailed to posts around town—and had yet to hit upon the magic formula to bring people in the door. Why should this be any different?

"Ho fatto questo." Diego pulled a flier off the chair next to him, handing it to Matteo.

"Learn to Cooking," Matteo read. "Give Classes With An Italian Chef How Easy It Is." He laughed. "OK, the grammar needs a bit of work. But maybe we could do something with this...."

"Not maybe. Can." Diego grinned. "I can."

Matteo looked around at the modern *enoteca* they had created. It had gone from the sadly out of date Little Italy restaurant they had found when they'd first arrived to something sparkling and modern and new.

They had sold their house in Bologna and mortgaged everything they had to make this dream come true. It would be a shame to lose it all and be sent back to Italy with their tails between their legs.

"Okay," he said, taking Diego's hand in his. "I'll tell you what.

Send me the file, and I'll clean it up a bit. We'll put these out around the neighborhood and see what happens. When do you want to start?"

Diego grinned. "*Domenica prossima?*"

"A week from Sunday, it is." He grasped the little golden cross his mother had given him before she passed away and said a little prayer to her. "*Ti prego. Mi manca, mamma.*"

Then they put away the dishes and turned out the restaurant lights. Matteo teased Diego with a kiss and then pulled him up the staircase at the back of the restaurant to their apartment.

On the table, the flier sparkled for a moment before becoming dark once more.

Wanna Read More?

https://www.otherworldsink.com/book/the-river-city-chronicles/

ABOUT THE AUTHOR

Scott lives with his husband of 25 years in a leafy Sacramento, California suburb, in a little yellow house with a brick fireplace and a couple pink flamingoes out front. He has always inhabited the space between the *here and now* and the *what could be*. Indoctrinated into fantasy and sci fi by his mother at the tender age of nine, he devoured her library. But as he grew up and read the golden age classics and more modern works as well, he began to wonder where all the people like him were.

After he came out at twenty-three, he decided that it was time to create the kinds of stories he couldn't find at Waldenbooks. If there weren't many gay characters in his favorite genres, he would reimagine them himself, populating them with a diverse universe of characters. He would subvert them and remake them to his own ends. And if he was lucky enough, someone else would want to read the things he wrote.

His friends say Scott's brain works a little differently – he sees relationships between things that others miss, and gets more done in a day than most folks manage in a week. Although he was born an introvert, he learned to reach outside himself and connect with others like him.

Scott writes stories that subvert expectations, that seek to transform traditional sci fi, fantasy, and contemporary worlds into something new and unexpected. He also runs both Queer Sci Fi and QueeRomance Ink with his husband Mark, sites that bring people like them together to promote and celebrate fiction that reflects their own reality.

His writing, whether romance or genre fiction (or a little bit of both) brings a queer energy to his stories, infusing them with love, beauty and power and making them soar. He imagines a world that *could be*, and in the process, maybe changes the world *that is*, just a little.

He was recognized as one of the top new gay authors in the 2017 Rainbow Awards, and his debut novel "Skythane" received two awards and an honorable mention.

He runs Queer Sci Fi, QueeRomance Ink, and Other Worlds Ink with Mark, and is the committee chair for the Indie Authors Committee at the Science Fiction and Fantasy Writers of America (SFWA).

ALSO BY J. SCOTT COATSWORTH

Liminal Sky: Ariadne Cycle

The Stark Divide | The Rising Tide | The Shoreless Sea

Liminal Sky: Redemption Cycle

Dropnauts

Liminal Sky: Oberon Cycle

Skythane | Lander | Ithani

Tharassas Cycle

The Dragon Eater | The Gauntlet Runner | The Hencha Queen (Mar 2024) | The Death Bringer (Sept 2024)

Other Sci Fi/Fantasy

The Autumn Lands | Cailleadhama | Firedrake | The Great North | Homecoming | The Last Run | Wonderland

Contemporary/Magical Realism

Between the Lines | Flames | The River City Chronicles | Slow Thaw

Short Story Collections

Spells & Stardust | Tangents & Tachyons | Androids & Aliens

Audiobooks

Cailleadhama | The Autumn Lands | The River City Chronicles | Skythane

www.ingramcontent.com/pod-product-compliance
Lightning Source LLC
Chambersburg PA
CBHW061239210726
48293CB00003B/824